Dear Reader,

I grew up in central Maine, about forty miles from the coast. My father was a game warden who taught me many things about nature. My husband grew up in Oregon, but he took to Maine eagerly in 1977, and we lived there another thirty-three years. The scenes in this book revolving around the Bauers' trip to the cabin had me alternately cringing and laughing as I wrote them. While I don't want to give away what happens, I remember some camping experiences that were not so different from Dan and Shelley's.

One of our favorite camping spots was on a little lake in northern Maine called Misery Pond. Only one campsite was available on this pond, and it was on a first-come, first-served basis. So if we were fortunate enough to find it vacant when we arrived, we had the pond to ourselves, except for any fishermen or hikers passing through during the day. The area is home to many moose, beavers, and other animals, and our children loved to go there.

But we did get our share of rainy days and minor mishaps. One year we camped at another, nearby small pond, Little Chase Stream Pond. As we drove in on the rocky forest road, our van got a flat tire. We were glad we had a spare! But we had to unload all our gear and change that tire before we could get out again.

Writing this book gave me plenty of opportunity to savor such memories. And I hope you'll enjoy *Setting Course* with our characters as much as I did!

Blessings,
Susan Page Davis

Setting Course

MIRACLES *of*
MARBLE COVE

SETTING COURSE

SUSAN PAGE DAVIS

New York

Acknowledgments

Every attempt has been made to credit the sources of copyrighted material used in this book. If any such acknowledgment has been inadvertently omitted or miscredited, receipt of such information would be appreciated.

"From the Guideposts Archive" originally appeared as "What Prayer Can Do: Empty Pew?" by Ida M. Saenz in *Guideposts* magazine. Copyright © 2008 by Guideposts. All rights reserved.

Cover and interior design by Müllerhaus
Cover photo by Shutterstock
Typeset by Aptara, Inc.

Printed and bound in the United States of America
10 9 8 7 6 5 4 3

SETTING COURSE

Chapter One

Beverly Wheeland jogged along the beach, enjoying the sea breeze. Her short ponytail bobbed as she slowed to a walk and mounted the boardwalk that led up to Newport Avenue. Her friend Diane was in her yard with her dog. Beverly waved and continued on, checking her pulse as she walked, until she reached her father's Victorian house at the other end of the short street.

Her father had lingered at the breakfast table, and when she entered the dining room, he was folding the latest edition of the *Marble Cove Courier* in half. The weekly paper had arrived on Saturday, but he liked to keep each issue around for several days and absorb all the town's news at a leisurely pace.

"Back already?" he asked.

"Yes. Would you like more coffee?"

"That would be nice."

Beverly carried her father's breakfast plate and coffee cup to the kitchen, refilled his cup, and took it back to the table.

"Old First is having an anniversary, I see," he said, peering at the bottom half of the front page. "I guess I missed that story on my first read-through."

"Yes, there's been some talk about it." She'd heard a few announcements at church services about the upcoming event and calls for volunteers. "It's the 250th anniversary of the church. Not the building, but the founding of the congregation."

"*Mmm*." He took a sip of coffee. "The old church burned, didn't it?"

"Yes."

"Ha!" He smiled at her over the folded newspaper. "It says here that it burned in 1789."

"There you go." Beverly gathered up his silverware and empty juice glass and turned toward the kitchen again.

"Do you suppose this building should be called 'Old Second'?"

She looked back at him and he winked, then returned to his paper.

The next time she returned, he had more information. "They're going to celebrate Founder's Day the end of June, and they want people to lend their memorabilia for a display."

"That's nice," Beverly said. "Do you have anything connected to the church?"

"I don't think so. It says Frances Bauer and Madeleine Bancroft are on the committee together." He grinned at Beverly. "Wonder how that will work out."

"Pretty well, I'd imagine." She shrugged. Both women were strong-willed and energetic. If they didn't butt heads, they'd probably do a great job.

"Maybe you should volunteer for the committee. You might learn something."

"That's not a bad idea." Beverly hadn't considered it since building her new business was keeping her fairly busy, but Father had a point. Helping out with the Founder's Day celebration might give her friends an opportunity to get back up in the old bell tower.

Her cell phone rang, and she took it from her pocket. The screen read "Jeff Mackenzie," and she stepped into the kitchen for a measure of privacy.

"Hi," Jeff said. "I wondered if you're free Saturday evening. I'll be on the mainland."

"Uh . . . sure."

Beverly liked Jeff and enjoyed his company, but she valued her time alone and the flexible schedule that allowed her to spend time with her friends. Dating again still seemed a little odd. But Jeff was like her in some ways—he usually called several days in advance, and this was no exception. He was giving her three days to prepare.

"Great," Jeff said. "I'll come by around five and pick you up. I thought maybe we'd drive up to Rockland."

"Sounds good." They signed off, and Beverly tucked her phone away. Their dates were becoming more or less regular, and though she didn't like to admit it, that made her a little nervous.

Right now she was still getting used to the new freedom of being a full-time consultant and the slower pace of her life in Marble Cove. Quickly she walked to her desk and outlined her tasks to accomplish. She always started her workday by making a to-do list. Today she would put in some time on summer promotional materials for the Landmark Inn. The owner, her friend Victoria Manchester, was eager to get some new print-ready ads to the coastal newspapers, and to have new brochures printed for her guests and people who inquired about the inn.

She'd crunched the numbers, and considering the amount of work she was doing for Victoria, she needed at least three more clients with similar needs for her targeted minimal income. Four or five would put her in the comfort zone, but she really hoped to land a couple of larger, corporate accounts.

A shiver of self-doubt crept over her. Could she really make it on her own? She wouldn't have the staff and resources now that she'd had for her job at the State House. Of course, she had savings, and if things got tight, she could consider selling her house in Augusta. But she wasn't nearly to the point of giving that serious thought.

She could make this business work. All it would take was some concentrated effort. Beverly set her jaw and opened an Excel file.

★   ★   ★

Margaret Hoskins was about to walk out the door to go and open the Shearwater Gallery for the day when her home phone rang. She answered it, glancing at the kitchen clock. She'd hoped to arrive at the gallery a little early this morning so she could take care of a few things before she opened.

"Mrs. Hoskins, my name is Rosalyn Neely, and I'm in charge of the Port Clyde Art Fair. It's coming up on Memorial Day weekend. Are you familiar with the fair?"

"Oh yes!" Margaret smiled at memories of strolling along the rows of art booths with Allan. "I've attended it several times, and I love the way you pull together such an eclectic group of artists."

"Thank you," Rosalyn said. "One of our members mentioned your name to me, and she wondered why you weren't on our list of artists yet. I took a peek at your gallery's Web site, and I do think you should be included in our show. Are you interested?"

Margaret clutched the phone. "Yes. Very interested." Was she going to gain some acknowledgment from the local art community at last? Ever since the condescending remarks she'd heard from a critic at her opening last year, she'd doubted whether she would ever be considered a "real" artist by those in the know—in spite of the fact that her work was now selling steadily.

"That's great," Rosalyn said. "You'll have space for an eight-foot table, which you have to provide yourself, and four feet on each side for displays. A lot of people use a smaller table and more vertical displays for their work. We ask that you exhibit at least eight pieces throughout the fair. If you sell some during the weekend, you either replace them with others or else ask the buyers to pick them up after the fair closes."

"All right." Margaret mentally counted the paintings hanging in her gallery. That shouldn't be a problem.

"Oh, and each artist is required to premier a new piece that hasn't been previously exhibited. Are you able to do that?"

"Well, it's short notice, but I think... Yes. Yes, I can." Margaret had a nearly completed painting that was earmarked for Matt Beauregard and Lighting the Way Greeting Cards. Matt would probably let her exhibit it first, along with the others she'd prepared for him this spring. And she could use the best of those for her debut piece if she didn't get a new painting finished in time.

"Wonderful. I'll send you a packet with all the details." Rosalyn took Margaret's mailing and e-mail addresses. "There's just one more thing," she said tentatively.

"Yes?" Margaret asked, wondering if there was some other requirement she had to meet. Or perhaps there was a hefty fee for the exhibitors.

"I have an opening for artists' ambassador for this event. I don't suppose you'd be interested in taking that responsibility?"

"I... well, I hardly know what to say." Margaret swallowed hard. "Wouldn't it be better to have someone with more experience?"

"Oh, I think you'd be great at it," Rosalyn said. "I know it's your first time, but I've had a good recommendation for you."

Margaret hesitated. She didn't want to get into something that would demand a lot of her time between now and the fair. "What exactly does it entail?"

"Oh, it's mostly helping out when the artists are setting up, and generally making things easier for them. You would need to arrive a little early and get your own exhibit set up so you'd be free to assist the others. And if anything comes up beforehand, where someone needs a little help, I might call on you."

"Well, I'm not sure."

"Oh, please?" Rosalyn urged. "I really need someone who lives in the area, who's dependable. I've held the position myself in the past, and I can tell you, it shouldn't be too demanding. Really."

"All right," Margaret said, still uncertain.

"Fabulous! I can't wait to meet you. Our next meeting is Saturday evening." She gave Margaret the time and address, and they signed off.

As Margaret replaced the receiver, her husband entered the kitchen.

"Not gone yet?" Allan asked.

"I'm running a bit late," Margaret said. "I just got a call from the organizer of the Port Clyde Art Fair. Allan, they want me to exhibit this year!" She turned to study his reaction, hoping he'd be pleased. She felt about to boil over, she was so excited.

His vibrant smile told her that Allan was on board.

"That's fantastic! It's Memorial Day weekend, though, isn't it?"

Margaret frowned. "Well, yes. That could be a problem."

"We'll make it work." Allan grasped her shoulders. "This is a great opportunity for you, Margaret. I'm all kinds of happy for you."

He bent and kissed her, and Margaret squeezed him for a moment.

"Thanks. You always say the right thing. But I'll have to fix it with Matt to let me show the paintings I'm doing for him before he takes them. And—oh!" She gritted her teeth. "Do you think that we'll have enough stock left in the gallery for the weekend if I take eight paintings to the show?"

"Now, don't you fret," Allan said. "I can frame a few more of those prints, and we can put one up in any spot where you take down an original."

"All right." Margaret still wasn't sure. "They want me to be a helper too. They call it 'artists' ambassador.' I hope it's not a very time-consuming position, but I'll definitely have to be at the show all three days."

"Okay. So we'll need to line up a little help at the shop. Adelaide can help me some, but maybe your friends would give us a hand. Do you think Diane or Beverly could fill in for a few hours?"

"Yes, I'm sure they'd be happy to, if they can. Diane is awfully busy working on her new book."

"Well, we'll work it out," Allan insisted. "Right now, I think you need to get down to the gallery and open the door."

"You're right." Margaret picked up her purse and car keys. She'd have to drive today to carry one of Allan's inlaid occasional tables to the Shearwater. "Oh, I should have given her my cell phone number. Rosalyn Neely was her name. If she calls again—"

"I'll tell her how to reach you. Now, skedaddle."

Margaret smiled at him and scooted out the door. By the time she reached the car, her lips were drooping again. Eight paintings, and at least one had to be brand-new. Would she have time to complete the painting she was working on and maybe do one more? The one in progress was a traditional-style seascape for Matt. She couldn't help feeling some of the area artists were a bit snobbish about style. The bolder, more abstract technique she'd experimented with might go over better. Her friends hadn't liked it as well as her usual style, but Margaret suspected some people would find it more meaningful. Could she do another of those in the next four weeks?

Whenever she pushed herself and tried to force the creative process, the painting never came out the way she'd hoped. She'd have to see how things went and trust God to give her the inspiration, skill, and energy she needed.

That calming thought flew out the window almost immediately. What was she thinking, agreeing to participate in an art fair on what might be the gallery's busiest and most important weekend?

CHAPTER TWO

Shelley hurried about her living room with a clothes basket, picking up toys, toddler shoes, magazines, and dishes. It wasn't yet 6:00 AM on Thursday, but she was already in high gear. She usually did this quick pickup in the evening, but last night she'd been too tired from baking all evening.

She had a full day ahead of her, as usual. She'd deliver her fresh-baked pastries to the Cove on Main Street and then come home to package up the baked goods she needed to ship for the online orders she'd received over the past couple of days. Then she had to do laundry and vacuum through the house. Of course, Aiden and Emma would be with her every step of the way, since Dan would be working all day.

She took the basket to the kitchen and set an empty coffee mug and a sippy cup on the counter near the dishwasher. Next stop, laundry room. As she pulled a few items from the basket she carried, she heard Emma give a little squeal. Shelley smiled. At least her little girl was waking up happy today.

In Emma's room, she placed her daughter's wayward shoes on the changing table and set down the basket.

"Good morning, sweetie!"

Emma grinned and stood in her crib. "Mama!"

Shelley pulled her into her arms and kissed her. "Let's get you dressed and see if we can find some breakfast."

Ten minutes later, Dan came into the kitchen, stretching.

"Hi," Shelley said. "Where is it you're working today?"

"Over in Boothbay. I'm meeting Wayne at his house, and we'll take his truck."

"Well, that's good." At least they'd save a little on gas. Dan's new boss was training him to be an electrician, for which he'd have to take a qualifying test later. The work involved traveling to new job sites, which sometimes made for long days. But the steady work and Dan's enthusiasm for the new skills he was learning made up for the inconvenience, in Shelley's mind. The work was legal, and it paid fairly well. Once Dan was certified, he'd earn even more. "Coffee's almost ready," she said. "Got time for pancakes?"

Dan glanced at his watch. "Probably not. Have you got something quicker?"

"Yeah, there are muffins over there." She nodded down the counter to a plastic container where she placed her imperfect baking products for family consumption. "I'll get you some orange juice. How about yogurt?" She hated to see Dan go out the door for a long workday without eating some protein.

Dan sat down at the table with his cobbled-together breakfast. While he buttered his muffin, he chattered to Emma, who sat in her booster seat eating slices of banana and Cheerios off her tray. She mirrored Dan's facial expressions and jabbered back at him.

"Do you think you'll be here long enough for me to run to the Cove before you go? If not, it's okay," Shelley added hastily. "It's just that I'll have to take the kids and it's so early—Aiden's not even up yet."

Dan glanced at his watch. "I'd better not dillydally. We have a long drive this morning."

"Okay." Shelley swallowed her disappointment, realizing that deep down she'd hoped he would offer to take her products to the Cove for her on his way out. For some reason, Wednesdays were always hectic for her. She bustled about and packed his lunch while he finished his breakfast and cooed at Emma. If he was working in a barn, he'd probably appreciate a thermos of coffee too. She filled the bottle and set it beside his lunch box.

She liked to have the baked goods to the Cove by now, as their early morning customers liked a fresh muffin or pastry with their coffee. But she'd have to call and let them know she'd be a little late today.

"I'd better get going." Dan pushed back his chair.

Aiden ran into the kitchen. His blue eyes were still droopy from sleep, and he wore his Spider-Man pajamas.

"Hey, buddy!" Dan scooped up his son and pretended to wrestle with him for a moment. Squirming and squealing, the four-year-old escaped.

"Daddy, can you go to the beach with me?"

"Not today. I'm working."

Aiden pouted. "You always work."

"That's a *good* thing," Shelley said.

"We're working on a farm today," Dan said, helping Aiden into his seat. "They want electricity in their new barn, and we're going to put the lights in for them."

"So the horses can see?" Aiden asked.

"Well, this is a dairy barn, so the cows will see. And the people who tend them."

"Moo," Emma said.

Shelley laughed.

"That's right, cows," Dan said.

Shelley went to the refrigerator for Aiden's juice. She'd hoped Dan would remember that their wedding anniversary was coming up on May 19, but so far he hadn't mentioned it. They'd been married seven years, and she hoped they'd get a chance to celebrate together. Dan wasn't big on romantic gestures, but he could be sweet and charming at times. She was sure that if he remembered, he'd do something for her. But she wanted him to think of it without her nudging him. Was that too much to ask? Maybe if she circled the date on the calendar, he'd see it and that would jog his memory.

They'd been so busy lately that it seemed they hardly saw each other, unless it was for scenes like this one—full of children and work and "have to" activities. Dan's apprenticeship workdays often stretched well into the evening, so that the kids often were in bed before he got home, and they starved all week for his attention. Shelley did too, but she tried not to be as demanding about it as Aiden and Emma were. Her home-based bakery kept her hopping. The Cove had increased its orders for baked goods with the tourist season looming, and she got more Internet orders now than ever before. She'd love it if she and Dan could slip off for a quiet getaway—even just one evening together without the kids would be lovely.

Still, he was under stress from working with new people in a completely new field. She had to give him a lot of credit for that.

"Here's your lunch." She held out the black plastic lunch box and thermos.

"Great." Dan stooped to kiss her.

He was out the door, and Shelley grabbed the telephone.

"Hi, Brenna. I'm running a little late. I'm sorry."

"Well, come as quick as you can," Brenna McTavish said.

"Will do. Oh, and I'll have the kids with me."

"Honk when you drive up, and I'll help you unload if I can," Brenna said.

Shelley hurried about the kitchen while the children ate. She had a couple of pies to deliver to Captain Calhoun's too, but those weren't as urgent. They wouldn't start selling dessert until lunchtime. But the Cove was another story. Maybe she should just go with Aiden in his pajamas. If Brenna helped her, the children wouldn't have to get out of the car while she unloaded the pastries. Not ideal, but better than stopping to get Aiden dressed.

As she unfastened Emma's safety strap, she heard tires on gravel in the driveway. Who on earth would come by this early? She looked out the window and moaned. Her mother-in-law was just getting out of her car.

*　　*　　*

Diane unclipped the leash from the collar of her yellow-Labrador/golden-retriever mix and let him romp down the beach. The tide had turned and was coming in, but hadn't progressed very far yet. They had plenty of time for a nice ramble. She walked on the firm, damp sand and kept an eye out for beach glass and unusual shells. Her walks with Rocky helped Diane in many ways—exercise, a change of pace, and a time to percolate her story ideas.

She enjoyed her new status as a published author, but she was learning that selling the first book didn't smooth out the rest of one's writing career. With her three-book contract signed, she now had two more books to complete, and she was a bit anxious about the one already in print. She had no idea how sales were going nationwide, but if they were booming, it seemed logical that someone from the publishing house would have mentioned it to her.

Was her mystery being marketed well? She wished she could get some hard sales figures, but she supposed it would be months before she had those. If only her editor would tell her that bookstores were ordering her book, she'd feel easier.

Rocky loped toward the Orlean Point lighthouse, and Diane smiled, steering her steps that way. She and her friends had solved a real-life mystery that centered on the lighthouse. Now they had a new puzzle. First Church of Marble Cove, affectionately dubbed Old First by the town's citizens, badly needed restoration, and Diane hoped she, Margaret, Beverly, and Shelley could help raise the funds for that.

They'd uncovered some clues about an old treasure belonging to the church's founder, Jeremiah Thorpe. Was the treasure still out there? Diane hoped so. If they could find it, maybe it could be used for the needed repairs on the beautiful old building. But the friends had forayed out with metal detectors twice already, and they hadn't turned up anything.

The strongest clue they'd found was a map made by Jeremiah Thorpe in the late 1700s. That was concealed in an old letter Diane had found in the church's original bell tower. If only they could get back up there and look around for more clues! But Old First's current pastor, Silas Locke, didn't seem to like the idea of the women poking around in the bell tower. In fact, he'd had the entrance nailed shut. Why would he do that? Diane had her own thoughts, though she hadn't been too vocal about it. Beverly attended Old First, and Diane didn't want to make her uncomfortable by casting aspersions on her pastor. But she still thought they would find more clues up there in the belfry if they had the opportunity.

Rocky came trotting toward her, wagging his tail and panting. Diane laughed and whirled as the dog danced around her.

"You silly thing. We'd better head back now so we don't get our feet wet." The tide still had a ways to go, but she needed to spend a solid block of time on her writing this afternoon.

She clipped the leash on Rocky's collar when they reached the end of the boardwalk and stepped briskly along toward home. Diane's house was on the end of Newport Street, nearest the beach. Next door was Margaret and Allan Hoskins' home, and she spied Margaret in the yard. She must have come home from the gallery for lunch.

Diane waved, and Margaret smiled. She stepped away from her car and walked to the low fence that separated their yards.

"Diane! Just the woman I wanted to see."

"Oh? That's flattering." Diane entered her own yard and let Rocky loose. She sauntered over to the fence, smiling at Margaret. "What's up?"

"I wondered if you could help out at the gallery on Memorial Day weekend. Not the whole weekend, but could you take a shift or two?"

"I think I could," Diane said. "I haven't made any plans yet. Expecting a big crowd?"

"Well, yes, I hope so, but you see, I've been asked to display at the art fair that weekend, and I'll have to be in Port Clyde all three days."

Margaret's eyes shone as she made her announcement, and Diane reached across the fence and squeezed her arm gently.

"That's a great honor, Margaret. Congratulations!"

"Thanks. Allan has been terrific about it, and he says he'll man the gallery, but three full days is a lot to ask."

"Well, you can put me down for two half days," Diane said. She wouldn't even stop to figure out how much that would set her back in her writing. This was obviously important to Margaret.

"Oh, thanks so much," Margaret said. "I know you're busy, and I appreciate your offer."

"No problem." Already Diane was thinking that she and Beverly and Shelley would need to get down to the art fair too. It was such a big honor, they couldn't let Margaret take this big a step without turning out to support her. She was still figuring out her work routine, but maybe she could plan a couple of "off" days into her writing schedule that weekend.

"How's your book doing?" Margaret asked. "Is it selling well?"

Diane drew in a deep breath. "That's the question I'd like answered. I guess it will be a while before I hear anything solid. I try not to think about it too much, but I do wonder."

"It's such a good story," Margaret said. "Anyone who likes mysteries would be crazy not to buy it."

Diane laughed. "Thanks for your enthusiasm."

"Well, that New York publisher liked it. And they should know, right?"

"Right." Diane wished she felt as sure as she sounded. If her first book didn't sell well, what would happen to the other two books? Would the publisher cancel her contract if the first book in the series flopped?

CHAPTER THREE

As Beverly walked the last block home after a run on the beach Thursday morning, her cell phone rang. When she realized the caller was a potential client, she was glad the man couldn't see how windblown and unprofessional she looked at that moment.

"My name's Thomas Sloan," he said, "and my wife and I own the Sand Dollar B and B in Pemaquid."

"How may I help you, Mr. Sloan?" Beverly asked. She was thankful she'd had a few minutes to cool down and didn't sound like she was gasping for air.

"We picked up a brochure for the Landmark Inn in Marble Cove, and I really liked the layout. We're interested in having you do some promotional materials for us."

Beverly smiled. This was exactly what she'd hoped would happen, and Victoria at the Landmark had been happy to let her put her business name and contact information on the back of the Landmark brochures she'd designed. It wasn't always possible to tell how a new customer heard about your services, but this time she could directly trace Mr. Sloan's path. Beverly's eyes lifted heavenward in a quick prayer of thanks.

"I'd be happy to drive over to Pemaquid if you want to discuss how I could help you." She paused on the walkway to her father's house and briefly outlined a few promotional ideas she could do for businesses like the Sand Dollar. When she mentioned the computerized financial programs she was proficient in, Mr. Sloan interrupted her.

"Say, we have a tax preparation program, but we've been wanting to get more of our record keeping onto the computer. Is that something we could do without a lot of fuss and feathers?"

"Absolutely," Beverly said. "Why don't I bring my laptop along when we meet? I can show you and Mrs. Sloan some programs that might save you a lot of time on bookkeeping and things like that."

She set a time for the next day. Mr. Sloan was enthusiastic, so she didn't mind making the drive on speculation. She had to follow any lead, and it sounded as though they had a picturesque location, so at the very least she would enjoy taking in the scenery.

Now she'd have to make sure Mrs. Peabody could make lunch for her father tomorrow and maybe stay and visit for a bit. As she hurried inside, she made a mental checklist of what she needed to prepare for the meeting.

Her father was catnapping in his recliner. Beverly went on upstairs and took a quick shower. Afterward she packed her briefcase with sample brochures, letterheads, and business cards. She'd need to make sure that demos of the programs she wanted to show the Sloans were loaded on her laptop. Half the battle in selling her services was demonstrating how much easier a client's work would be after she finished her magic with their computer setup.

Next, she checked her camera bag. Her digital camera and the card to save her photos on were all set, but she'd need new batteries.

She went down to the living room. Her father was stirring in his chair and reached for the TV remote.

"I'm going to walk downtown," Beverly said. "Is there anything you'd like me to pick up for you?"

"Oh yeah, there's something I'd like, but I don't know if you'd get it for me."

"What?"

Her father smiled sheepishly. "Some of those cookies Shelley Bauer makes. You know—the oatmeal-raisin ones."

Beverly nodded. "The sugarless ones. I'll see if they have any at the Cove today." She generally tried to keep him on a strict diet, but half a dozen, rationed out, wouldn't wreak havoc on his blood sugar.

When she got to the Cove, Shelley was there picking up a check. Since her commercial kitchen was completed, Shelley could do all her baking at home, but she still supplied the Cove daily with fresh baked goods.

"Well, hi, Beverly," she called.

"Wow! No kids?" Beverly walked toward her, looking around for the stroller.

"My mother-in-law offered to stay with Aiden and Emma while I do a couple of errands."

"Nice." Beverly smiled. "Tell me you've got some of those sugar-free oatmeal cookies today. Father has a hankering."

Shelley laughed. "I sure do."

Brenna smiled at her from behind the counter. "How many would you like, Beverly?"

"Half a dozen. Thanks!"

While Brenna bagged the cookies, Beverly turned to Shelley. "I have a meeting with a possible client tomorrow, thanks to the Landmark Inn's brochure."

"Really? That's fantastic!" Shelley beamed at her. "So many people have commented on the one you made for my business. A lot of folks say it makes their mouths water just looking at the picture of my lemon bars."

"Mine too," Beverly said with a laugh.

"I'm going to pop into the gallery and see Margaret. Want to go with me?"

"Sure, but just for a minute. I need to get some double-A batteries and get home again."

They left the Cove together, and Shelley put her trays and boxes in her car. They walked a few steps to the shop next door—Margaret's gallery. Allan was inside, mounting a painting on the side wall, with Margaret supervising.

"Well, hello, ladies," Margaret called.

"Is this a new painting?" Beverly asked, eyeing the piece as Allan set it on its hanger. The long shadows and dusky tones on the lighthouse walls told her it was a twilight view.

"I don't think I've ever seen this one," Shelley said.

"Me either. I like it." Beverly looked expectantly to Margaret for information.

"Thanks," Margaret said. "It's one I did for Matt Beauregard last month. I'm doing a batch of four for him. But we figured we may as well hang this one until he picks it up."

"It will fill the empty spot from the last one she sold," Allan said with a wink.

"Did you sell a painting today?" Shelley asked.

"Not mine, but one of the other artists'," Margaret said.

"Oh, that one with the old hay rake, wasn't it?" Beverly asked. "I loved that one."

Margaret nodded. "Yes. I called and begged for more. The artist promised me three new canvases before Memorial Day."

"Great. Looks like you got some deliveries today too." Shelley nodded toward two wooden crates on the floor on the other side of the room.

"Oh yes. That's pottery," Margaret said. "I hope there are some small pieces. They make good impulse purchases. Of course, I love the bigger bowls and vases too."

Beverly was glad she'd taken a few moments out of a busy day to share in her friends' excitement. The three of them were all beginning new ventures, and Diane Spencer was too, with her fiction writing. And all of them, while at varying points along the road, had taken significant steps toward success. She felt as though that called for some sort of acknowledgment. She was going out with Jeff on Saturday evening, and she was a little nervous about that. She was always happy to spend time with him, but she also worried that he wanted to be more serious than she did—at least yet. Slipping an event in earlier in the day might give her just the distraction she needed.

"I just had an idea." Shelley and Margaret both looked at Beverly expectantly. "I was thinking... Would you two like to come to my house for lunch on Saturday? If you're not too busy, that is. I thought we could congratulate each other on our new successes. I'll phone Diane too, of course. What do you think?"

"I think it sounds great," Shelley said. "Dan should be home then. If he is, I'll be there."

"Me too," Margaret said. "Well, maybe I should check with Allan first."

He turned around and gave her an approving nod. "Sure. I'll sit in for you here for an hour or two on Saturday. And you all can celebrate Margaret's birthday."

"Your birthday?" Shelley almost squealed the words. "Margaret, why didn't you tell us?"

Margaret shrugged. "I don't know. It doesn't seem that important. And it's Sunday, anyway, not Saturday. The sixth."

"Well, your family will probably want to celebrate on Sunday," Beverly said.

Allan nodded with a smile. "That's right."

"So we'll have our own little party on Saturday," Shelley said.

Margaret's face was flushed pink. "Don't you dare go to any trouble. But, Beverly, I'd be happy to accept the invitation."

Beverly smiled. "Thank you. I'll look forward to it. Now I'd better go get my batteries and hoof it for home, as Father would say."

*   *   *

By the time the minicelebration rolled around on Saturday, Margaret felt a pleasant anticipation. Her friends would make the occasion feel special. She realized she'd dreaded her birthday—whenever she thought about turning sixty-eight, she felt ancient. But Shelley had seen it as an excuse for a party. Maybe spending time with her friends would help her feel younger.

She drove from the gallery to Beverly's house to save a couple of minutes over her walking time. She wanted as much time as possible to spend with her friends without overtaxing Allan and Adelaide while they filled in for her. The Shearwater occasionally got a little busy during the lunch hour, as people working in town sometimes stopped in to browse.

Diane and Shelley were just climbing the steps to the Wheelands' Victorian house as she pulled into the driveway. Shelley was carrying a plastic cake carrier, and Diane held a rectangular container. They waved as Margaret got out of the car, and Diane rang the bell as she hurried up the flagstone walk to join them.

"Can you believe this weather?" Shelley said, glancing up toward the cloudless sky.

"It's wonderful," Margaret said. "Next thing you know, we'll have to start mowing the lawn."

"You mean May isn't always this balmy in Marble Cove?" Diane asked.

Margaret smiled at her naïveté. "Honey, just you wait. Some years, May is cold and miserable as can be here."

"Well, I'll take this one," Diane said.

The door swung open, and Beverly smiled at them. "Hi. Come on in."

As usual, Beverly was immaculately dressed, and her shoulder-length, dark hair was very becoming, though she maintained a no-nonsense style. Her beige pants and top in variegated shades of brown would have been nice enough to wear to an office job, but Margaret knew Beverly had dressed even more professionally when she'd worked at the State House.

"Happy early birthday, Margaret," Beverly said.

"Oh, thank you."

The three callers followed Beverly to the dining room. The table was laid with old china and flatware—Beverly's mother's, Margaret assumed—on a snowy linen cloth.

"What a lovely table," Diane said. A centerpiece of grape hyacinth and greenery drew the eye.

"Thank you," Beverly said with a faint smile. "Those flowers came up in one of Mother's old beds."

"What a nice way to remember her. Is your father joining us?" Margaret asked, noting only four places were laid.

"No, he insisted on eating early so the four of us can have 'girl talk.' He's in his library." Beverly looked around at them almost shyly. "Won't you all have a seat?"

"Let me help you in the kitchen," Diane said.

"All right. You can help me carry things in."

The luncheon menu was simple but elegant—the main dish was a chicken salad with grapes and celery on lettuce beds. Margaret wondered how long Beverly had worked on it. "Beverly, this salad is delicious," she said after one bite.

"I'll say," Shelley added with a smile. "You'll have to give us your recipe."

"Thank you." Beverly flushed slightly. "The breadsticks aren't homemade. I bought them frozen."

"Well, they're very good," Diane said. "No need to apologize for them."

Beverly nodded, but darted a glance at Shelley, the professional baker.

"How did your business meeting go, Beverly?" Shelley asked.

"Quite well, thanks." Beverly looked around at the others. "Someone saw one of my brochures and called me. I drove to Pemaquid yesterday and took some pictures of their B and B. It's a beautiful old house overlooking the water. The owners liked my suggestions, and it looks like I'll be setting up a computer accounting program for them, along with a computerized check-in system."

"Wonderful," Diane said. "I'll bet that will save them a lot of time and trouble."

"What about brochures?" Shelley asked.

"Well, they had some that were printed last year that they're using this summer, but if all goes well, I'll design a new one for them to begin using in the fall. They need to raise their off-season prices a little."

"I sympathize with them," Margaret said. She'd had some trying moments figuring her overhead into her pricing at the gallery.

"Oh, these folks also want me to put together some print-ready ads for them. It's too late to meet any of the magazine deadlines for the season, but they thought they'd place a couple of ads in the Boston and Hartford papers to see if they could draw in some business from there."

"We get a lot of summer people from down that way," Shelley said.

"I hope they get lots of guests and you get lots of business too," Diane said.

"Thanks." Beverly shrugged. "I'll need to find a few bigger clients as well, but this is a start."

"Bigger, as in bigger businesses?" Shelley asked.

"Yes. My original plan was—and still is, really—to do corporate financial planning and analysis, that sort of thing. It's what I'm best at, and it would be much more profitable."

Shelley's eyes were round. "I don't even know what that means."

They all laughed, and Diane said, "We don't have to understand it, as long as Beverly does."

"And how's your writing going?" Margaret asked.

Diane smiled but gave a halfhearted shrug. "Okay. I hoped I'd be finished with my second book by now, but I've had a little trouble making all the clues come together."

"You'll get it," Margaret said.

"Thanks. I'm a little antsy, I guess. I wish I knew how the first book is selling. That's probably distracting me from doing my best on the next one. I just need to concentrate." She looked around at them all. "I've been meaning to ask, have you ladies given any more thought to the Thorpe treasure?"

"I've thought about it some," Shelley said, "but I've been too busy to *do* anything."

"Yeah, me too," Diane said. "I'd really like to get up into that bell tower again."

"It seems as though Reverend Locke doesn't want us to go up there," Margaret said. She looked to Beverly. "Old First is getting ready for the Founder's Day celebration, right?"

Beverly drew a breath. "Well, yes. I don't know a lot about it yet."

"Dan's mom is on the committee," Shelley said. "She came over the other day and she was all wound up talking about it. But I'm not sure that will help us find out anything about Jeremiah Thorpe."

"They *are* gathering material for a history of the church," Beverly said. "I guess they've asked folks to bring in any memorabilia they have so they can exhibit it for Founder's Day, and they'll put together some sort of booklet or handout."

"Well, that's something," Diane said.

Margaret nodded. "We might learn more about Thorpe through what the committee turns up. After all, he was the founder of that congregation."

Diane winced. "Yes, and I'm starting to feel seriously guilty about those letters I took from the bell tower in February."

"Maybe we ought to give them back," Shelley said.

Margaret smiled at her inclusiveness. No one had pointed a finger at Diane over the incident. She hadn't intended to steal the old letters from the church. She'd just been distracted by the pastor's sudden appearance and forgotten she had them inside her zippered jacket. And the whole group had cooperated in trying to glean clues from the letters about the founder's rumored treasure.

"I admit I'm chicken," Diane said.

"They probably should go back to the church," Margaret said. "They would be something the committee could add to the Founder's Day display."

Beverly nodded soberly. "That's true, but I'd hate to give up that hand-drawn map we found."

Diane reached for her water glass. "Well, we have a digital file of the map, and I don't suppose we can keep anyone else from seeing it if they read the letters."

"True," Beverly said. "And we really should take them back. I was thinking about volunteering to help with the Founder's Day exhibits. Maybe I'll learn something that will help us figure out the whole Thorpe thing."

"That's wonderful," Diane said. "I wonder if I could do anything."

"I'm sure they'd accept all the help they can get."

"Now, Margaret, it's your turn," Diane said with a smile. "I know you're getting ready for the art fair. How is that coming?"

Margaret gave her a big smile. "Well, I do have some news about it."

"Tell us about it," Shelley cried. "Here we are yakking away about that old map. What's going on?"

"I think you all know I was asked to exhibit at the Port Clyde Art Fair, but I'm not sure I told you that the organizers want me to be the artists' ambassador for the event."

"Wow, congratulations," Diane said.

Shelley nodded. "Yeah. But what does that mean?"

Margaret chuckled. "I'm not sure I know. They said it's helping the artists who are going to exhibit if they have questions, and making sure things run smoothly on opening day when they set up, and maybe on takedown day. Sort of acting as a liaison between the artists and the organizers." She shrugged. "There's a meeting tonight, so I should know more the next time you see me."

"Do you have to go far for that meeting?" Beverly asked.

"To Port Clyde." Margaret winced. "That's the one bad thing about it. It will involve some meetings. But I'm honored that they asked me."

"Sure," Beverly said. "I think it's great."

"Thanks. I have to admit I'm a little stressed about the added responsibility."

"You'll feel better once they explain the details to you," Diane said, "and it's not that long a drive."

"I know you'll do a good job," Shelley added.

"Now, you let us know when you need us to cover for you at the gallery," Diane said. "I'm planning on being there when you need me."

"Yes, make a schedule for Memorial Day weekend. I'd be happy to help out as well," Beverly said.

"Thank you," Margaret told her. "I'll try not to take too much advantage of all your generosity, but Allan was relieved when I told him he'd have some help."

Shelley stood. "I think it's time for dessert. Beverly, could you assist me, please?"

"Let me help," Margaret said.

"Oh no. You're the guest of honor." Shelley smiled sweetly and headed for the kitchen with Beverly.

"I knew it," Margaret said. "She baked a cake, didn't she?"

"What did you expect?" Diane asked with a chuckle.

A moment later, Shelley entered carrying a layer cake with half a dozen candles blazing on top. Beverly held the door for her, then brought in a stack of dessert plates and a carton of ice cream.

Shelley set the cake before Margaret. On top, she had piped lavender ropes around a bouquet of purple and lilac flowers and the words HAPPY BIRTHDAY.

"That's beautiful," Margaret said. "Thank you, Shelley."

"You're welcome! Blow out the candles."

"I'll try."

Shelley laughed. "I made it easy on you—one for each complete decade."

"Oh, that was very discreet." Margaret drew in a deep breath and easily puffed out the six flames.

"And my gift for you is over there." Shelley pointed to the plastic container Diane had carried in. "Cookies for home or the gallery, however you want to use them."

"Thank you so much."

Beverly set a small wrapped package on the table beside her. "Here's mine."

"And mine," Diane said, laying an envelope on the tablecloth.

Margaret felt like a schoolgirl as she tore the wrapping paper off Beverly's gift. The package held a soft leather case for her business cards.

"Oh, thank you! That's perfect!"

Beverly smiled and nodded, looking pleased. Diane's card held a gift card to a stationery store in Rockland.

"I checked, and they have some art supplies. I'm sorry your favorite store in Augusta closed, and I thought this one might have some things you'd find useful."

"I'm sure they will," Margaret said. "Thank you all!"

She looked at each of her friends and smiled. As much as she appreciated their presents, these three wonderful women were among the biggest gifts she could ever have asked for in life.

Chapter Four

Rocky barked joyfully when Diane unlocked the door to her little house at the end of the street.

"How's my good boy!" she gushed, stroking his silky head and scratching behind his ears. "You want to go for a *walk*?"

He *woofed* and pranced around her, tail wagging rapidly.

"All right," Diane said with a laugh. "Just let me get the leash."

She had just clipped the line to Rocky's collar when the phone rang. She frowned at the dog.

"Sit. Now, you be good for a minute."

Rocky whined but stayed put while she reached for the phone.

"Diane, it's Frieda. I have some news—what I hope you'll think is good news."

"I can hardly wait to hear it." Diane sat on a kitchen chair. Sometimes it paid to sit down when her agent called. A Saturday call was unusual and must be significant.

"There's a large chain bookstore in Augusta that would like to do a signing with you next week. What do you think?"

Diane blinked. "Wow. That wasn't at all what I was expecting. Uh—sure, I guess so."

"Good. The publicist is going to call you, probably on Monday, but I wanted to give you a heads-up because it's short notice."

"I appreciate that."

"Now, you don't have to take anything with you, unless you have a favorite pen you want to use. But you just need to show up about fifteen minutes beforehand, and they'll set you up with a table and your books."

"That sounds good," Diane said. "Thank you."

Frieda gave her the time for the event and the telephone number for the store's customer representative. Diane hung up feeling a bit dazed and at the same time excited. She looked at Rocky, who had lain down and was licking one of his paws.

"Wow," she said.

Rocky barked, and Diane laughed.

"All right, Rocky, let's go." She grabbed the loop on the end of the leash and let him lead her to the door. Already she felt a bit nervous about the book signing.

"Stop being silly," she told herself. "You can't stay jittery for a week. Calm down."

Rocky turned and looked at her anxiously.

"Sorry, boy." She patted him. "Just talking to myself."

When they reached the promenade, she unclasped the leash. "There you go. I know you want to run."

She watched him tear out over the beach, barking wildly at a seagull. It took flight before he was within ten yards of it. Diane laughed. In a few weeks, the beach would be crowded with tourists and she'd have to keep a tighter rein on Rocky. But for now she could let him run free while she strolled along in his wake, sending up a prayer of thanks for the past year she'd had here in Marble Cove, her new home, her dog, her friends—and her book signing.

★   ★   ★

Getting ready for a date with Jeff always put Beverly on edge. The man was too handsome, if that was possible. He had movie star good looks, with his dark hair and vibrant eyes. Couple that with his romantic vocation as a photojournalist, and most women would find him very desirable.

That fact also made her uncomfortable, as she frequently caught females staring at Jeff when she was out with him. She never mentioned it, and she wasn't sure he was conscious of the stir he could cause just by walking into a crowded restaurant, with his hair wind-tousled and his casual clothing hanging on him as it would on a model.

Evenings were still quite cool, and she opted for a navy blazer over black pants and a tailored blouse. As she buttoned the last button and glanced in the mirror, she realized she'd dressed as if she were going to the office. She pulled off the blazer and tossed it on the bed. She turned to the closet, then slowly went back to the bed and picked up the blazer. Somehow she couldn't leave it in a heap. She hung it up, with the shoulders hitting the rounded parts of the hanger just right, and replaced it on the closet rod. Off came the blouse. She rummaged a bit and found a long-sleeved print tunic. Over it, she put an unconstructed gray wool jacket. Her reflection looked a bit informal and outdoorsy. Probably perfect for an evening with Jeff.

The door knocker sounded, echoing through the old house, and she hurried down the stairs.

Her father had beaten her to the door and was letting Jeff in.

"Hi," Jeff said, with that heart-stopping smile waitresses swooned over.

"Hello," Beverly said. "Did you have a good trip?"

"Yes, thanks."

Her father said, "I was just saying to Jeff that I wish he'd take a picture of you for me, Beverly."

"Of me? Whatever would you want one for?"

"I want a nice new one, is all. The ones I have are old."

On the contrary, Beverly thought. *They are young, while I am old—or getting older.* Forty-three probably didn't seem old to her father.

"All right," she conceded, "but not tonight."

"No," Jeff said. "I didn't bring my camera tonight. We'll do it soon though, Mr. Wheeland."

That seemed to satisfy her father, and Beverly picked up her purse. With any luck, Father would forget about it.

"All set?" Jeff asked.

"I think so. Father, you'll call me if anything comes up, won't you?"

"As if I can't take care of myself for one evening." He shook his head, frowning.

"Well, I thought about asking Mrs. Peabody to come over," Beverly admitted.

"Don't you dare! She's a wonderful cook, but I see her enough as it is. I shall enjoy a quiet evening here by myself. I have a new book on the Popham Colony, and I anticipate some good reading."

Beverly smiled. He was right—he was perfectly able to take care of himself. Ninety-five percent of the time, that was. It was that other five percent that worried her, and she never saw his crises coming. But he was doing well this week, and his blood sugar had checked out in the middle of the normal range this afternoon.

"All right, we'll see you later." She pecked him on the cheek and walked out the door with Jeff behind her.

"Will you be warm enough?" Jeff asked. "That's quite a breeze off the bay."

"I'm sure I'll be fine." Beverly let him open the door of his Subaru Forester for her.

On the way to Rockland, they talked sporadically. First Jeff confirmed that she was up for seafood, and then they discussed the relative merits of a couple of restaurants with which they were familiar. There were occasional lulls in the conversation, and while Beverly didn't mind companionable silence, she tried to fill in the gaps.

"How's the mileage on this thing?" she asked.

"It's good. I think I made a good trade." Jeff spent the next few minutes reviewing the merits of his SUV, then he asked her if she had any new clients.

Beverly was glad she had the Sloans to tell him about, and the work she'd started for the Sand Dollar B and B. She felt fairly relaxed by the time they reached the restaurant. Ever since she had met Jeff, she had found him very easy to talk to once she overcame her own natural reserve.

Over broiled scallops, she asked him how his photo essay for the magazine was coming, and Jeff warmed to the topic.

"I spent three days by myself on one of the little islands out beyond Vinalhaven. Just me and the birds. It was great."

Beverly could understand that feeling. She thrived on solitude. Jeff was more sociable, though, and while he always seemed happy to make his solo treks, he was equally content to return to civilization.

They both turned down dessert but ordered coffee. After the waitress brought it, Jeff smiled at her across the table, over the glowing jar candle.

"Beverly, I've been thinking a lot about us while I was out on the island."

"Oh?"

"Yes. I care about you a great deal."

She said nothing, but her pulse raced. She liked Jeff a lot too, but his tone was so grave, she was afraid he was headed into territory she wasn't ready to explore.

"I wondered if it wasn't time we made some sort of declaration," he said.

"I—what do you mean?" Surely he wasn't going to propose. She felt she hardly knew him. That was silly, though. She'd known him several years, and during the last six months, they'd seen each other quite a bit.

"Well, I just thought it would be nice to know we're seeing only each other. An exclusive relationship."

He shot The Smile her way, on high beam, and her heart lurched.

"I guess I'd like to know I'm the only man in your life." He chuckled. "Except for your dad, of course. We're too old for any 'going steady' nonsense, but I guess I'm a bit old fashioned. I'd like to know you aren't seeing anyone else."

Beverly swallowed hard. She hadn't dated anyone but Jeff for the past year. Well, Dennis Calder, whose grandfather lived across the street from her and her father, asked her to have coffee with him now and then, and Jeff had seen Dennis flirt with her, but she'd never reciprocated. She considered Dennis a friend at most, though she knew he would like a deeper relationship.

Was that why Jeff was bringing this up? Did he wonder how she felt about Dennis? She'd figured Jeff would know she wouldn't date anyone else now, but the whole conversation made her nervous and uncomfortable. Not dating anyone else was different from telling a man you wouldn't.

"Well, I . . . " She looked away from Jeff's intent gaze. Those eyes! What sort of commitment was he asking her for? He had recently invited her to join him at a conference in San Francisco, and she'd declined because it seemed to imply a level of deep commitment. He had graciously accepted that. But now, only a few weeks later, he was pressuring her again.

"Jeff, I...I'm just not sure I'm ready for this."

The hurt in his eyes almost made her snatch the words back. To add, "*But* let's give it a try." Almost.

She had to get over this. Really, wasn't six years long enough for a widow to move on? She didn't want to hurt Jeff. She really did like him, more than any other man she knew. But would she freeze up every time he got close to her for the rest of her life? That wouldn't be fair to him. Locking into an exclusive relationship with someone who made her that nervous didn't seem like a good idea. Yet, anyway.

"I'm sorry," she said.

He shook his head. "Don't be."

"It's not..." She licked her dry lips. "I might be able to say yes someday. But right now, I'm feeling a little pressured. I just..."

"You don't have to explain." Jeff picked up the check. "Are you ready to go?"

He paid the bill and they went out into the parking lot. The wind had picked up, and Beverly shivered, drawing her wool jacket close.

They rode in silence for the first ten miles, and her heart slipped lower and lower. She'd wounded him—something she never wanted to do. Her stomach began to ache, and she didn't think it was from the scallops.

Finally, Jeff glanced over at her in the dim light cast from the dashboard.

"I'm sorry I made you feel pressured, Beverly. I thought you felt the same way I do."

"I'm not sure that I don't. I enjoy your company, Jeff."

He was silent for a moment, then slapped the steering wheel with his palm. "I feel like you're sending me mixed signals. I can't tell if you like me or not."

She gulped. "I'm sorry. That wasn't my intention." After a long minute, she ventured, "I do like you. Very much. Could we just give it a little more time?"

"Sure." Jeff cleared his throat but said no more.

Fifteen minutes later, he pulled up at the Wheeland house. Before Beverly had her seat belt unfastened, he was out of the vehicle and going around to her side. She waited for him to open the door. They walked up to the front porch together, and she turned to face him.

"Thank you, Jeff. I enjoyed dinner."

His face was too serious for her to feel things were settled, but he nodded.

"I'll call you before I go off again."

"All right. That sounds good."

He hesitated, then reached out and squeezed her hand gently. "Good night."

She watched him go down the path to the SUV, and her heart felt heavy in her chest. Jeff was such a nice guy—she was fortunate to have him in her life. She didn't want to drive him away, but he'd entered her life at the wrong time—and re-entered it when she was still fragile inside. She wasn't sure she knew how to fix this.

CHAPTER FIVE

Dan went to church on Sunday with Shelley and the kids, but that was about the only time she saw him all day. He'd gone to help his dad with a repair project at the elder Bauers' house after church. Shelley had hoped they'd have some time to talk, but instead she cleaned up the kitchen and put the kids down for their naps alone.

Since it was quiet, she decided to do her baking prep work for the day. She tried to do as little baking as possible on Sundays, but she had to have fresh pastries ready for the Cove no matter what. Mixing the dough calmed her, and she prayed silently as she worked.

By the time Dan came home, Aiden was up, but Shelley still had half a batch of Danish pastries to bake.

"Can you take Aiden out for a few minutes?" she asked. Dan's face fell, and she wished she'd greeted him more cheerfully. "Sorry. I'm almost done, but I'm afraid he'll wake Emma up."

"Okay," Dan said. "Half an hour is it, though. I need to study some of that material Wayne gave me."

He helped Aiden find his shoes and jacket, but before the door shut behind them, Shelley heard Emma babbling over the baby monitor. Maybe if she ignored her, Emma would go back to sleep. Shelley knew that was wishful thinking. As she turned back to her work, Emma's voice came clearly.

"Ma-ma-ma-ma-ma!"

Shelley sighed. No ignoring that. She pushed the button on the monitor. "I'll be right there, angel."

Quickly, she slid another tray of pastries into the oven and headed down the hallway.

Emma had soiled her diaper and her outfit and the crib sheet, so it took a while to clean her up. To Shelley's dismay, when they finally got back to the kitchen, the smell from the oven was a bit acrid.

"Oh no!" She plopped Emma in the playpen and dashed to get the pastries out of the oven. They weren't burned, but they were definitely overbaked. She sighed and set them on a cooling rack. "Looks like we'll be eating well-done Danish for the next couple of days."

When Dan and Aiden came in, Emma was crying to be released from her playpen, and Shelley was rolling out another batch of pastry dough.

"You're not done?" Dan asked, peeling off Aiden's jacket.

"No. Emma made a big mess, and I left a batch of Danish in too long. They're still edible, if you want one, but I had to mix up more dough." The pastries were one of her most labor-intensive offerings, since she had to repeatedly roll and layer the dough to give it the flaky texture her customers loved.

"Well, I really need to study," Dan said.

"I know. I'm working as fast as I can."

"I thought you'd do that tonight."

"I would have had it done if Emma hadn't needed so much attention. Guess I should have waited until tonight. I just—" She blinked back the tears in her eyes. She'd hoped to reserve the evening for some one-on-one time with Dan. Fat chance she had of getting an anniversary date with him if she couldn't arrange a simple evening here at home. The only times they were both in the house, they were frazzled and exhausted. "Where are you headed in the morning?"

"We've got a job in Bangor. We should be up there the next few days."

Her heart sank. Dan would have to turn in early tonight in order to be up early and ready for the long drive.

"Okay. Maybe I can refrigerate this dough and bake it later. I hate to wait, though. The oven's all hot."

Emma's wails escalated, and Dan picked her up.

"Hey, little girl, what's got you so miserable?" He rocked Emma in his arms. "I don't suppose Adelaide could come over and play with the kids while you finish?"

"*Hmm*, I think Margaret said they were going somewhere this afternoon."

"That's right, they were gone when Allan and I finished in the workshop."

Shelley closed the refrigerator and turned off the oven. She walked over and held out her arms to Emma. "Come on, I'm all yours now."

"Thanks," Dan said, passing Emma over.

Aiden appeared in the living room doorway with a toy truck in one hand. "Dad, can you play trucks with me now?"

"Afraid not, buddy. I need to study for a while."

Shelley shook her head. "Look, Dan, I wasn't going to say anything, but do you realize our anniversary is coming up in a couple of weeks?"

"Huh? Oh." He turned toward her, holding the big three-ring binder of electrical safety codes that Wayne Stover had sent home with him. He looked a little apprehensive. "So?"

"So, I was hoping we could do something special."

"Oh. Well, I don't know, Shell."

She grimaced. "Just one evening. I figured if I mentioned it now, maybe we could work something out by then."

"Well, we'll see how things look then, okay?"

She wasn't happy, but she could see that this wasn't a good time to discuss it. She wished she hadn't brought it up.

"Come on, Aiden," she said. "Bring your truck into your room, and I'll bring Emma. We'll stay in there for a while so Daddy can do his homework."

★   ★   ★

Beverly ran into Diane on Sunday afternoon when she went to jog on the beach. Diane was just heading out with Rocky, so Beverly invited her to stop by her house in an hour to talk about their progress, or lack of it, on the Thorpe treasure.

Diane brought the packet of letters with her, carefully wrapped up, and gently placed them on the Wheelands' dining room table.

"I don't know why I brought these. We've photographed them and read them and tried to make something of them. I guess it's time to get rid of them. I wanted to make sure you and the others feel that way too."

"Yes, they should go back to the church," Beverly agreed. "We can consult the copies we made any time. Stop feeling so blue about it."

"I'll try."

"How about some tea?" Beverly asked. Her friend looked glum, and she hoped a change of subject would help.

"That sounds really good," Diane said.

Beverly paused at the library doorway. "I was going to ask my father to join us," she whispered to Diane, "but it looks like he's dozed off."

They moved on to the kitchen, and Diane got out the mugs and tea bags while Beverly put the teakettle on.

"I don't have any of Shelley's treats left," Beverly said ruefully.

Diane gave an exaggerated wipe of her brow. "Whew! I've been indulging in them far too often lately. I won't blame Shelley, but I put on a few pounds this winter. Rocky and I have been trying to walk them off since the weather turned warmer."

"I know what you mean," Beverly said. "In some ways it's a blessing that Father's diabetic. It makes it easier not to keep sweets in the house."

A few minutes later, they sat down in the dining room with their tea.

"How's the new book coming?" Beverly asked.

Diane smiled a bit grimly. "Not bad. I think it's going to work. Hey, I've got a book signing set up for Saturday up in Augusta."

She seemed more cheerful when she made that announcement, and Beverly smiled. "Fun! I might be able to drive up. I need to go over to my house and check on a few things anyway."

"Well, don't make a special trip for me," Diane said. "But if you do show up, it'll be nice to see someone I know." She took a sip of her tea.

"So how are things with you and Jeff?" Diane arched her eyebrows. "How did your date go last night?"

Beverly sipped her tea and took her time placing her cup on the saucer. "He's…he's fine. Still working on the shorebirds assignment."

She must have signaled her uneasiness somehow, though she'd tried to speak in a normal tone. Diane was so intuitive. She seemed to be able to read her friends' moods and fears, though she wasn't the prying type.

"Beverly, any time you want to talk, I'm available."

"Thanks." Beverly didn't know what else to say. This tension with Jeff was something she needed to settle in her own heart.

The back door opened, and Diane looked toward the kitchen.

"It's Mrs. Peabody," Beverly said. "She's here to fix supper for us. Excuse me just a minute, won't you?"

"Of course."

Beverly hurried to the kitchen and found Mrs. Peabody removing her coat. Her snowy white locks were a bit windblown, and she had an apron over her dress.

"Hello." Beverly tried to muster a cheerful tone. "Looks like you're ready to work."

"Yes, I am. I'm doing chicken and dressing tonight and I need to get started. How's the mister?"

"He's fine. Catnapping in his chair right now. Diane is here."

"Oh?" Mrs. Peabody peeked into the dining room and gave Diane a little wave. "Nice you're having company. You won't know I'm here."

"I'm not worried about you," Beverly said.

"I just had a thought." Diane spoke from the doorway behind her, and Beverly turned. Diane waved a hand in dismissal. "If you've seen enough of me for one day, Beverly, feel free to say no, but I was thinking I ought to return those letters today."

"Ah." Beverly glanced at Mrs. Peabody, whose sharp eyes darted between her and Diane. It might be best not to say too much in front of the neighbor since she was sometimes referred to as "Mrs. Busybody."

"I could go with you now, Diane, if Mrs. Peabody's all right with that."

Mrs. Peabody turned toward the counter. "I'm fine. You know I don't like my kitchen full of people while I'm working."

"Thank you." Beverly threw Diane a quick glance, hoping she wouldn't disclose their destination. "We shouldn't be gone more than an hour."

"Oh, at the most," Diane said.

Beverly went to the coat closet for a lightweight jacket, and Diane carried their teacups out to the kitchen.

"Shall I just leave these here?" she asked Mrs. Peabody.

"Leave them wherever you like," the older woman said, "and get off to wherever it is you're going."

Diane didn't take the hint but scurried back to the dining room for the packet of old letters, and they were soon outside.

"Let's take my car," Beverly said.

"I could run over and get mine—"

"Nonsense. It's not far to Reverend Locke's house. Oh, and thank you for not telling Mrs. Peabody where we're going. She attends Old First, you know. I figured it was best not to let her in on this part of our day."

"No problem." Diane grinned and slid into the passenger seat.

★   ★   ★

Diane had felt a sense of sadness in Beverly as they'd talked about Jeff and had their tea. Beverly often kept things inside, which Diane suspected meant that she was working through it on her own, and Diane respected her reticence. She knew Beverly well enough by now to realize she would open up in her own time. She had shared things with Diane previously, and just needed to process things on her own before sharing with friends.

As they drew near to the minister's house, her nerves kicked in, and she realized she was doing the same thing—fretting over something. Here was a chance to share her anxiety with a true friend.

She smiled at Beverly. "I hate to admit, but I'm a little intimidated by Reverend Locke."

"I know what you mean." Beverly pursed her lips for a moment. "He was so angry when he found us in the cemetery that night. He's been polite to me since then, but still, I get a little nervous around him too."

"That makes me feel a little better. But you're not on his 'bad' list the way I am."

Beverly chuckled. "Aren't we all? But seriously, I'm sure he doesn't think of you that way."

"Well, he might after I tell him I've had these old letters since February."

Beverly turned in at Locke's driveway and parked beside his car. "Would you like me to take them in and explain to him?"

For a brief moment, Diane considered taking her up on the offer. It would be the easy way out. But she'd never be able to look Pastor Locke in the face again.

"No, I'd better tell him myself. But I won't say no to having you beside me for backup."

"I wouldn't dream of letting you go in there alone."

They got out of the car and walked up onto the porch. There was no doorbell, so Beverly knocked.

"Well, ladies! Welcome." Silas Locke eyed them curiously as he swung the door open. "May I offer you some coffee?"

"No, thank you," Diane said. "We just came to give something to you."

"Oh? Well, please, have a seat."

They went into his living room, and Diane perched on the edge of the green tweed sofa. Beverly sat beside her, and Reverend Locke sat down in a comfortable-looking, oxblood red leather armchair nearby. Most of the furniture looked like vintage 1970s stuff, but the chair was newer, and a couple of good nautical prints hung on the walls.

"I admit I'm mystified," the minister said.

Diane opened her tote bag. The blood rushed to her cheeks as she delved deeper and took out the packet of old letters.

"It's these. They're letters of Jeremiah Thorpe's."

Pastor Locke's eyes widened, and he reached out hesitantly. "Really? Letters in Thorpe's own hand? How wonderful." He took them and then looked quickly at Diane and Beverly. "Are you bringing these for the Founder's Day exhibit, or—"

"I'm returning them," Diane said. "You'll probably want to exhibit them, though. They're quite interesting."

"I don't understand. Returning them? These don't belong to me, but I'd be delighted for a chance to examine them."

"They belong to the church," Beverly said calmly, and Diane was thankful for her matter-of-fact demeanor.

"The church? But—I've never heard anything about any letters. I didn't know they existed."

"We found them that day we explored the old bell tower," Diane said sheepishly.

He stared at her for a moment, then looked at Beverly. "But that was months ago."

"Yes," Diane said. "It was February."

"You didn't say anything at the time. Mrs. Spencer, you surprise me."

"I'm sorry," Diane mumbled.

"She didn't realize what they were at first," Beverly said. "We've examined them since then, and we decided they definitely belong to Old First."

Locke studied her for a moment, then turned his gaze on Diane. "Why did you take them out of the church in the first place? It seems so...so inappropriate."

"It was a mistake," Beverly said.

"Yes." Diane threw her a grateful look. "I didn't mean to carry them off. I had them when you came and—and you asked us to leave. It all happened so fast, I didn't think about it at the time. A while later, I realized I'd carried them off. But as Beverly said, I didn't know what we'd found then. And now we do know, and I'm returning them."

"My goodness." He looked at her with disapproval. "It certainly took you long enough."

"Well, yes. When we discovered what they were, we all wanted to read them, you see. That is—my friends and I—"

Diane took a breath and stopped talking, afraid she was digging herself into a deeper hole.

"When we realized what Diane had found, we were all excited about it," Beverly said. "It didn't occur to us that these needed to come back to the church right away. I mean, they'd been up there for years and years. Centuries, even."

"Still, they probably have great historic value," Reverend Locke said, eyeing Diane sternly. "You had no right to take them, or to hold on to them so long."

"But I never intended to *keep* them," Diane said. "It was…well, I just want you to know it wasn't intentional, and I'm sorry."

"I see."

Diane wasn't sure he *did* see, but at least the worst was over.

"Jeremiah Thorpe was an interesting man," the pastor said, fingering the aged paper.

Diane hadn't talked about it with Beverly, but she didn't want to tell him about the map. Reverend Locke would probably read all of the letters minutely, and when he did, he might see the map. But there was nothing she could do about that.

"He was intriguing," Beverly said. "This talk about him and a treasure…"

Diane glanced at her sharply, but Beverly let the sentence trail off and waited, as though she hoped Reverend Locke would reveal his thoughts on the matter. *Beverly might make a good police officer*, Diane thought. Beverly didn't seem the least bit intimidated by Locke's manner.

Locke cleared his throat. "Well, yes, of course I've heard the stories. But I don't believe there ever was a treasure. Or if there was, it was no doubt found a long time ago. These letters, however, should be properly preserved. I hope you haven't damaged them too much."

"We were very careful," Diane said, though she felt a pricking of her conscience as she remembered how she and Beverly had worked over the one containing the map.

"Frances Bauer might have some ideas on preserving them," Beverly said, which seemed to Diane a neat way to distract Reverend Locke from her "crime." "She's on the Founder's Day committee, isn't she?"

"Oh yes, she is. And you're probably right. She likes antiques, and she may know something about the subject."

"Well, that's all we really wanted," Beverly said, shifting forward as though about to rise.

That seemed like a capital idea to Diane, and she grasped her tote bag and stood.

"Thank you for...for your understanding," she said.

"Thank you for bringing these back," Locke replied, but he didn't look happy.

As he escorted them to the door, Diane feared he would speak again, perhaps feeling the need to give her a stern lecture. But he was quiet, and she stepped outside with a rush of relief. Beverly wished him a cheerful good-bye, but Diane tried to avoid his disapproving gaze.

At last the two women were in the car. Diane let out an exaggerated breath. She'd felt very uncomfortable in Reverend Locke's presence, even if he was Beverly's pastor. "Whew. I'm so glad you were there. I felt like a naughty kindergartener caught stealing the teacher's red pencil."

Beverly chuckled. "He wasn't happy, but it could have gone worse."

"How? If he called the police?" Diane snapped her seat belt into place.

"Oh, I don't think he'd do anything like that."

"He'll probably see the map, of course."

"Does it matter?" Beverly asked.

"I think it does." Diane pondered the ramifications as Beverly started the car and backed out the driveway. "I look at it this way: if the four of us found the treasure, we'd use it to restore Old First, right?"

"That's the plan," Beverly said soberly. "I mean, it would rightfully belong to the church, wouldn't it?"

"I'm not sure, legally. If it was on church property, certainly. But we've seen that some property lines have been changed, and streets are even different than they used to be. What if it turned up on private property? Wouldn't the property owner have a say?"

"I don't know about that," Beverly said.

"Well, anyway," Diane continued as they turned onto Newport Avenue, "we know what we'd do with the treasure if we found it. My question is, what if Pastor Locke finds it? What will *he* do with it?"

Beverly raised her hand in a wave to Albert Calder, her across-the-street neighbor, who was sitting on his front porch. "Well, I don't know what he'd do with it, but we're making a huge assumption there."

"Oh?" Diane asked.

Beverly nodded as she turned in at her driveway. "Yes. We're assuming there still *is* a treasure."

CHAPTER SIX

Shelley was just about to place Emma in the stroller Monday morning when her phone rang.

"Hello, Shelley. It's Beverly. We're all meeting at the Cove for coffee on Margaret's break time. Any chance you can join us?"

"Uh…well, I was going to take the kids for a walk. I might have to bring them. Dan's in Bangor today."

"Bring them along," Beverly said.

Shelley wasn't sure that was such a good idea, as the women would probably want to talk, and Aiden and Emma would get restless. But she agreed to stop in and pointed the stroller toward Main Street. At least she'd done her pastry run early this morning while Dan was getting dressed in the gray light of dawn.

When she entered the Cove, Margaret and Adelaide rose from a table near the back, where they'd been sitting with Diane and Beverly.

"Hi," Margaret said, smiling. "Adelaide came to help Allan at the gallery during my break, but she said she'd be happy to help entertain the kids."

"Wow, okay," Shelley said, looking around at the crowded coffee shop. "We probably shouldn't stay long, though."

"I can take them next door," Adelaide said eagerly.

"Oh well—I don't know." Shelley looked anxiously at Margaret. "What do you think?"

"*Hmm.* The gallery's only a few yards down the sidewalk, and there weren't any customers when we left." She turned to Adelaide. "Take the stroller around to the back door, all right? And if there are customers, don't let the kids go out into the gallery." To Shelley, she said, "I'll give Allan a quick call and let him know they're coming."

Shelley helped take the stroller outside and watched anxiously as Adelaide started off on her short trek. To her relief, Aiden stuck close to Adelaide, "helping" her push the stroller. Down the street, Allan appeared in the Shearwater's front doorway and waved. Shelley waved back and went inside.

"Your husband is a saint," she said to Margaret as she joined the other women at the table.

"He said he didn't mind, as long it wasn't for long."

"Okay, ladies, you heard that," Shelley said. "Fifteen minutes max. What's up?"

"I'll start," Diane said. "Yesterday, Beverly and I went over to Reverend Locke's house, and I gave him the Thorpe letters."

"What did he say?" Margaret asked, reaching for her coffee cup.

Diane grimaced.

"He wasn't happy," Beverly admitted. "He gave Diane a bit of a scolding, I'm afraid."

"That's not fair," Shelley said. "Diane found those letters! If she hadn't, he'd have no idea they were there. And she didn't have to take them back."

"Well, I felt as though I did have to," Diane said. "And he was right—I should have told him the day I found them."

"You didn't mean to take them," Beverly said evenly.

"True. At least I don't think I did. Maybe subconsciously— oh, I don't know!" Diane shook her head and took a big bite of her cheese Danish. "*Mmm*, these are good!"

Shelley smiled, glad her baking marathon on Sunday was appreciated. "Thanks. So, Pastor Locke was really mad?"

"No, I wouldn't say mad," Beverly said.

Diane added, "Not *really* mad. But, you know, he was quite adamant that there's no treasure, and it's just a story. I admit it made me wonder if he might know something."

"Something about the treasure?" Margaret asked.

"Well, yes. I mean, he's been there at Old First for a long time. I'm surprised he'd never found those letters himself."

"So...did you get the feeling he might be hiding something?" Margaret asked. Margaret had known Reverend Locke the longest, and she found his recent behavior puzzling.

"I don't know. Maybe I just don't want to feel like such a slimeball for taking the letters."

"Maybe we should do a background check on him," Shelley said.

"I don't think I'd be comfortable with poking into his past," Beverly said slowly. "I mean, he is my pastor. I'm new at the church, but I'm trying to have a cordial relationship with him. So far, so good, but I wouldn't want to upset that."

"Beverly's right," Margaret said. "He's always been respected, and even liked, here in Marble Cove."

Diane sipped her coffee thoughtfully. "Yes, and I'm sure the church's pulpit committee investigated him before they took him on as their pastor."

"But still, how can he be so sure there's no treasure?" Margaret asked. "I wonder if the old church records have anything to say about it."

Diane's eyebrows rose. "Could be. Maybe he knows something about the treasure and is trying to sidetrack us so we'll quit looking for it."

"For that matter," Shelley said, "maybe he's already found the treasure and wants to keep it for himself."

The others all laughed, and Shelley felt her cheeks flush. "Okay, so that's not likely. But I do wonder sometimes."

"Well, not to change the subject," Margaret said, "but I went to an art fair meeting in Port Clyde last night."

"How did that go?" Beverly asked quickly, and Shelley felt that she was glad for a new topic.

Margaret made a sour face. "Not too badly overall, but I did learn something that put me in my place."

"What are you talking about?" Diane asked, elbowing her lightly. "Your place? What does that mean?"

"It means I was second choice for the artists' ambassador post. They asked someone else first, and he turned them down. That's when they came to me."

"Aw, phooey," Shelley said. "That's nothing. Who was the other artist?"

"Blake Harris. He's very well known."

"So he's probably too busy," Diane said.

"Maybe he did the job in the past, so they asked him again, but he felt he couldn't do it this time," Beverly suggested.

"I'm not sure," Margaret said. "I just know it took the wind out of my sails, learning I wasn't first choice."

"But still," Shelley said, "a lot of artists are exhibiting, right?"

"Yes, more than forty."

"There you go. You were second out of forty-something. That's not so shabby." They all chuckled, and Margaret reached over to squeeze her hand. "Thank you, Shelley. That puts things in perspective."

Shelley glanced at the clock. "I'd better go over and see if Allan is tearing his hair out. I wouldn't want him to have a bad experience with the kids. Thanks, ladies. This was fun."

She hurried out the door and headed for the gallery. Poor Margaret. Shelley could tell from the extra lines on her face that she was still stressing over the art fair developments. Margaret was a wonderful artist, but she had moments of self-doubt. When other artists criticized her technique, she began to question her abilities and, in fact, her own worth.

"Mama!" Aiden ran toward her across Margaret's small office, his arms upraised.

"*Sh*." Adelaide put a finger to her lips and approached with Emma in her arms. "My dad has a customer."

"Oh, okay," Shelley whispered. "We'll sneak out the back. Thanks so much for watching them, Adelaide."

She grinned. "We had fun. Aiden made a picture." She turned and scooped a sheet of copy paper off the floor and held it out to her.

Shelley took it and gazed down at the mishmash of green and red scribbles. It might be a Christmas scene. Or not. She bent down and held it in front of Aiden.

"I like your colors, honey. What is it?"

"It's an astronaut on Mars."

"Oh, of course. I see it now." Shelley shared a smile with Adelaide over his head.

*   *   *

Beverly worked all morning after her trip to the Cove. She'd promised to have the newspaper ads ready to show the owners of the Sand Dollar by Wednesday. It took longer than she'd expected to resize her photographs and get the layout just right. She barely heard Mrs. Peabody come in and start bustling around the kitchen.

About noon, her father came into her office and stopped near her desk.

"I'm having lunch now, Beverly. Are you hungry?"

She looked up from her screen. "Oh, I guess I am. I'm not really at a good stopping place, though."

"Oh, come on. You've been sitting there for almost three hours."

She realized he was right and pushed her chair back. "Time for a break. All right, I'll be right with you."

She tried not to think about the job while they ate together, instead asking her father about his plans for gardening and letting him catch her up on the local news he'd heard via Mrs. Peabody.

After lunch, she went back to her desk, though she longed to take a run on the beach. She promised herself that treat when she was finished for the day.

She sent the ads by e-mail to Thomas Sloan, and then she opened the hotel software she'd downloaded and began to customize it for the Sand Dollar.

A knock on the front door snagged her attention an hour or so later.

"Beverly, can you get that?" her father called.

She glanced at the time in the corner of her screen. Mrs. Peabody must have gone home long ago, after her kitchen cleanup. Beverly didn't mind getting up to answer the door—she would probably benefit from moving around more frequently. But she hoped this interruption didn't turn into one of those hard-to-end conversations she sometimes got into with the neighbors, as much as she liked them.

She swung the door open to find Jeff standing on the porch, all six feet of him. He looked very dashing in his cargo pants, chambray shirt with button tabs on the sleeves, and dark glasses.

He gave her a tentative smile. "Hi. I'm heading out in the morning, and I wanted to say good-bye." He held up a small, square camera bag, "And I thought maybe we could snap that photo your dad wants."

"Oh. Well, come in." Beverly moved aside and put a hand up to her hair. She hadn't looked in a mirror since early this morning. She was glad to see Jeff, but she wished she'd had a little warning.

"Can I get you some coffee?" she asked, walking toward the kitchen.

"Well, I thought maybe we'd do the picture first. I admit I'd like one myself. I don't have one of you, and sometimes I get pretty lonesome when I'm off on a shoot."

Beverly grimaced. She hated having her picture taken, and the thought that Jeff might show it to someone else bothered her. "Could we wait on that? Maybe next time you're home. I've been working all day, and I'm sure I'm a mess."

"You look beautiful," Jeff said softly.

The wistfulness in his voice and expression twisted her heart. Why couldn't she just love him? But no. The very thought shortened her breath and made her feel queasy—or guilty, she wasn't sure which.

"I—I'd rather wait. If I have time to prepare for it, the photo will be much better."

Jeff sighed and set the camera bag on the counter. "All right. Next time. I'll call you first, so you can feel more prepared."

She could feel her cheeks flush. Jeff deserved someone better than her. Someone more demonstrative, more spontaneous. Some days she wondered why he even liked her—though she could think of several reasons why she liked him. His patience was one, but even Jeff might grow tired of waiting for her to respond to his overtures.

"Thank you," she said, and managed to smile. "How about that coffee?"

"Oh, no thanks." He looked at his watch. "I should probably get going. I still have a few things to pick up and pack."

She knew he'd have lingered if she hadn't refused to let him take her picture. Now he was as uncomfortable as she was and wanted to get away. But what could she say to change that?

"I thought I heard your voice, Jeff." Beverly's father stood in the doorway, smiling at their guest.

"I'm sorry," she said. "I ought to have told you. Jeff is going out on another expedition to the islands."

"Ah. Beautiful out there."

"Yes, sir," Jeff said.

"When will you be back?"

"Probably not until next week." Jeff glanced at Beverly. "Well, I'll get going then."

"I hope you have a good trip," she said.

He didn't reach toward her or ask her to walk out with him. Should she go anyway, at least as far as the porch? So much was still left unsaid between them.

"Thank you." He turned to go.

"Do let us know when you're back," she said, suddenly bereft. It wasn't at all what she ought to have said, or what she honestly would like to have said, but she couldn't come up with anything better without a great deal of thought—especially not with Father standing beside her.

Jeff waved and closed the door behind him.

Beverly let her shoulders slump.

"Aw, he'll be back soon," her father said, moving toward the coffeepot.

"I hope so," Beverly whispered.

Chapter Seven

Margaret spent Monday at the gallery, and when no customers were present, which was often, she went to the back room. She worked some on the canvas she would use for her next painting.

She planned to do a study of Marble Cove from near the shore, with the quaint buildings of the town peeping out from between the trees and Old First's steeple towering over the rest. It was a subject she'd wanted to paint for some time, and she thought a lot of folks would like that—folks who lived here especially. But would it be sophisticated enough for the art fair? The required debut piece should stand out. She needed to weigh each decision she made about her painting this month against that.

Several customers came in after lunch, and a married couple purchased one of Margaret's *giclée* prints. It was her first sale of the day, so that encouraged her a little. Traffic in the gallery and sales would pick up after Memorial Day, she knew. Her original paintings usually went to tourists with bigger budgets than the local folks had.

After an uninterrupted hour in her studio, Margaret laid down her brush and studied the beginnings of her painting.

It would come out well and would be a pleasant scene, but it would not be daring enough for her debut piece at the fair. She put her brush in a jar of water to clean off the acrylic paint and went to her desk. There was one friend who could understand her struggle as an artist—and who might be able to give her advice. She found Louellen Lumadue's number in her address file and punched in the numbers.

"Margaret! I'm so pleased to hear from you," Louellen said. "Tell me what you're doing this spring."

Louellen was quite well known for her art, and her vibrant use of color and theme had inspired Margaret in the early stages of her own career. In January, Margaret had the opportunity to meet Louellen and to encourage her during a difficult time in her own artistic journey.

"I've kept the gallery open, but I'm gearing up for the summer traffic. I expect to have a lot of new pieces come in over the next couple of weeks. Can you send me anything?"

"Yes, I think so. I've got a couple of paintings that might go well in your gallery. But what about your art? How is that coming?"

Margaret frowned. "I'm not exactly sure how to answer that. In some ways, it's going well. The Lighting the Way Greeting Card Company is still buying paintings regularly, and my prints are selling steadily. I'm going to exhibit at the Port Clyde Art Fair on Memorial Day weekend."

"Oh, that's a wonderful show," Louellen said. "You'll get a lot of exposure."

"Perhaps," Margaret said. "It's the first year I've been invited."

"It's quite an honor."

"Yes, I think so, and that's got me a little scared."

"Ah. I understand."

"I thought you might." Margaret sat back in her desk chair. "I'm flattered to be invited—they've even asked me to act as artists' ambassador—but I'm apprehensive about my work."

"You're afraid it's not good enough?"

"Well, yes." Margaret was slightly taken aback. "What do you think? Will I measure up? Some very prestigious artists take part in this show."

"Oh yes, I know. I exhibited there twice myself in years gone by. But what makes you think your work isn't good enough?"

"I don't know. I suppose I'm afraid the other artists—and critics—will feel it's only 'greeting card' quality—not fine art."

"That's ridiculous. Great masterpieces are made into greeting cards, and there's a reason for that. People *like* them."

Margaret chuckled. "Thank you. That does give a little perspective, I guess, but we both know I'm no Rembrandt."

"But you're very good," Louellen insisted. "You know me. Would I tell you this if it weren't true?"

"I've always known you to be painfully honest," Margaret said with a wry smile.

"I strive to be. You know, Margaret, you showed me a couple of pieces last winter that I felt had real depth and feeling in them—more so than those you usually put out. I'm not saying your lighthouses and seascapes aren't lovely—they are. But sometimes the artist reaches deep inside herself and finds something beyond the usual. You told me you'd tried some different techniques, and you found that inspiring."

"Yes. I'm not very confident when I do that, but it stretches me."

"Sometimes we have to go to a place where we're not comfortable to bring out real feeling in our work. Oh, I don't mean a physical place—you understand."

"I think so," Margaret said. "And for the past few months I've concentrated on putting out more of what Matt Beauregard wants, which is fine, as you say, but I haven't tried anything really ambitious—or risky—for quite some time now."

"That's it!" Louellen's voice rose in excitement. "Oh, Margaret, you are such an encouragement to me."

"I am?"

"I know you called me for a pep talk, my friend, but you've made me think about my own work too. I've been enjoying my painting so much more lately. But even so, just talking to you like this makes me want to try something new. Something challenging. Something that will touch my soul."

"That's what I need to do," Margaret said thoughtfully.

"Yes. Put new colors on your palette, my dear. Find a scene that speaks to your heart and let it flow onto your canvas. Look at your subject from a different angle of the mind. And try to express how it makes you feel, not just what you see."

"I think I will try that." Margaret smiled. "The worst I can do is produce a lousy painting, right?"

"And if that happens, start over from a new place."

"Yes. I'll try it. I have some traditional pieces I have to finish, but for my debut piece for the show, I think I'll at least try what you're saying. If it's not working—well, we'll see what happens."

"Good," Louellen said. "Let me know how it turns out."

Margaret hung up feeling refreshed and motivated. For her primary exhibit, she would start fresh, with no preconceived idea of the style she would use, and with a few unexpected colors on her palette. She wasn't sure she could find that elusive place her friend talked about, but she knew she would enjoy the search.

★   ★   ★

Diane walked along Main Street with Rocky on his leash. She didn't often take him downtown, because she couldn't take him into most of the shops. But she'd worked all morning on her book, and she needed to pick up a few things. Rocky had whined for a walk so pitifully that she'd decided to take him along instead of making him wait another hour alone at home.

She stopped at the Crow's Nest and left Rocky tied to a bench outside for ten minutes while she picked up a book she'd ordered and briefly browsed the shelf of new releases. After a visit to the Hermit Crab for a card to send Jessica and another stop at the post office, Diane headed home with the intent of popping in at the Shearwater Gallery, if it wasn't busy, to say hi to Margaret.

She opened the door and looked in. There didn't seem to be anyone in the main room, and soft jazz music played over the speaker.

"Margaret?" she called.

Margaret came to the doorway that led to the studio and broke into a warm smile. "Diane! Come on in."

"I've got Rocky, so I'd better not. Just wanted to say hi."

"Oh, bring him in the back. He's usually very well behaved."

If she only knew, Diane thought. But it was true that, while Rocky had occasional "moments," he would usually lie down quietly and wait for her if she told him to.

He looked around eagerly as they crossed the gallery, sniffing and panting a little.

"Easy, boy." Diane guided him into the next room.

Margaret sat down at the stool near her easel and waved toward her desk chair. "Have a seat."

"Thanks." Diane looked down at Rocky. "Lie down." The dog plunked down and rested his chin on his paws, gazing up at her with adoring brown eyes.

"Aw, that is so sweet," Margaret said. "He loves you."

Diane sat down. "He's really getting good about obeying my commands." She turned to the dog and crooned, "Rocky, you're such a good boy, aren't you!" Rocky's tail thumped rapidly and he rewarded her with a toothy canine smile.

"I'm so glad you have him. He seems like a wonderful companion for you."

Diane reached down and stroked Rocky's silky head. She'd found him, abandoned and injured, shortly after her move to Marble Cove. Now she couldn't imagine life without him.

"Are you getting ready for the art fair?" she asked.

"Trying." Margaret smiled. "How about you—how's the writing going?"

"Pretty well." Diane was chipping away at the rough draft of her second mystery. "I had to run a couple of errands, but I'll be back at the keyboard in a little while. You know, every time I come into town and see Old First, I think about that old bell tower. I wish the four of us could get up there."

Margaret gave a sheepish chuckle. "I'm starting a painting with the steeple as my focal point, and I was thinking the same thing. It would be nice to know if there's anything else up there that would shed light on the treasure stories."

"Well, maybe we can go in during the Founder's Day celebration, or while they're getting ready for that. You'd think the church members would want to know what's up there."

"I guess they're not as curious as you are."

Diane laughed. "Well, maybe Reverend Locke will be, now that he knows I found the letters up there. The celebration isn't until the end of June, so I guess I need to be patient. It's frustrating, though, not being able to investigate now."

"How does Beverly feel about it?" Margaret asked. "She seems not to want to rock the boat with Pastor Locke."

"That's true, and I don't want to upset her. She's such a dear. But she doesn't think we should ask him to let us up there again. He wasn't happy with us the first time."

"Still, the church doesn't belong to Silas Locke," Margaret said, arching her eyebrows.

"True. But it's not fair to put Beverly in the middle of this, when she's the only one of us who attends church there and she's uncomfortable with the situation. It's probably better to let it alone for a while."

"I suppose so," Margaret said. "We're all busy anyway. Shelley and Beverly both have demanding businesses, and you and I are up to our necks in our new ventures."

"Speaking of which, I'd better leave you to yours and get back to mine." Diane stood and wiggled the leash. Rocky bounded to his feet.

"If it will ease things along, I'll go with you to ask Pastor Locke when the time comes," Margaret said. "That way, if he refuses, he won't associate the request with Beverly."

"Thanks." The front door of the gallery opened, ringing a bell that hung on it. "Sounds like you have a customer," Diane said. "Rocky and I will slip out the back door."

★   ★   ★

Beverly had a hard time concentrating on her work Monday. She placed a few phone calls to new contacts but couldn't settle down to work on the computer. After trying for most of the morning, she gave up. Lunchtime was nearly upon her, and she could smell something good wafting up from below. Mrs. Peabody must be nearly ready to feed them.

She went downstairs and walked to the library door. Her father looked up at her.

"How are you doing?" she asked.

"Pretty well," he said, laying his book aside. "I could use a glass of water."

"I'll get it." Beverly strode to the kitchen. Mrs. Peabody glanced at her and gave a curt nod. Beverly walked to the counter and opened an upper cupboard door. As she reached for a glass, an object on the counter next to the toaster caught her eye.

"Oh!"

Mrs. Peabody pivoted. "What?"

Beverly touched the black case. "Jeff must have left his camera bag here." How could she not have noticed it yesterday, or even this morning when she got breakfast?

"Is that what that is? I thought it was something of yours."

"No, it's Jeff Mackenzie's." Beverly didn't have Jeff's number memorized, so she carried the camera bag up to her office, where she got her cell phone from her purse and scrolled to Jeff's listing. She heard four rings, and then the call went to his voice mail.

"Hi," she said a bit shakily. "It's Beverly. You left your camera bag. I'm not sure if you need it or not, but... Well, it's here."

She closed the phone. Why did she sound so businesslike, so cold, in her message? Why couldn't she put a little warmth in her voice? Any other woman could have. No wonder he'd been so glum when he left. Had she driven him away for good?

She sighed and hurried back down the stairs.

"Whatcha doin'?" her father called.

She stepped into the library. "Sorry. I had to run back upstairs. One glass of water, coming right up."

*   *   *

Shelley scrambled around the kitchen Tuesday morning, attempting to pack Dan's lunch, fix Aiden's cereal, and tend a pan of scrambled eggs and sausage all at once. Sometimes the early morning routine was chaotic. So far she was holding her own, but then, Emma wasn't up yet. That in itself had given her an advantage.

Even as the thought hit her, Emma's chatter came over the baby monitor. Shelley turned to the check the eggs.

"Mama, I need more milk," Aiden said.

"Just a second, hon." She got the milk jug from the refrigerator and added a generous dollop to his bowl of cereal. Glancing regretfully toward the counter, where she had the sandwich makings spread out, she sighed. Dan's lunch would have to wait a few minutes.

She was about to head for Emma's room when she stopped in her tracks. Over the baby monitor came Dan's deep voice, low and coaxing.

"Hey, little girl, what's the matter? You want to get up?"

Shelley smiled. Hooray for Daddy! She would let Dan handle getting Emma up while she finished putting his sandwich together.

Five minutes later, Dan entered the kitchen with Emma tucked against his chest with one arm. With his other hand, he held his phone to his ear.

"Yeah, that's great," he said into the phone as Shelley heaped a plate with eggs and sausage and slid a blueberry muffin in on the side. "Thanks a lot."

Dan laid his phone on the table and plopped Emma into her booster seat. "This little lady is hungry, Mama."

Shelley bent down and smiled at Emma as she buckled her in. "Good morning! What do you want for breakfast, Emma? Want some scrambled eggs?"

"I want eggs," Aiden said petulantly.

"You'll get some, don't worry." Shelley straightened and sprinkled a few pieces of dry cereal on Emma's tray.

Dan had sat down and was reaching for the butter dish.

"Coffee?" Shelley asked.

He glanced up at her. "I can get it."

"That would help me a lot." She opened the dishwasher to grab a plastic bowl for Emma.

"That was Phil Caswell on the phone," Dan said.

"Oh? What did he want?" Shelley had met Dan's high school friend several times, but she didn't know him well.

"He says we can use his and Mindy's cabin next weekend if we want."

Shelley froze and stared at him. "A cabin? Next weekend?"

"Yeah." Dan gave her a lopsided grin and stood with his coffee mug in his hand. "As in our anniversary weekend. What do you think?"

"Wow. Do we have to pay?"

"Nope. It's free."

Shelley huffed out a breath. "I don't know what to say. It sounds great."

"Doesn't it? It's on a lake, and he's got a boat there in case we want to putter around or fish or something. He said there are dishes and all of that stuff. Sheets and towels too. And there's a fireplace we can use if we get cold."

"Ma-ma-ma," Emma squawked, reaching toward Shelley.

She looked down at the bowl in her hand. "Oh, you want your eggs, don't you?"

"Me too," Aiden said. "Daddy, can I go in the boat?"

Dan's smile faded. "Oh, I don't think so, buddy. Not this time. I think this is just for Mama and me." He looked questioningly at Shelley.

She opened her mouth and closed it again. The thought of a weekend alone with Dan was too good to be true. And yet it would be hard to leave the kids behind. Who would they stay with? Dan's mother would probably jump at the chance to have them overnight, but Shelley wasn't sure she could bring herself to leave them with Frances again for that long. A few weeks ago, they'd left the kids overnight at Dan's parents, and Frances had cut Aiden's hair very short without asking first. Shelley wasn't sure if she was ready to trust her just yet.

Dan poured his mug full of coffee and went back to the table. "I've got to tell you, I asked Phil about this a week ago, and I've been waiting for him to get back to me. He wasn't sure what weekend he and his wife were going up there. So when you mentioned our anniversary, I almost spoiled the surprise."

Shelley laughed and tousled his hair. "You did great keeping it a secret." She put some scrambled eggs in Emma's bowl and chopped them into small pieces with the spatula.

"So what do you think?" Dan asked.

"I'm overwhelmed. And happy. I'm sorry I thought you didn't care about our anniversary." She put the bowl on Emma's tray and got a plate for Aiden.

"Well, think about it and let me know," Dan told her. "I should probably call Phil back by tonight and finalize it. I know you can't leave your business for long, but if you can set it up with that other baker I figure we can go for two nights. Couldn't the Cakery lady substitute for you?"

"Yeah, Liza Cramble," Shelley said, putting Aiden's sausage and eggs down in front of him. "I'm sure I can work something out. I'll call her this morning." She grinned at Dan.

"And Mom?"

"Why not?" She would wait until the kids were napping before she talked to Frances, though. Shelley sent up a quick prayer for serenity. Maybe this would really work, and they'd finally have some time off together.

CHAPTER EIGHT

Margaret walked along the outside of the cemetery fence, looking for the best place to set up her easel. She soon decided she was too close to the church. The little park across the street was better, but there was still too much of the twenty-first century in her view—telephone cables and traffic signs. She wanted to paint a view of the town that was timeless.

Her cell phone rang. She was tempted to ignore it, but her conscientious nature wouldn't allow it.

"Hello?"

"Ms. Hoskins?"

"Yes," Margaret said.

"This is Barry Towers. I'm an exhibitor for the Port Clyde Art Fair. I was told that you're the one to call when we have glitches."

"Oh. Well, if I can help you, I certainly will."

Barry explained that he'd had unexpected surgery over the weekend. While he hoped to be well enough to attend the art fair, he wanted to cover all his bases.

"So, if I'm not up to it, could my wife bring my paintings and set up for me? I hope to be there all three days, but

I may be limited in my activity, and it might just be too much for me to set up and sit outside all day."

"Oh, of course," Margaret said. "In fact, we've got several high school students who will be helping out. On Saturday they'll be there to assist with the setup. They can carry artwork and help put up tables and booths, that sort of thing."

Their conversation soon ended, and Margaret sensed satisfaction on both sides. Barry would have the assistance he needed, and she had been useful to one of the other artists. She would make a special point of ensuring that Mr. and Mrs. Towers were greeted on opening day and that their setup went smoothly.

She pushed the little cart that held her art supplies down the sidewalk, toward the shore, until she could barely see Old First's stone walls through the foliage of the maples around it. The steeple rose, tapering toward the clouds, dominating the panorama.

Perfect.

She set down her paint box and canvas and unfolded the easel's legs. The afternoon had turned out quite warm for early May, and she was glad. This, in her opinion, was the best time of year in Maine. The annoying insects weren't out yet, and neither were the tourists. Though she appreciated the prosperity the "summer people" brought to Marble Cove and the rest of the Maine coast, she did enjoy these more peaceful times when the residents could enjoy their beautiful home without fighting for elbow room.

The leaves on the maples and birches were still a fresh, yellowy green, and on some of the maples the winged seeds still hung in thick clusters. On a windy day, they would work free and whirl to earth like miniature helicopters coming in for a landing.

She set her canvas in place and positioned her camp stool. When she sat down, her vista changed subtly, and she frowned. Maybe she would have to stand to capture the steeple at just the angle she wanted.

The next hour flew as she made a sketch of her composition and roughed in the principal lines on her canvas. As she began to apply layers of paint for the tree trunks, her old doubts resurfaced. Even if this painting came out exactly as she hoped, she didn't feel that it would be her primary piece for the art fair. She still didn't know what that artwork would portray, and she had to figure that out soon. With only a little more than three weeks left, she was starting to feel pressured—about the special painting, and about the ambassador's position.

A call from Rosalyn Neely that morning had told her they now had fifty exhibitors, and a few more seemed to be added each day. Where were they all coming from? And why hadn't they signed up earlier? She'd thought the registration would have been closed by now. That many artists could run her ragged when the fair weekend came.

She remembered Louellen's words. Even though this wasn't an experimental painting, maybe she should give her feelings a little freer rein with it. She gazed up at the steeple.

How did the sight of this marvelous old building make her feel? Part of the church was more than two hundred years old. There was something comforting about that. She liked knowing she could walk where people had walked more than two centuries ago, and that she could touch the same stones and boards and hardware that Jeremiah Thorpe had touched.

She began to fill in the foliage on the trees around the steeple, making the leaves a bit hazy and surreal. She would portray the steeple itself and the part of the church's stone wall that was visible very precisely, but she would let the scene around it blur a little.

"My, that's going to be lovely," a strong feminine voice said from directly behind her.

Margaret turned on her stool. "Oh, Maddie. I didn't hear you. Do you really think so?"

Madeline Bancroft, the superhousewife who made women like Shelley feel inferior, eyed the canvas critically and nodded. "I do. Of course, you're just beginning, and I can tell it's still a bit rough, but I think I can already see how it will shape up."

Margaret smiled at the way she hedged on her compliment. "Well, thank you. Beautiful day, isn't it?"

"Gorgeous," Maddie said, "though I don't dare to put my garden in quite yet. The weatherman says we could still get a frost."

"Well, I'm going to soak up all the sunshine I can." Margaret started to turn back to her easel and paused. "Aren't you chairing the Founder's Day committee?"

"Yes, with Frances Bauer. It's going to be a wonderful tribute to the church's founder and Old First's contribution to the town over the years. I'm going to the church now to meet with Frances. We need to decide where to place the exhibits."

"Do you think you'll have a lot?" Margaret asked.

"I do. We've asked everyone to bring in anything related to the church's past, and some very exciting items have come in." Maddie's eyes sparkled. "Lila Compton's granddaughter dropped off a box yesterday. I can't wait to see what's in it."

"That sounds interesting."

Margaret's mind raced. Maybe she could talk Beverly or Diane into volunteering to help with the exhibits. She itched to offer herself, but she had too much to do this month already.

"Are you taking volunteers?"

"We sure are. As more material comes in, we'll need lots of help." Maddie gave a little wave. "I'd better get over to the church. Can't be late for anything where Frances is concerned."

Margaret picked up her brush with a lighter heart. Her friends would be tickled to hear about this.

★   ★   ★

Victoria Manchester's call caught Beverly at her desk, where she was working on the registry program for the Sand Dollar.

"I want to offer a discounted package at the Landmark for the month of June," Victoria said. "Dinner, an overnight stay, and breakfast. What do you think?"

Beverly pictured the gorgeous ocean view from the porch of the rambling shorefront hotel, and the guest rooms Victoria had redecorated in a charming country style. "If you price it right, that should draw in some new customers to the Landmark."

"Well, that's my problem," Victoria said. "As usual, I'm not sure where to begin with the pricing. It needs to be a bit of a discount from buying the components separately, but not so much that I lose money."

"True, but if you only break even, you might come out ahead in the long run, since you'll gain new customers and get some word-of-mouth advertising out of it."

Victoria laughed. "New Landmark lovers. That's what I want."

"Okay," Beverly said. "How are things going in the kitchen now?"

"Beautifully. I hired more staff, and Louis has gotten the buying down to a science."

"Good," Beverly said. It sounded like an improvement over the chaos she'd seen on Valentine's Day. "I'll look at the prices you're offering on a regular basis and crunch some numbers for you to see how much you can shave off for the special package. I'll get back to you later today, all right?"

"Fantastic," Victoria said. "That would give me plenty of time to get ads to the radio stations and the *Press Herald* and the *Boston Globe.*"

Beverly loved her enthusiasm, but sometimes her client's ideas weren't cost-effective. She was glad to see that Victoria was thinking this one through before jumping in.

She finished the section of the program she was working on for the Sand Dollar and found a good place to break off for a few hours. A cup of coffee would brace her before she dived into Victoria's request. She got up and went to the library doorway. Her father was sitting in his recliner, reading.

"How's the book?" Beverly asked.

"Very good. This author documents everything. You don't have to read the footnotes, but I find them fascinating. I had no idea there was so much out there on the Popham Colony."

Beverly smiled. Her father had been an excellent teacher, but he was an even better learner. Even now, he delighted in learning new things about history, especially Maine's, and she couldn't help catching some of that eagerness. She supposed she had him to blame for her love of antiques.

"Wasn't it earlier than Jamestown?" she asked.

"No, the same year—1607. Too bad the colony failed."

"I guess they weren't prepared for our winters."

"You got that right. Thanks to the jet stream, our winters are harsher than England's, even though we're a little farther south than they are."

She smiled. "Well, I'm glad I live now, not in the 1600s. I'm getting some coffee. Can I bring you some?"

"Thanks, that would be nice."

She went to the kitchen and had just poured two mugs full when the back door opened and Mrs. Peabody came in.

"Good morning," Beverly said with a smile.

"Well, hello, Beverly. It *is* a good morning. I hope the sun stays with us all week." Mrs. Peabody took off her jacket and hung it on a hook near the back door. She eyed Beverly soberly. "I'll be fixing whole wheat macaroni and cheese today, with fruit salad and steamed broccoli."

"Sounds lovely. Your macaroni is one of our favorites." Beverly knew a hint when she saw it—Mrs. Peabody was saying she wanted the kitchen to herself for the next couple of hours. "I'll be at my desk if you need anything."

Mrs. Peabody sniffed, as if she'd ever need to ask for assistance. "What are *you* working on today?"

"A new promotion at the Landmark Inn for Victoria Manchester."

"Oh. I haven't eaten there since she took it over. They say the food is good." The elderly woman sounded a bit dubious.

"I have, and it is. She has a very good chef working the dinner shift." Beverly picked up the mugs. "Oh, I meant to tell you, on Saturday I'll be going to Augusta. Diane Spencer is having a big book signing up there. I wanted to make sure you'd be available to fix Father's lunch that day."

Mrs. Peabody frowned. "Augusta, huh? I haven't been up there in ages."

Beverly thought she knew when her last jaunt had taken place—the previous August, she and her father had taken Mrs. Peabody and her sister up there to meet Edward Maker. Was she hinting that she'd like to go again? Beverly hesitated, and thought, *Why not?*

"Would you like to ride up there with me?"

"What? All the way to Augusta?"

"Yes." Beverly smiled at her. "I'm going to support Diane. She probably won't see many people she knows up there. We could stop in at the bookstore and then have lunch together—my treat."

Mrs. Peabody blinked and brushed her hands down the front of her apron. "Why, you wouldn't have to pay for my dinner, Beverly."

"I'd like to. We could have 'Girls' Day Out.' What do you say? It would be fun."

"Well...sure. Might be nice to drive by the capitol and the Blaine House again."

"We could do that," Beverly said—not that she needed to see her old workplace again, but she would be happy to oblige Mrs. Peabody.

"But you said your father's not going."

"No. I asked him, but he wasn't crazy about the long drive. He went to Diane's launch party at the Crow's Nest a couple of weeks ago, and he decided to bow out on this one."

"What about his lunch?"

Beverly did some quick thinking. "We can leave it for him, or I could ask somebody to bring something over."

"I'll fix it," Mrs. Peabody said firmly. "Uh...he'll be all right alone for that long?"

"Sure he will, but we can call and check in on him," Beverly said.

"All right, that's settled then." Mrs. Peabody nodded and opened a cupboard door.

Beverly felt she'd been dismissed. She carried the mugs to the library and gave one to her father, then went upstairs to her desk. She pulled up Victoria's files for her menus, brochures, and pricing schedules. With a little online research and a call to the wholesale seafood supplier Victoria bought from, she was able to arrive at some cost estimates for the meals her friend would offer in the package deal. She called Victoria for approval and then began laying out a print ad for the newspapers. She smiled, musing that she'd never dreamed that starting a business consulting firm would reveal a knack for graphic design and copywriting too.

She'd just finished the rough draft for a radio spot announcement when Mrs. Peabody came to call her for lunch.

Beverly rose and stretched. She could print out the ads after she ate, to make sure they looked right in print. Then she'd have to e-mail them to Victoria, and if she liked them, Beverly would send them off to the papers and call the radio stations. She loved this new work and the feeling that she was helping small business owners on a personal level.

As she turned away, her gaze fell on Jeff's camera bag, which she'd left on top of her printer. She'd meant to try to call him again this morning. Risking Mrs. Peabody's wrath for taking another minute before reporting to the dining room, she called Jeff's phone number. As before, it rang, then went to voice mail. She didn't wait for the beep but hung up without leaving another message. Sooner or later, he'd get the one she left yesterday and call her back.

Chapter Nine

The Shearwater Gallery was a whirlwind of activity on Thursday morning. Several customers came in, and though Margaret tried to keep the crates of new stock she was unpacking confined to the back room, that wasn't always possible. Adelaide had come along to help for a while, and she happily helped clear away the packaging materials.

Around ten o'clock, just after Allan had come to get Adelaide to take her to the community center, Diane breezed in with an offer to help out.

"Bless your heart," Margaret said. "I actually had a bit of a rush this morning and I'm still trying to get new items out on display. Bernadette Lassiter is bringing me a new batch of her jewelry any minute, and I need to set up the spinner display Allan made for it."

"Let me help you carry out anything you need, and then you go ahead and work," Diane said. "I'll make a new pot of coffee and wait on anyone who comes in while you put things right."

"That sounds wonderful." Margaret showed her the boxes she needed to take into the front part of the gallery. As she situated the new walnut display for the jewelry exhibit on one end of the counter, the bell on the door chimed. Bernadette and another woman entered carrying several small boxes.

"Hello." Margaret straightened and turned to greet them. "Bernadette, I'm so glad you brought in some new pieces. I can barely keep your jewelry in stock, and I know it will do well with the summer crowd."

"Thank you." Bernadette was a young artist who lived in the community, and today she was wearing a gauzy off-the-shoulder top and a long batik skirt, with myriad rings and a long strand of colorful beads. The woman with her was dressed in neat navy pants and a bulky knit sweater.

"This is my sister-in-law, Angela," Bernadette said. "She offered to help me bring everything in. I think we got it all in one load."

Margaret smiled at Angela. "Thanks for helping."

"No problem." Angela, who looked several years older than Bernadette, glanced around the gallery. "This is the first time I've been here. Bernadette's been telling me about it. May I look around?"

"Of course." Margaret gestured to Diane. "My friend Diane Spencer can answer any questions you have while Bernadette and I get her new pieces cataloged."

Diane smiled. "I'd be happy to. And I was just going to make fresh coffee. Angela, why don't you look around? I'll be right over there by the refreshment table if you need me."

Bernadette leaned toward Margaret and whispered, "She's down from Bangor. I knew she'd like your style."

Margaret took that to mean that Angela did not particularly like Bernadette's style of painting, which was much more modern and fluid than Margaret's. When Bernadette had first approached her, Margaret had declined to carry her paintings in the Shearwater because they didn't blend with the other artwork she offered. But the young woman's jewelry was another story since it complemented the coastal art Margaret featured.

Bernadette opened a rectangular, flat white box on the counter. "I can't wait to show you this new line. I got started about six weeks ago, and I couldn't stop. I'm calling these Bernadette's Ocean Drops."

Margaret stared down at the lovely array of opaque green, blue, and amber lumps strung together to make necklaces and bracelets. Some were interspersed with shells, and others had metallic or carved wooden beads between the dull, glassy stones.

"They're beautiful!" She reached out a hand to lift one of the necklaces and study the green pieces. "It's beach glass."

"Yes." Bernadette was so excited, she gave a little hop. "I had quite a bit that I'd found and saved, but once I got going on these, I had to buy more. And I had to find someone who could drill holes in them for me, but I think they came out rather well. Don't you adore them?"

"I do." Each piece of colored glass had tumbled in the waves until the sand smoothed it into an irregular but beautiful lump, as lovely in Margaret's mind as any cut gem. "And the colors are perfect for our setting." Her gaze flickered over the water and earth hues Bernadette had used in her creations.

"I'm so glad you like them. All of the bracelets are elasticized."

Bernadette had brought a list of all the new pieces, and they spent the next half hour pricing the jewelry and setting out about half of what she'd brought.

"I'll keep the rest in the storage room," Margaret said. "Thank you so much for bringing these to me."

"Isn't she the most creative person you ever saw?" Angela asked.

Margaret looked up quickly, realizing she'd hardly given Bernadette's sister-in-law another thought once she'd seen the new jewelry.

Diane stood next to Angela, smiling and holding one of Margaret's framed giclée prints. "Angela wants to buy one of your prints, Margaret. Shall I go ahead and wrap it?"

"Oh yes, by all means," Margaret said. "I'll come ring it up."

"Thanks." Angela held out a small blue pottery bowl. "I can't leave this on the shelf, either. It's just too cute."

Margaret went to the counter, pleased to have a nice sale that morning. While she and Diane worked, two more people entered the gallery and began to browse.

Before long, Bernadette and Angela were heading out the door and Diane grinned at Margaret. "Do you want to wait on the next customers, or are you ready for coffee?"

"I'd love a cup," Margaret said.

Diane had hardly put a mug in her hand when Margaret's phone rang.

"Hello, Margaret," came Matt Beauregard's cheery voice. "Just wondered when I can pick up the next four paintings."

"Well, three are ready, but I still need to do another session or two on the last one. But I was wondering if you could possibly wait and pick them up after Memorial Day weekend."

"Oh? *Hmm*, let me check our production schedule. I was hoping to get them this week."

"If you have to, I'll understand," Margaret said. "It's just that I've been asked to exhibit at least eight paintings at the Port Clyde Art Fair, and if your four are gone, that will leave my gallery very bare for the weekend. You know what Memorial Day weekend means to the tourist trade."

"Of course. I suppose I could get them on Tuesday after the holiday, but no later."

Margaret let out her breath in relief. "Thank you so much. I guarantee they'll be wrapped and ready for you that morning."

Matt chuckled. "You're our best seller this season, Margaret. Our card with your *Safe Harbor* painting on it is breaking sales records. The whole line is doing well, though."

"That's great news. I'm proud to be working with you."

"The honor's mine, Margaret. Is one of the new paintings by any chance similar in theme? I was thinking of doing a new sympathy card with one of your lighthouses, but of course, it has to have the right feel to it."

"Oh. Well..." Margaret mentally ran through the lineup she would deliver to him in this batch. "There's one that may be suitable for that, but you'll have to see them to decide."

"Yes."

His voice was a bit wistful, and Margaret felt guilty for asking him to wait.

"I'll tell you what, Matt. I'll take some pictures with my digital camera. That way I can e-mail them to you so you can see what I've got."

"That would help me a lot. Thanks, Margaret."

She hung up feeling more stressed than she had before.

The browsers were going out the door empty-handed. Diane came over with a gentle smile.

"Everything all right?"

"Yes. Matt's going to let me keep his four new paintings for the show, but I need to send him photos as soon as possible." She grabbed the notepad she kept on the counter. "One more thing to do. I'd better speak to Allan about it. Oh, and Maddie Bancroft called me and invited me to go over to Old First this evening to help unpack items that have come in for the Founder's Day displays, but I don't see how I'll have time. Beverly was going with me. I'd better call her and tell her I just can't make it."

"I could go with Beverly," Diane said.

"Could you? I hate to back out on that, but with so much going on here and my preparations for the art fair—"

"I'm sure Maddie will understand if you send a substitute. And I'd love to see what people are sending in about the church's history."

"Bless you," Margaret said.

The door opened, and Shelley maneuvered Emma's stroller through the doorway. "Hello, Diane. Hello, Margaret!"

"Miss Diane!" Aiden ran to Diane, who bent to return his greeting.

"Hello, Aiden! What do you have there?"

"My truck." He held up the small toy so Diane could admire it.

"And I brought a snack," Shelley said. She handed Margaret a small bakery bag and stooped to unbuckle Emma. "Oh, she's sleeping."

"Better leave her alone," Margaret said.

"No, if I do, she won't nap this afternoon." Shelley undid the harness and lifted the little girl out. Emma blinked and burrowed her face into Shelley's collarbone with a whimper.

Margaret opened the bag and passed out cookies. "I've got my coffee. Will you ladies join me?"

Since there were no customers at the moment, they settled in the back room.

"I can't stay long," Shelley said. "I wanted to tell you what Dan did."

Diane eyed her cautiously. "Good or bad?"

"Good. Great, in fact. He's arranged a weekend getaway for our anniversary. A friend is lending us his lakefront cottage."

"That's fantastic," Margaret said.

Diane nodded. "Very classy. You two need a break."

"Yeah, but..." Shelley frowned.

"What's the matter?" Diane asked. "This is a good thing, right?"

"Yes. I've got someone to cover for me on baking for the Cove. I'm looking forward to getting away. It's just that I'm—" Shelley glanced around to see where Aiden was. He had wandered a few steps away and was running his toy truck over the wide boards of the old building's floor. "I'm not sure I'm ready to leave the kids with Dan's mom for that long," she whispered.

"Oh." Margaret nodded. She'd gone through similar feelings over the years when it came to finding short-term care for Adelaide. "I understand, but I would think Frances would take very good care of them."

"She would." Shelley scrunched up her face. "The last time we left them overnight, she cut Aiden's hair—something that didn't sit too well with me—but we've gotten past that. It's just…I can't explain it, really. She always makes me feel so…like a bad mother. And the kids love going to her house, but after they've been there an hour or two, that's enough and they want to come home. Another overnight would probably be stressful for them. And Dan wants to go for *two* nights."

"I'm sure it would be good for both of you," Diane said.

"So am I." Margaret squeezed Shelley's arm. "Maybe you need to take a chance. The kids might surprise you."

"Maybe," Shelley said. "Frances is really busy right now, anyway. She's cochairing the Founder's Day committee, you know, with Maddie Bancroft."

"Yes," Diane said. "In fact, I'm going to try to go over to Old First with Beverly tonight to help go through things for the exhibits."

"Great. Maybe you'll learn something about the treasure."

"Wouldn't that be something?" Diane's conspiratorial smile made her look as young and eager as Shelley.

"Anyway," Shelley went on, "Frances is quite preoccupied with all her lists of things they need to do to get ready. I'm not sure this is the best time to trouble her with the kids."

"If you feel very strongly about it, maybe you could cut it back to one night," Margaret said.

"I guess I should talk to Dan about it."

"Absolutely," Diane said. "He might have some ideas, and I'm sure he wants to know how you feel."

"Aiden," Shelley called, "don't run your truck on the wall."

The little boy looked around at the sound of his name. He left his truck on the floor and walked over to Diane, shoving his hand into the pocket of his pint-sized jeans.

"Look, Miss Diane." He held up a good-sized periwinkle shell.

"Oh, that's a pretty one." Diane took it and held it toward the light for a moment, then handed it to Margaret.

She peered at it. "Oh yes. I love the brownish stripe on the white."

Aiden grinned up at her. "You can have it."

"I can? Why, thank you," Margaret said. "Did you get it on the beach?"

Aiden nodded, smiling.

"We went down there earlier. I'm trying to tucker them out for their naps," Shelley said.

"I saw a starfish too." Aiden gazed up at Margaret. "But Mama wouldn't let me have it."

Shelley smiled sheepishly. "It was in a little tide pool. I don't like him to take things like that when they're obviously alive. Guess I'm too tenderhearted."

"Well, shells are different," Margaret said. "The critter's usually done with it by the time you pick it up off the sand."

"You're right. And you can't actually *see* the animal." Shelley looked at her watch. "We'd better get going. Margaret, I know you're going to do a great job on those paintings for the art fair. You always get the mood of the scene just right."

"Yes, you do," Diane said. "And if you want to try something new, just relax and go for it. You have enough of your regular-style pieces to use if it doesn't turn out well, but if it does, you might have a new masterpiece."

Margaret looked down at the shell in her hand and turned it over. "Thank you. You're both good friends. You make me feel almost competent."

They all laughed.

Diane said, "Shelley, let me help you with the stroller."

While they bundled the children out the door, Margaret went back to her desk. She'd unpacked all the new merchandise to display, and the gallery looked well stocked at the moment. Louellen's paintings hadn't arrived yet, but if they came before Memorial Day weekend, they should have plenty of pieces to hang here while she went AWOL with her eight for the fair.

She fingered the white and brown shell and set it beside her laptop. In her mind, she could see Aiden splashing into the tide pool to capture the hapless starfish, squealing when he felt its rough body move in his hand.

Maybe she would include some wildlife in her premier painting for the show. Some of her landscapes incorporated birds, and a few had pictured marine mammals breaching, but what if she tried to see the beach from Aiden's point of view?

Diane bustled back in and shut the door firmly. "There. What else can I do for you?"

Margaret stood and smiled. "I honestly think I'm all set for a while. Thank you so much." She gave Diane a hug.

"You ought to paint this afternoon," Diane said.

"Do you think so?" Margaret considered the possibility. Allan would be here soon to stay at the gallery while she went home for lunch. It was possible he'd stay a couple hours afterward. Adelaide would be at the community center most of the afternoon. Maybe she could finish Matt's fourth painting, and work some more on the one of Old First. Or maybe she'd do some sketching and let the beach ideas Aiden had inspired flow. She could do that here in her studio, even if Allan couldn't give her time to walk down to the shore. "I think I'll try to work it out so I can do that."

"Well, you deserve a break from the gallery," Diane said.

"I don't know about that, but I do know it's good to dive in when the inspiration hits, and today I feel pretty good."

"Attagirl." Diane picked up her purse and headed for the back door. "I know I'm going to dive into my book this afternoon. We'll both strike while the iron's hot."

Margaret watched her go and then hurried into her studio. Her friends had propped up her spirits. It was in moments when she was alone that her confidence fled. Well, she wasn't going to sit around and let that happen today. She would pack up her cart so she'd be ready to go outside and paint if Allan could cover for her, and then she'd lay out her sketching materials for roughing out ideas at her desk. One way or another, she would get some time in to paint today.

CHAPTER TEN

While the children had their afternoon naps, Shelley phoned Liza Cramble, owner of the Cakery. Liza was glad to bake for the Cove on Shelley's anniversary weekend, and she asked Shelley if she could bake six pies and a carrot cake the first Saturday in June for a restaurant the Cakery supplied. Pleased that they'd reached a mutually beneficial tradeoff, Shelley gathered her courage to call her mother-in-law.

No one answered Frances' home phone, so Shelley called her cell phone.

"Hi, Shelley," her mother-in-law said. "What's up?"

Shelley could hear background noise, and she wondered if she'd chosen a bad time to try to reach Frances. "Should I call you back? I was just going to ask about maybe having you watch the kids—"

"When? I'm in Rockland right now. Decided to stock up on groceries and paper products today."

"Oh, not now," Shelley said. "It'll be a couple of weeks from now. Dan and I want to get away for our anniversary if we can."

"You know I'm always happy to take the children," Frances said.

"Yes, you've been very generous that way." Shelley gulped. "We can talk about it later if you want, but—uh—"

"Mama!"

She whirled around. Aiden stood in the kitchen doorway, trailing behind him the towel he used for a superhero cape. Shelley held up a finger to him, indicating he should wait until she got off the phone.

"Oh, Frances, Aiden just got up from his nap."

"Really? It's early, isn't it?"

"Well, yes. He's growing right up on us." Shelley wasn't even sure he'd actually gone to sleep. It was getting harder to keep him on the nap schedule, and she supposed he'd give it up entirely soon. "Anyway, why don't you call me later about this, when you're home and—"

"So are you just planning to go out to dinner?" Frances asked.

"No, Dan's friend has offered us his cabin for the weekend, and—" Shelley glanced at Aiden. His eyes were huge, and his mouth hung wide open. He hadn't caught on to the extent of their plans before, as she'd hoped he wouldn't, but now he'd obviously caught the word "cabin." She turned away. "Uh, Frances, I need to go, but let's talk about this later, all right?"

"Okay," her mother-in-law said.

"Thanks. Bye." Shelley hung up before Frances could say another word and turned to face her son. "So, big guy, you haven't been to sleep, have you?"

Aiden padded over to her in his bare feet. "We have a cabin?"

"No, no, honey. I was just telling Meemaw that Daddy has a *friend* who has a cabin, and he—"

"And we're going there?" Aiden's blue eyes shone with anticipation.

Shelley winced. "Well, no, not exactly." A distraction was definitely in order until she could think things through. "So, would you like to color a picture?"

"No. I want to play camping."

"Camping?"

"At the cabin."

"Oh." Shelley sighed. "All right, you can use two blankets off your bed to make a pup tent. But you have to be quiet, okay? I don't want you to wake Emma up. She needs her nap."

Aiden nodded solemnly. "'Cause she's a baby."

"No, she's a toddler now, but she still needs her rest."

"Can Prize go in my tent?"

Shelley smiled. "Of course. It's a pup tent."

Aiden giggled. "Will you come see it?"

"Yes, I'll come in a few minutes. Don't yell for me, okay? *Sh.*" She put her finger to her lips.

Aiden nodded and trotted off toward his room.

Now what am I going to do? Shelley wondered. Why couldn't Aiden have gotten excited about going to Meemaw's instead of the whole cabin thing? Maybe that was how they should approach it—tell him how he and Emma would have a special weekend with their grandparents. Maybe then he wouldn't be too disappointed, especially if she enlisted Dan's father to do something special with the kids that Saturday.

But Aiden would still be disappointed that he wasn't going with them. She decided she'd better pray about it and talk to Dan before she went any further with the planning.

She stayed busy for the rest of the afternoon, taking the children to the beach for a while and then doing a little housework and laundry while they played in the living room. She put Emma in the playpen while she started cooking supper and let Aiden take Prize into his room again. Although she'd hoped he would forget about the cabin, he wanted to play camping again, and she had a feeling he wouldn't let it go.

Dan arrived home about six o'clock. She'd given up waiting and fed the kids a half hour earlier. When Aiden heard the truck drive in, he ran to the door and opened it.

"Daddy! Daddy!"

Dan swung him up in his arms and came to the kitchen carrying Aiden and his lunch box. "Hey, buddy! What are you so excited about?"

"I want to go camping at the cabin," Aiden shouted.

Shelley winced, and Dan shot her a questioning glance.

"Sorry," she said, pulling a pan from the oven. "I was talking to your mother about—you know—S-I-T-T-I-N-G—and he heard me say 'cabin.' He hasn't thought of anything else since."

"Oh." Dan frowned and set down his lunch box. "Do we need to talk about this A-L-O-N-E?"

"Wouldn't hurt." Shelley set the chicken casserole on the table. "They've already eaten. Why don't you get washed up, and we can eat now? But we'll—you know—have a discussion—later."

"Right."

More than three hours later, Dan came into the kitchen, where Shelley was baking muffins, cookies, and pies. She had her ingredients and utensils spread out over her work island and the counter. Dan surveyed the room and shook his head.

"How do you keep track of what you're doing?"

"I don't know."

"Don't you ever put the baking powder that was supposed to go in one recipe into the wrong bowl?"

"Don't think so." She plopped a row of cookies onto a shiny baking sheet. "So—the kids are down?"

"Yup. Seems like they get livelier every day."

"I know, and Aiden didn't even have a nap today. That's how he heard about the cabin. I thought he was asleep, so I called Frances to tell her about our anniversary plans, and he came out here."

"So, what now? Do we just tell them Mama and Daddy are going to the cabin, but they can't go?"

Shelley didn't like that idea. "I was thinking maybe we could ask your dad to do something extra special with them while we're gone."

"Like what? Take them to Story Land?" He was referring to a popular nearby theme park.

She laughed. "Nothing that extravagant. Besides, I want to wait until Emma's old enough to remember it before we do anything like that. It would be a waste of money now."

"Well, I can talk to Dad, if you want, and see if he has any brilliant ideas."

"Okay, thanks." Shelley sighed. She was tired, and just thinking about breaking the news to Aiden wore her out. "Do you think they'd do all right with your folks for two whole days?"

"Beats me. They've only slept at Mom and Dad's overnight a few times."

"Yeah, and the last time didn't turn out so well."

Shelley and Dan looked at each other, and then laughed, remembering how Dan's mom had taken it upon herself to cut Aiden's hair.

"It's going to be hard to leave them behind," she said.

"Yeah." Dan opened the refrigerator and took out a can of soda. "Aiden would love to go to the lake. He could have a ride in that boat. We could go fishing..."

"And swimming." Shelley could picture him sticking his toes in the water and squealing. She whirled and stared at Dan. "What are we thinking? It would be so much work to take the kids."

"Yeah. But we'd get some fun time together." He came over and slid his arm around her waist. "What do you think?"

"I don't know. We...well, we wouldn't have any alone time. You and me, that is."

"True." He bent down and kissed the side of her neck. "But the kids would have so much fun. And we could take pictures of the fish Aiden catches."

Shelley giggled. "Which side are you on?"

"Does there have to be sides?"

Shelley laid down her spatula and put her arms around his neck. "I guess not. If you're game, so am I."

"Let's do it, then. Let's take them."

His eyes twinkled, and Shelley knew she couldn't spoil his anticipation. Between the two of them, Dan and Aiden would be wound up from now until the trip.

"I fixed it with Wayne," Dan said. "I can have Friday off, so we'll get a three-day weekend."

"That was nice of him." Shelley kissed him lightly, then frowned as she thought of the one downer in this whole scenario. "What about your mother? I didn't have time to give her all the details, but I did say we hoped she'd sit for us so we could go away."

The light in his eyed shifted to low beam. "Okay. *Hmm.*"

Shelley could envision the scene when Frances learned her grandchildren weren't going to spend the weekend with her after all. "How are we going to tell her?"

★　　★　　★

Diane let Beverly lead the way when they entered the old church that evening. Her adrenaline kicked up as they walked through the side door and she couldn't help wondering if there was anything else of interest up in the old bell tower.

They found Frances Bauer and Maddie Bancroft in the fellowship hall. Maddie was opening a cardboard carton that sat on a table with several others, and Frances stood beside her with a pen poised over a clipboard.

"Hello, ladies," Maddie sang out in her clear soprano voice. "Welcome!"

"Can you use a little help?" Beverly asked.

Diane followed her into the room.

"We sure can," Maddie said.

"I think you know my friend, Diane Spencer," Beverly said. "She came in Margaret Hoskins' place. Diane is very interested in the town's history."

"Hello, Diane," Frances said, looking her over.

Diane wished she'd worn nice slacks, not her jeans, but after all, she expected to get dirty handling old artifacts.

"Hello, Frances," Diane said. "Margaret sends her regrets. How can I help you ladies on this project?"

"Just tell us what needs to be done," Beverly added, "and we'll pitch in."

"Well, we're cataloging the items people have dropped off so far. The notebooks and loose items are all on our list, but we're going through this box from Lila Compton. It has a lot of old bulletins and financial reports. We may display a few of them, but there are a lot of duplicates of items we already had." Maddie looked toward another box, farther down the table. "Now, that stuff was brought in by Elsie Roux.

She said her husband Hank got it at an estate sale. I have no idea what's in it."

"Me either," Frances said. "I haven't dared peek. Perhaps you ladies could open it and take a look. If there are things related to Old First, we'll need a list describing each item carefully, so that it can't possibly be confused with what someone else brought."

"We can do that," Diane said, opening her purse to look for a notepad.

"Oh, there's another clipboard over there in my tote bag," Maddie said, pointing to where she'd left her bag and sweater on a chair. "Feel free to use it."

"Thanks." Diane went over and easily located the clipboard. She pulled it out and found that Maddie had stocked it with lined paper, and a pen rested in a clip at the top. She joined Beverly at the table, near the box belonging to the Rouxs. "Do you want to take things out or write them down?"

"Why don't you take them out and describe them, and I'll write them down," Beverly said.

Diane handed over the clipboard and opened the flaps of the carton. "Looks like a few old books and a couple of pamphlets. About... *Hmm*, I'd say seven items."

She took out a thin, cream-colored booklet with a line drawing of the church on the front. "A Brief History of Old First."

"That sounds like the 1970 pamphlet," Maddie called. "Let me see."

Diane held it up so that Maddie could view the cover.

"Yeah, I think it's like one we have already. Someone put it together back then, and it has some good information in it, but it's limited. We hope to find more."

"A few people have brought in news clippings about past events," Frances said. "At this point, we're looking for anything that's unique, or at least different from what we already have."

Diane laid aside the pamphlet and picked up the other small item.

"This looks like a business listing for the town." She opened it. "Ah, there's a section on churches, and Old First is listed. Pastor David Reed. Who's he?"

"Oh, that's from the fifties, I think," Frances said. "Probably not worth displaying, but write it down. We've talked about doing a display of memorabilia for each pastor, and there may not be much for him."

Next, Diane removed a book with a frayed navy blue cloth binding. The scuffing was so bad along the edges that the "boards" showed through the fabric in several places. "Well, this is an old hymnal." She opened to the title page. "Copyright 1929. Oh, and it has 'Property of First Church of Marble Cove' handwritten in the front.'"

"That is old," Beverly said.

"Do we have one of those?" Maddie asked Frances, glancing over at the book.

"I'm not sure, but there are quite a few old hymnbooks in the choir room. We can check and see if it matches any of those."

"Do you think somebody took it home?" Diane asked.

Frances shrugged. "Sometimes people bought their own. And when the church purchased new hymnals, they would sometimes let members take one of the old ones."

"That makes sense." When Beverly had completed her description, Diane reached into the box again and took out another old book. This one had a brown cover that had once had a gilt design on the front, but most of the gold was rubbed off. She opened it carefully and noticed what looked like a Scripture reading. The pages seemed stiff and brittle. Diane said softly, "This looks ancient. Even older than the hymnal." She held it out to Beverly.

"Wow. It does." Beverly's brow furrowed as she gently turned to the front. "It's an old prayer book."

"Is that like a Bible?"

"Sort of. It has Bible passages in it, but also official prayers of the church. The Anglican church, that is."

"Anglican? Like the Church of England?" Diane stared at her. "So this could be... *really* old."

"I'd say so."

Frances and Maddie were discussing an item they had found in their box.

"That seems very fragile," Frances said, eyeing a paper that Maddie held. "Maybe we shouldn't display it."

"Well, we could put it in a glass case so no one could touch it."

"Maybe we should put it in a plastic bag right now," Frances said. "Then the oils on our hands won't damage it. I'll go get something from the kitchen."

Diane immediately felt guilty for touching the old prayer book with her bare hands. Frances bustled out of the room.

"What did you find?" Beverly asked.

"It's a letter of membership transfer from the late 1800s," Maddie said, "but it's coming apart where it's been folded and creased."

"Well, we have something that may be even older," Beverly told her.

Maddie stepped over close to her.

"See? It's a prayer book," Beverly said. "I think it's very old. My father could probably tell us something about it."

"Would you like to take it home with you and ask him about it?" Maddie asked.

Frances bustled back in as she spoke. "What is it?" she asked.

Maddie quickly explained what Diane had found.

"Oh. Well, I don't think it should leave the church without the owners' permission," Frances said.

"I didn't think of that." Maddie made a regretful face at Beverly. "Sorry. Maybe I can call Mrs. Roux and see if she would mind."

"It's probably best to keep it here," Frances said. "Just catalog it for now. We'll make sure it's kept in a safe place."

Maddie eyed her thoughtfully. "Well, I could ask Mrs. Roux. If she didn't mind, perhaps Beverly could learn more about it by studying it for a few days."

"I'd love to research it and see if we could pinpoint when it was published," Beverly said.

Diane nodded. "Me too. I love old books, and if this one belonged to someone here at Old First..."

She and Beverly looked at each other. No one said the name "Jeremiah Thorpe," but Diane knew they both had the same thought. Of course, since Hank Roux bought the box at an estate sale, it might have absolutely nothing to do with the building. Still, the hymnbook had come from here.

"Do you know where the sale these things came from was held?" she asked.

"No," Frances said. "I don't think Elsie mentioned it."

"I'll call them and let you know, Beverly," Maddie said. "They probably won't mind if you borrow it."

Frances didn't look happy, but she said nothing.

Beverly glanced at Diane and then nodded. "That would be fine. Thank you."

CHAPTER ELEVEN

Diane sat at a small table in the bookstore in Augusta, facing the entrance. The magazine racks were at her back, and beyond them lay the coffee shop. She supposed it was a good location—most of the store's customers would see her either as they headed for the coffee shop or after they'd checked out and were making for the exit.

But not many of them paid her any attention, despite the signs, the stack of shiny new books in front of her, and the perpetual smile on Diane's face. Most of them smiled back, but then they kept going. A half dozen or so stopped at the table and actually looked at the books and spoke a few words to Diane. One gray-haired man, bless his heart, eagerly carted away one of her books and returned after paying for it to have her sign it. Diane could have kissed him.

She scanned the store continually, looking for likely prospects. Maybe they should have put her table in the mystery section. Two women entered the store, chatting nineteen to the dozen. Diane renewed her smile, though her cheeks were starting to ache.

"Oh, look," one of the women cried. "It's a real author."

Diane laughed. "Yes. Hello, I'm Diane."

"Hello." The second woman picked up a copy of her book. "*The Lighthouse Goes Dark*. It looks scary."

"Well, it's a murder mystery," Diane said.

"Is it set in Maine?" the first woman asked.

"Yes, it is."

"Fun!"

"Come on, Jodie," the first woman said. "Let's get our coffee and browse afterward."

They ambled off toward the coffee shop. Diane tried not to let her shoulders droop in case someone else was watching.

"Hi. How's it going?"

She jerked her chin up and stared into Leo Spangler's eyes.

"Leo!" Diane jumped to her feet. "Wow, it's great to see you. I sure didn't expect you to come all the way up here today."

He shrugged. "It's not that far. Thought it might be nice for you to see a friend walk in."

"You don't know the half of it." She leaned toward him. "It's been really slow."

"Sorry to hear that." He fingered the top book on her stack. "I'm going to buy one."

"Didn't you buy one at the Crow's Nest?"

"Well, yes, but I liked it so much, I thought I'd send a copy to my sister. Her birthday's coming up."

Diane's insides melted. "That is so sweet of you. Thank you!"

He picked up the book, smiling. "So, when does your next one come out?"

She grimaced. "I'm still working on it. That's been slow too. I hope to finish it soon, though."

They chatted for a few more minutes, and Leo looked around. "Well, I guess I'd better go pay for this. I'll see you in a minute."

He headed for the checkout line, and Diane sat down again. *Thank You, Lord, for sending a friend when I needed one*, she whispered.

The door opened and two women came in—Beverly, with her head bent solicitously toward her companion, Mrs. Peabody.

Diane laughed out loud. *Well, Lord, I feel ashamed for being so downhearted. Thank You!*

She rose to greet her friends. "Look at you! How wonderful that you're here!"

Mrs. Peabody grinned at her, and Beverly wore a rather satisfied smile.

"Hello, dear," Mrs. Peabody said, reaching for Diane's hand. "We're having a girls' day out. It was Beverly's idea."

"I'm certainly glad to see you." Diane looked at Beverly. "I take it your father isn't along?"

"No, he stayed at home, but we promised to look through the history section for him and see if they have anything new on Maine or the French and Indian War." Beverly brushed back her dark hair. "Have you sold a lot of books?"

"Not many," Diane confessed. "The manager said they did run a short piece in the *Kennebec Journal*, but nobody knows me up here."

"Well, hello, ladies."

Beverly and Mrs. Peabody turned in surprise to find Leo behind them with his newly purchased book.

"Dr. Spangler," Beverly said. "How nice to see you. Did you come specially for Diane's signing?"

Diane thought his face flushed slightly.

"No. Well, yes. But I thought I'd do a few errands in town while I'm here." He held the book out to her. "Would you mind signing it to Ellen?"

"I'd be happy to."

Diane clicked her pen open and signed her name with a flourish. Leo really was a dear.

Beverly and Mrs. Peabody headed off toward the back of the store to find the history section. Leo lingered for a few more minutes. At last another customer hesitantly approached Diane's table.

"Hello." Diane smiled and held out her hand. "I'm Diane. Are you a mystery reader?"

"Yes, I am," the woman said with a smile. "In fact, I've started writing one myself." She cast a questioning glance at Leo, as though wondering whether she interrupted an important conversation.

"I should get going," Leo said. "I hope all goes well, Diane."

"Good-bye. And thanks again for coming, Leo." She turned back to the woman, smiling. "It's exciting to start putting your story on paper."

The customer's eyes brightened. "I have it all thought out in my head. It's just getting the details down that's hard."

They were still talking about writing when Beverly and Mrs. Peabody came back. The woman left with a copy of Diane's book in her hand. Beverly had also bought a copy, as well as a nonfiction book for her father.

"I don't think Jeff has read this yet," Beverly said, holding out Diane's book.

"Why don't I just sign my name?" Diane suggested. "That way, if he does have it, you can give it to someone else." She hoped her friends wouldn't feel they had to come to every book signing and buy more copies, but it did feel good knowing the store would have a few more sales to ring up.

"If we wait to eat, can you have lunch with us?" Mrs. Peabody asked.

"Oh, no, thanks," Diane said, pressing her hand. "I still have more than an hour here, and it's already nearly one. You must be hungry."

"Well, make sure you eat something before you head for Marble Cove," Beverly said soberly. "Keep that blood sugar where it belongs."

"I will." Diane pulled out an energy bar from her bag. "I'll eat this to tide me over."

"We'll see you back home then," Beverly said. "We're having lunch and then doing a little shopping."

Mrs. Peabody's eyes sparkled. "I probably won't buy much, but it will be nice to see some different stores for a change."

At the end of her time at the bookstore, Diane kept up an enthusiastic exterior while thanking the manager, but she felt as though FAILURE were stamped on her forehead. Four books—that was all they'd sold beyond the two her friends had bought. A total of six. Not good. Next month the store would probably have her leftover books on the bargain table at half price just to get rid of them.

She had promised herself a nice, albeit late, lunch if the signing went well. Instead she took the car through a fast food restaurant's drive-through for a chicken sandwich and iced coffee. She didn't want to waste another minute in town. Time to get home and get to work on the next book.

She pulled out of the parking lot and headed for the bridge. She caught glimpses of the capitol dome, with the statue of Wisdom on top, holding up her torch. She could use a little wisdom right now. Diane pulled up at a stop light. The blue state flag flapped in front of the state office building near the street. She let out a huge sigh. She was bluer than the flag right now. Why did she ever think she could be a writer?

★   ★   ★

Beverly stopped by her house in Augusta to pick up a couple of marketing books she'd left there and take a quick look around. She had an electronic security system and a landscaper who kept up the grounds, but now and then she liked to eyeball the place.

"I won't be a minute," she said to Mrs. Peabody.

Her companion's eyes were wide as she studied the front of the house. "Beverly, this is beautiful. I had no idea!"

Beverly hesitated. The house Will had designed *was* lovely. She was considering selling it now. She wasn't at all vain about the house, and she didn't want to seem that way, but seeing it might give Mrs. Peabody some pleasure.

"Would you like to see inside?"

The old woman drew a quick breath, and her eyes brightened. "Really? I'd love to!"

"Come on in, then. I had a colleague staying here for a while, but she found another place, so it's empty right now." Beverly gave her a quick tour, trying to see the simple elegance of the craftsman's house with fresh eyes. Mrs. Peabody seemed particularly impressed by built-in cabinetry and the ultra-modern kitchen. Beverly left her for a moment to poke about and discover the pull-out pantry while she retrieved her books.

"Such an exquisite home," Mrs. Peabody said as they buckled into their seats again. "Of course, your father's house is nice too. I like an old, cozy house. This one is a showplace, though."

"That's exactly what it is," Beverly said. "My husband designed it, and he liked to show it off to his clients."

"Ah. Sort of like a car dealer driving a Cadillac?"

"Kind of." Beverly smiled and decided to turn the topic away from the house and Will Parker. "Are you contributing anything for the exhibits at Old First's Founder's Day?"

"I took a few things to Frances the other day. Nothing much—some old bulletins and such. Say, Beverly..."

Mrs. Peabody leaned toward her conspiratorially. "I know you and your friends are interested in that Jeremiah Thorpe fellow. Couldn't help hearing you and Diane talk about some letters and maps the other day."

"Well, yes, that's correct." Beverly wondered how much her neighbor had gleaned. She might be old, but she still had keen ears.

"I've heard stories over the years." Mrs. Peabody said.

"Have you?"

"Sure. Rumors, legends—whatever you want to call them."

"What sort of stories?"

"Oh, you know. People say Thorpe brought a chest full of treasure from England to help him establish the town and the church. But they say it went missing shortly after he got here."

Beverly thought about that as she drove out of the city. "Well, I don't put much stock in that. I mean, it's been more than two hundred years. Don't you think someone would have found it by now?"

"Plenty of people have tried," Mrs. Peabody said. "I suppose Thorpe probably used it up—I mean, he *did* get the church built and all that. If there was ever a box full of money, he must have used a lot of it. Someone probably started that story later on, about a treasure still being out there, just for fun."

"You may be right." But Diane would be disappointed if she was.

Beverly dropped Mrs. Peabody at her house and then went home.

"Look what I brought you," she said to her father, taking the book from her shopping bag. "I hope you haven't read this one."

His eyes glinted as he surveyed the cover. "*Hmm, The Plymouth Company in Maine.* Nope, I haven't. Looks like a good one. Thanks!"

Beverly stooped to kiss his cheek and left him in his recliner while she unpacked the rest of her purchases. One could never have too many books about colonial Maine.

As she put a new ink cartridge away in her desk drawer, she again noticed Jeff's camera bag. He'd left it on Monday— five days ago—and she hadn't heard a word. Should she be worried about him? She was pretty certain this camera wasn't the main one he used on his assignments, but still, he ought to have responded to her call about it. She picked up the phone and put in his number. It rang a few times and cut to voice mail. She decided she'd better leave another message in case he had missed the first one.

"Hey, Jeff, it's Beverly. I'm wondering if you need the camera you left here. I…hope you're having a good time and getting some great pictures." She gulped. "Let us know how you're doing."

Uncertain whether she'd said enough, or perhaps too much, she clicked off and stood staring for a moment at the camera bag. Was he angry with her? She knew she'd hurt him. But she certainly hadn't meant to drive him away.

Chapter Twelve

Monday morning found Diane out on the beach with Rocky. They'd spent two hours out here Sunday afternoon, and she'd told herself she wasn't procrastinating. She was recharging after the disappointing day in Augusta.

But she was still blue, and nothing seemed to lift her from the doldrums. Church services hadn't refreshed her the way they usually did, and even a call from Jessica hadn't helped. She had several online interviews to write up this week, but she was finding it hard to dredge up the enthusiasm she needed to engage the readers.

The chilly wind off the bay kept her from going too far down the beach this time. The lighthouse was still in the distance when she called to Rocky and turned back. On the boardwalk, she met Shelley and the children, with their little dog Prize following them and exploring new scents.

"It's awfully chilly today, isn't it?" Shelley stooped to tuck an afghan around Emma's neck.

"It is," Diane said. "It's so windy and cold down there that Rocky and I are going back. I'm not sure you should take the kids very far today."

"Well, I don't want them to get chilled." Shelley frowned as a new gust hit them and Aiden clapped both hands on his head to keep his hat in place. "That's it. We'll try again tomorrow." She turned the stroller and walked with Diane back to the end of Newport Avenue.

"How did the book signing go Saturday?"

"Not so well." Diane clipped Rocky's leash on as they reached the street.

"I wish I could have gone," Shelley said.

"Oh, honey, you've got your hands full. Beverly and Mrs. Peabody drove up, though. It was good to see them. And Leo Spangler."

"Dr. Spangler went?" Shelley's eyes widened. "Wow, that's cool."

"It was nice of him." Diane smiled ruefully. "Guess I'm a little glum because of the poor sales. I should be inside polishing off the new book."

"You must be close to finished," Shelley said.

"Well, I've still got a ways to go. The plot doesn't seem to flow like it should." Diane shrugged. "Maybe it's because I'm worried about the first book. I keep wondering what will happen if that doesn't sell well—if they'll still want the other two books."

"They wouldn't cancel them, would they?" Shelley turned to check on Prize. "Aiden, call the dog."

"Come here, Prize," Aiden shouted. The little dog trotted to him, and Aiden petted her. "Good dog. You stay with me."

"I don't know what would happen," Diane said. "I need to quit worrying about it—I know it's depressing me and keeping me from doing my best work."

"Well, I think you should call your agent," Shelley said. "She'd probably have some information on how things are going, wouldn't she? Or at least she could give you an idea of what will happen."

Diane frowned. "You're probably right. I hate to bother Frieda. I haven't worked with her long, and I'm not really sure I should just call her with something like this. I don't want to come across as whiny, you know?"

Shelley nodded. "Sure. You don't want her to think you're high maintenance."

"That's it." Diane smiled for the first time all day. "I'm so new at this, I don't even know if writers should call their agents out of the blue or not."

"Well, maybe you could e-mail her first. Ask if she's got time for a phone call. Tell her you're concerned about how the book is selling. I'll bet she'd call you right away."

"Maybe." Diane nodded with new resolve. "Thanks, Shelley. What's the worst thing that could happen?"

"That's the spirit!" Shelley pointed the stroller across the street. "See you later!"

"Thanks!" Diane waved and turned toward her home with Rocky at her side. Shelley was a big encouragement. But her own question nagged at her. What *was* the worst thing that could happen? Frieda might be too busy to take her call. Or she might feel Diane was being pushy. Or naïve.

Or unprofessional. She blew out a big breath. Shelley's idea of an e-mail first seemed like a good one. The humiliation wouldn't be quite so bad if it came via her inbox.

★　★　★

The week was a hectic one for Shelley, and she was ready to tear her hair out by the handful Thursday morning. Departure time for the cabin was only twenty-four hours away, and she had a list of forty-seven things that she needed to do before they left. She tossed an apple and a plastic bag of cookies into Dan's lunch box and crossed Make Dan's Lunch off the list.

Dan sat at the breakfast table between Emma's chair and Aiden, drinking his coffee.

"I think Emma's stinky," he said.

"Oh, bother! I don't suppose you can change her?"

Dan eyed the clock over the rim of his mug. "I've got to get going."

Shelley shoved the mayonnaise and cold cuts into the refrigerator and slammed the door. "Couldn't you have done it earlier?"

"I just smelled her." Dan pushed his chair back and rose.

Probably he couldn't wait to get out of her range, Shelley thought. "Right. Do we want to take swimsuits, or will the water still be too cold?" She wouldn't dream of swimming in the ocean this early, but lake water rose in temperature quicker than the Atlantic did. She sort of hoped they could swim this weekend, but if Dan said they could, she'd have to dig out swimwear they hadn't used for nine months and buy a new one for Aiden. He'd outgrown everything he wore last summer.

"It's generally warm enough by Memorial Day," Dan said. "But that's not for a week or so."

"*Hmm.*" Shelley thought she might tuck their suits in just in case it was unusually warm at the cabin. Aiden could wear shorts into the water.

"But I heard it's going to rain this weekend," he said.

"Really? That's the pits!"

He shrugged and picked up his dirty dishes.

"Here's your lunch."

Dan's path to the sideboard led him behind Emma's chair.

"*Pe-ew!* Don't let her sit in it."

Shelley glared at him. "Like I'm going to leave her messy all day."

"I'm just sayin'."

"You're always sayin'. Go on. You'll be back by six, right?"

Dan paused in reaching for his baseball cap. "Uh, no, I've got to work late tonight. Wayne said we'll need a few extra hours to finish up this job."

"Oh, wonderful!" Shelley scowled as she unbuckled Emma's safety harness. The poor little thing really did smell bad.

"It's because I'll be off tomorrow, remember?" Dan asked testily.

"Yeah, yeah."

"Look, Shell, you want to go, don't you?"

Emma started to cry as she lifted her. Shelley felt like joining her. "Yes, I want to go. I just didn't realize how much I'd have to do first. I've got orders I need to fill today, and the laundry, and the packing—"

"Well, we'll relax when we get there," Dan said.

"Sure." Suddenly the weekend getaway didn't seem like so much fun. Shelley envisioned herself cooking all the meals, washing the dishes, keeping track of the kids—all the things she did at home except bake pastries. "I was hoping for some 'you and me' time, but that's probably not going to happen."

Dan turned, his face set in displeasure. "Look, it was your idea to take the kids, remember?"

Shelley huffed out a breath and held Emma out away from her shirt. She had a feeling the diaper was leaking or the little girl wouldn't smell so foul. "Maybe it wasn't such a good idea."

"Yeah? Well, I've already told Mom we're taking them, and I can't ask her again to keep the kids at the last minute. Do you want to do that?"

Shelley gulped. Frances had just about bitten Dan's head off when he'd told her they'd changed their minds and were taking the children to the cabin. The last thing she wanted to do was beg her mother-in-law to keep them now.

"No. Just go. Everything will be fine."

Dan hesitated. "You sure?"

"Yeah."

He walked back over and kissed her perfunctorily. "I'll see you later."

"Call me?"

"Sure."

He went to the door with Aiden tagging after him and clamoring for attention. After he'd ruffled the boy's hair and promised him a boat ride if it wasn't raining at the cabin, Dan said, "Bye, buddy," and shut the door.

Shelley's shoulders ached. Emma was wailing now, and her odor wasn't getting any better. "Aiden, feed Prize." Shelley headed for Emma's room. At least when she'd changed her, she could cross off Dress the Kids.

Twenty minutes later, with Emma clean and in the playpen and Aiden playing in the backyard with the dog, she threw a load of laundry into the washer. She needed to find their sleeping bags in case they decided to use them instead of the sheets. And did she really want to root through boxes for swimsuits? That had better wait until she'd packed four boxes of cookies to ship to customers. They'd stop at the post office after she'd delivered pies, muffins, and a jelly roll to the Landmark and the Quarterdeck. Tears streamed down her face as she measured the detergent. She closed the lid of the washer and went to the kitchen counter, where her list lay. She crossed out item 3. At the bottom, she wrote: 44. Get My Sanity Back.

Chapter Thirteen

Diane carried her mug of strong Canadian tea to her desk and sat down at the keyboard. She was determined to get on with the new book, but in order to do that, she had to stop obsessing about the first one. She took a cautious sip of tea. Somehow its flavor, aroma, and warmth comforted her. Her e-mail program held a new message from her agent— *Call me anytime.* That was a relief.

Diane picked up the phone and called New York. Within seconds, Frieda Watley answered with an upbeat, "Good morning, Diane! How are things in Maine?"

Diane smiled, if only because Frieda had answered so quickly and sounded so positive.

"Not too bad, but I did have some questions."

"Sure, what about?"

"Well, uh..." Diane grimaced. "The traffic was pretty light at my book signing on Saturday."

"I'm sorry to hear that," Frieda said. "These things do happen."

"Yeah, I know. It kind of got me down, though. I've been wondering how the book is selling. Are people actually buying it? And are stores ordering it in?"

"I'm sure they are."

Diane sighed. "I don't want to be a worrywart, but this is sort of…well, I think it's affecting my writing. I sit down at my desk and I think, 'What if the first book tanks? Will my contract be canceled?' Things like that."

"First of all, no. I don't think you need to worry about having your contract canceled. The publisher believes in you. They want to help you grow an audience. That may take some time, but they definitely want to get your next book out."

"So do I," Diane said grudgingly. "I guess I've just got to quit dwelling on the sales end of it."

"I'll tell you what," Frieda said. "I'll see if I can get some information for you. But you do understand that it's very early? That you won't get a royalty statement for several months?"

"Yes, I know. And I don't want them to think I need to have my hand held every step of the way." Diane gave a nervous chuckle. "But that's what I'm doing, isn't it?"

"I wouldn't say that," Frieda replied. "In fact, you haven't bothered me at all. There's nothing wrong with asking for an update now and then."

"Thanks. I admit, I wasn't sure if I ought to call you or not. I've been thinking about it all week and finally got my courage up to ask you if that was okay."

"Diane, anytime you're having doubts, feel free to call me. And if you have a question, I don't mind if you call or shoot me an e-mail. If I'm in a meeting and can't talk then, I'll get back to you as soon as I can."

"Thanks. That really makes me feel better."

"All right, you go back to work, and I'll see if I can get anything solid for you from your publisher. They probably won't have any firm numbers yet, but the company should be able to at least give you a report on their marketing efforts."

"Sounds good. Thanks, Frieda."

Diane hung up and clicked open her manuscript file. No matter what, she was resolved that when Frieda got back to her, she'd be able to say she'd made progress.

*   *   *

Beverly tried to concentrate on the program she was setting up for the Sand Dollar. She wanted it to work flawlessly when Mr. and Mrs. Sloan tried it out. A few more hours and the registry program would be ready. She still had some work to do on their billing and accounting program.

Mrs. Peabody was fixing lunch, and occasionally Beverly heard the rattle of dishes or her father's voice. When his and Mrs. Peabody's conversation got loud enough so that she could make out the words, she raised her head and listened, frowning. Were they arguing? She heard her father say something about a cup of tea, but he sounded a bit peevish.

She rose and went downstairs, pausing hesitantly in the kitchen doorway. Her father stood near the microwave, leaning against the counter, and Mrs. Peabody was working at the counter, ten feet away.

"Well, I'd rather do it than have you out here poking around," Mrs. Peabody said.

"Ha! I guess I can poke around my own kitchen if I want to," Father said. "Been doing it for a long time."

"What's the matter?" Beverly asked.

"I'm just getting a cup of tea," her father said.

"And getting in the way," Mrs. Peabody added. "Go on, you. I'll bring it to you."

"It's almost ready now."

The bell on the microwave rang, and her father said triumphantly, "It's all yours. I'm taking my tea and getting out of your hair."

"Good," Mrs. Peabody said. "It's about time. I'm making something you like for dinner. So there."

"That's the kind of payback I like." He smiled and took a mug from the microwave, holding it carefully as he lurched toward Beverly.

"Here, I'll carry it for you." She reached for the mug.

"I can do it."

"I know you can, but you need to use your cane, and you'll have less chance of spilling if I bring this into the library for you."

"Oh, all right." Her father let her take the mug and continued out of the room, muttering unintelligibly.

"I'm sorry," Beverly said to Mrs. Peabody.

"Oh, he's all right," the old woman said. "Seems we're all set in our ways. I just like to have the decks clear when I'm cooking. He knows that. And I'd rather stop what I'm doing for a minute and fix his snacks than have to work around him."

"I think he's just trying to stay as independent as he can. He doesn't like to have someone do everything for him."

"True. And I suppose it's good for him to get up out of that chair once in a while."

"Yes, I'm sure it is. Thanks for understanding." Beverly headed for the library, glad that Mrs. Peabody, at least, was mollified.

Her father had settled into his favorite chair again, and she took the mug over and set it on a coaster on the end table. "There you go."

"Why does she have to carry on so?" her father asked, shaking his head.

"She's not so bad, is she?"

"Well..."

"Isn't her cooking worth it?"

"I suppose so. But if she's not fussing at me, she's wanting to tell me a story. Chatters on with these endless tales of her grandchildren."

"Oh, come on. There are worse things." Beverly knew there were times when her father and Mrs. Peabody had some enjoyable chats.

"*Hmpf.*" He set his cane down and reached for the mug. "Now she's telling me that the treasure old Jeremiah Thorpe was supposed to have never existed."

"Oh, I don't know," Beverly said, thinking of her conversation with Diane. "I'm not sure the treasure is still out there, but why would the stories persist if it didn't exist?"

"Don't ask me." He picked up his mug, blew on the surface of the tea, and took a sip.

"Well, on Saturday she was telling me in the car that she thought there was a treasure, but that Thorpe probably used it up. She's probably just trying to get your goat."

"Think so? Sometimes I do think she takes the opposite side of a discussion just to keep me talking."

Beverly smiled down at him. "All set?"

"Yes. Thank you."

She went back to her desk, hoping this signified a cease-fire. Usually they got along all right, but when their personalities clashed, she felt tense, and today was no exception. She rubbed her forehead. Would she be able to concentrate? Other things were worrying her too, one of them being Jeff.

She hadn't heard from him all week. Was he deliberately avoiding her and not answering her calls? If she only knew he was all right, she'd feel better. She'd expected him to call days ago.

The house phone rang, and she picked it up.

"Beverly? It's Dennis. I'm at my grandfather's, and I wondered if you like to go over to the Cove with me for a cup of coffee."

"Hi. Um, sure, that sounds good."

The Calder house was just across Newport Avenue. Dennis lived in the condominiums at Sunrise Shores, but he stopped over frequently to see his aging grandfather.

"Great. Meet me outside?" Dennis asked.

"Just let me grab a sweater."

Beverly snatched a warm brown ombré sweater from the closet and a five-dollar bill from her wallet. She didn't want Dennis to pay for her coffee or he might start thinking she was interested in dating him. He was a nice enough guy, but Beverly had enough on her plate with Jeff and starting a new business and caring for her father. Still, she enjoyed talking to Dennis now and then, and he seemed to appreciate the friendship too.

She went downstairs and stopped at the library door. "That was Dennis on the phone. I'm going over to the Cove with him, but I'll be back within an hour."

Her father looked up absently and nodded. "All right, dear."

Beverly felt slightly guilty as she left the house and crossed the street, but she told herself it was for no reason. Jeff wouldn't mind her having an innocent cup of coffee with a friend, and her father would be fine while she was gone. Her work wouldn't suffer if she took a short break. What was she stressing about?

Dennis waited outside his grandfather's house, smiling as she approached.

"Hi. How are you doing?" he asked.

"Not bad. Mrs. Peabody and Father were having a little dustup earlier. I admit I'm glad to get out of the house for a few minutes."

"Ah, what we go through with our elders," Dennis said with a chuckle.

They ambled to the coffee shop, and Beverly stepped up to the counter and ordered black French roast.

"Care for a muffin?" Dennis asked.

"No, thanks."

Beverly waited while Brenna fixed her coffee and got Dennis a blueberry muffin and a latté.

"Don't you ever let yourself indulge?" he asked as they settled at a table near the window.

"Sure," Beverly said, "but not often."

He nodded. "It shows." He held up one hand in quick protest. "Sorry. I meant…well, you're obviously in good condition. I know you run a lot."

"Just trying to keep in shape." She took a sip of her coffee and hoped he'd change the subject. Soon they were chatting about Mr. Calder's and Beverly's father's foibles and having a good chuckle over Mrs. Peabody's crustiness.

"You know she's a marshmallow inside," Beverly said.

"No, really? Sorry, but I just can't see that. However, I haven't been around her nearly as much as you have."

Beverly smiled. "I took her to Augusta Saturday. Diane Spencer was having a book signing. Afterward, Mrs. Peabody and I went shopping. It was quite entertaining."

"That's nice," Dennis said. "So, how's your business coming?"

"Pretty good. I got a new client this week, and I'm setting them up with a hotel registry program and some accounting software."

"Great." He began to tell her about his latest project.

Beverly's mind drifted as Dennis talked. Where was Jeff? On one of the islands, for sure, but did anyone know precisely where? It seemed very odd that he'd never responded to her initial message, or the one she'd left more recently. Could he be hurt? She got a mental image of him lying on the rocky shore of a tiny, unpopulated island. Maybe he'd fallen down a cliff. He might have broken bones. She couldn't shake off the picture of Jeff, injured and stranded, with no one but the seabirds to hear his cries for help.

She realized Dennis had asked her a question.

"I'm sorry—what did you say?"

"I asked if you'd like a refill."

"No, thanks." Beverly glanced at her watch. "I'd better get back. I can still get a little work in before lunch."

"All right." Dennis seemed to have picked up her mood, and on their walk home they hardly spoke.

When they reached the parting of their ways, Beverly smiled up at him.

"Thanks. I really needed a break."

"Same here," Dennis said. "Say hi to your dad for me."

As Beverly turned up the flagstone walk, her thoughts went back to Jeff. He was a grown man, and he was most likely fine. But what if he wasn't?

CHAPTER FOURTEEN

Margaret's mind wandered as she ate breakfast with Allan on Friday morning. Things were piling up on her, and she wished this week had an extra day in it.

"Something on your mind?" Allan asked as he brought a plate of bacon to the table and took his seat.

"*Hmm?* Oh yes. I've got that art fair meeting tonight. I'll have to leave as soon as I get home from the gallery."

"How's your painting coming?"

She knew he meant her artwork in general, not a particular painting. "Not bad, but I need more time." She gave him a rueful smile. "My usual plea."

"Well, maybe I can come tend the gallery this afternoon, and you can get out and paint."

"Are you sure? I know you've been busy in your shop."

Allan shrugged. "I don't have any custom orders right now. Why don't I go over after I eat lunch? You can come home and eat and then go work wherever you want. We could eat at Captain Calhoun's tonight before your meeting."

"Do you think so?"

"Sure. At closing time, I'll get Adelaide and meet you at the restaurant."

"Perfect." Margaret left for the gallery thinking about everything she wanted to get done that day. She'd finished the last of Matt Beauregard's four paintings; maybe Allan could hang the last one this afternoon. She knew just where she wanted it. Her portrayal of Old First was still in progress, and if she wasn't going to use it for her premier piece at the art fair, she needed to get cracking on something new. She liked the composition, but even if it turned out well, it was still in the unexciting style that sold steadily—but earned lukewarm critical comments.

A few customers came into the gallery during the morning, and to her delight, Margaret sold a painting by Dorothy Granger, one of the first artists to exhibit in her gallery. She couldn't resist giving Dorothy a call to tell her that a check would soon be in the mail. In between that and waiting on the other people who drifted in, she had time to catch up her bookkeeping and order some new supplies. Around eleven o'clock, she went to her studio to pack up the materials she would take with her that afternoon.

She still hadn't decided what to paint for her debut piece. Every time she thought about it, her nerves began to flutter again. She wanted to have a piece so good that she'd feel confident when she displayed it at the fair. How likely was that? Even when others praised her work, she never felt completely satisfied with it.

Dear Lord, please help me, she prayed silently. *I want to honor You through this experience, both through my paintings and through my job as artists' ambassador. Please guide me as I work on my paintings. I just don't know what to do!*

When she opened her eyes, her gaze fell on the brown and white shell Aiden had given her. Again she saw his glowing eyes and felt his excitement when he told her about the starfish in the tide pool.

The idea she'd had earlier came back. The lighthouse in the distance, with the tide pool in the foreground, making up the bulk of the picture. Shells and a starfish, or perhaps a crab, would highlight the scene.

She still liked the concept, and she grabbed a sketch pad. In the next ten minutes she quickly sketched four different perspectives. The one she liked best had a child crouching barefoot at the edge of the pool, reaching for the starfish. She was sure the people who liked her usual style would find it engaging, though a little different. Still, it wasn't what she wanted for her debut painting at the fair.

Among the boxes of new merchandise, cases of prints, and unframed paintings in the storage room, she knew there was a basket of shells she'd collected over the years. She had displayed it last summer on one of Allan's tables, beneath a seascape.

The bell over the front door jingled, heralding the arrival of a customer, and Margaret set Aiden's shell squarely in the middle of her desk to remind her to look for more shells later. When she was free again, she would look for the shell basket. Maybe the shapes and colors would spark some inspiration.

By the time Allan arrived at noon, she had prepped a new canvas and sorted carefully through the shell basket, setting aside the ones that had the most intriguing lines and colors. She didn't dare get excited yet, but she was beginning to think the shells had inspired two very different paintings— the tide pool scene and one that combined shell shapes and hues in an abstract. Would it work? Perhaps not. But she could hardly wait to try.

★   ★   ★

Diane enjoyed a leisurely walk on the beach with Rocky. A brisk breeze swept in from the sea, and clouds gathered to the west. She wondered if they were in for a storm. Dan and Shelley had set out that morning for their getaway with the children strapped into their car seats. Diane hoped poor weather wouldn't ruin their weekend.

When she and Rocky turned homeward, she had to bend her head and push against the wind. Rocky seemed happy to go back too, which was unusual. They tumbled into the house, and Diane shoved the door shut behind them.

"Well! I think we need a cup of tea and a dog biscuit." She unbuttoned her jacket and peeled it off. Rocky barked once and sat watching her intently. Diane laughed. "You understand every word, don't you?"

She put the teakettle on, then got down his box of treats and tossed him one. Rocky caught it in his mouth and retired to his bed to chew on the tasty biscuit.

Ten minutes later, Diane settled in at her desk with her tea and brought up her e-mail. A message from Jane Veers had come in, and she clicked on it, eager to see what her editor had to say.

> *Diane, hope things are going well for you. I spoke to Frieda, and I wanted to reassure you that our marketing team is hard at work promoting your book. One of the team members will be contacting you soon about some publicity opportunities for you. Getting your name out there through interviews and blog posts can be very effective, and they'll also discuss social media with you. We're excited about your book!*

Diane exhaled slowly. That sounded promising. She wished they'd lined up more interviews and appearances earlier, though. As much as she hated speaking before groups, she could see the value of it.

The phone rang, and Rocky let out a single *woof.* His nails clicked on the wood floor as he walked to the door of her office. Reaching for the phone, Diane waited for him to show his face at the doorway.

"Go lie down, boy."

He turned and padded back to the kitchen, and she answered the call.

"Diane, it's Frieda."

She sat back in her chair. "Hi! I was just reading an e-mail from Jane and telling myself to breathe."

Frieda chuckled. "I hope the message was encouraging?"

"Yes, it was. Thank you for your help."

"You're welcome. From what I gathered, bookstores are placing orders for your book—both chain stores and independents. The orders aren't huge, but they aren't bad for a debut book. I think you should take satisfaction in that and move forward with the next book."

"I know you're right," Diane said. "I think the book signing the other day just got me down. I felt so discouraged and...and rejected."

"That's normal. You know, the poor turnout might be because the store didn't do much advance publicity. They only called you a week before the event, and they might not have gotten a notice into the paper. It's never easy to pinpoint what works and what doesn't in a case like that, but I have some ideas you might want to try next time."

"Oh? I'm willing to do anything that will help bring out people and boost sales."

Frieda spoke at length about innovative ways Diane could drum up readers and attendees at her appearances, and by the end of the conversation she felt equipped with some great new ideas.

When they'd finished talking, Diane went out to the kitchen with her empty tea mug. Rocky sat up on his cushion and whined hopefully.

Diane laughed. "We just came in half an hour ago, silly boy. Tell you what: I'm going to put in a good, solid chunk of time on my book. Then, before supper, we'll take a quick turn around the neighborhood. But you have to cooperate."

Rocky wagged his tail and laid his head on his paws. Diane bent and stroked his glossy head for a moment.

"Good dog. Now, if only you knew how to brainstorm."

Her phone rang, and she answered it, wondering what else would keep her from actually writing today.

"Diane, it's Beverly. Maddie Bancroft just called me and said we can get the prayer book and keep it for a few days. And I wondered—do you think it would be any help to talk to Mr. Roux about it personally? He might know a little more than he told her and Frances."

"Great idea!"

"Okay," Beverly said. "I'll see if I can get the prayer book later today, and we can try to set up something."

Chapter Fifteen

Margaret spent almost two hours on the tide pool painting. She sat in a folding canvas chair on the beach, gazing past her easel toward the lighthouse. It was tiny in the distance, but that was part of her plan. She roughed in the major lines of the composition. The edge of the beach, with gentle waves washing in, drew the eye toward the center of the painting. The rocks surrounding the tide pool would give texture and contrast to the main attractions—the starfish and the shell dwellers. The child would have Aiden's blue eyes and freckles, and a deep maroon T-shirt that would harmonize with the background colors but not steal all the viewers' attention. His hand reaching down into the water would pull their gazes to the starfish, and viewers would want to pluck it out and examine it, just as the little boy did.

When she got up at last to stretch her legs and take a walk, the tide was much farther out than when she'd arrived. The breeze was getting chilly, and she noted that the morning's scattered clouds had thickened. She hoped she still had another hour or two left to work.

She wandered about the rocks, seeking out pools of trapped water. She found a couple and snapped photographs with her digital camera. They might help her with the pool in her painting.

When she returned to her easel, she was ready to try something new. She took out a fresh canvas and added blobs of orange, purple, and vibrant blue to her pallet.

She planned to represent the tide pools with lines and blurred images that would suggest the sea creatures, not the precisely realistic view she sometimes created, or the softer, more impressionistic look she often used in landscapes and ocean views. This would go beyond the gentle blending of strokes she used for foliage.

As she reached for her brush, she saw a shell poking out of the damp sand near her foot. She picked it up and brushed the sand off. The spiral shell was a pure, almost chalky white. She turned it over and saw that the animal was gone and the shell was empty. The opening of the tunnel was a pinkish tan, smooth and glossy compared to the rough exterior.

That was what she wanted. The contrast in the texture, as well as the color.

An hour later, a gust of wind made her easel and canvas shudder, and her hair whipped about her face. She looked up and realized the clouds had closed in and darkened.

Quickly she gathered her things and put her brush into her protective case. The canvas went into a special box to keep the paint from touching anything while she carried it. Her shoulders ached as she lugged her paint box, easel, and canvases to her car.

She wasn't certain yet whether she'd begun to find the essence of this painting. Maybe she'd be able to tell when she looked at it later, inside the gallery.

⋆   ⋆   ⋆

"Wow, look at our cabin!" Aiden went running through the rooms with Prize barking at his heels, and Emma toddled along behind them, squealing with joy.

"Let's hurry and get everything inside," Dan said. He set down the cooler he'd brought in and headed back outside.

Shelley took a quick glance around the kitchen and then followed the children. "Emma! Aiden! Wait until Mama and Daddy can go with you." All she needed was for one of them to get hurt first thing. Sure enough, Emma was halfway up the stairs that had no risers at the backs of the treads. She was small enough to fall right through one of the gaps. Shelley scooped her up. "Aiden, where are you?"

"Up here!" He popped out of a doorway on the landing above her. "It's super cool, Mama."

"Good. Come on down and help Daddy and me get our things in. And we can't let Emma go up those stairs alone. She could fall and get hurt."

To her surprise, the dog poked her head out of the doorway at Aiden's side. Apparently Prize hadn't had a problem with the steps.

When they got back to the kitchen, Dan was piling grocery sacks and duffels in a heap on the floor.

"The wind's picking up," he said.

"Sorry. I had to get Emma. Those stairs look dangerous. We're really going to have to watch her."

"Okay. Hey, Aiden."

"Yeah, Daddy?"

"You come help me," Dan said. "Mama and Emma can put the food away. You can carry your backpack and a pillow, can't you, big guy?"

"I sure can." Aiden strutted out the door with Dan.

"Bring the playpen next if you can," Shelley called after them. She carried Emma into the next room and took a quick look around. There were no bedrooms on the first floor—just the kitchen, living room, a bathroom, and a large screened-in porch facing the lake. She ignored the sagging sofa and rickety-looking shelf unit. The cabin was rustic, but the view was priceless.

She turned and frowned at the stairs. They would all be sleeping up there. She was glad she'd brought the collapsible play yard. That would keep Emma confined some of the time, but Shelley foresaw an ongoing battle to keep the toddler away from those steps.

"But where is it?" Aiden wailed in the kitchen.

"It's probably still in the car," Dan said. "I'll go back and check."

Shelley turned and carried Emma back to the doorway. "What's up?"

"Aiden's looking for his sleeping bag. It wasn't with the other stuff in the back."

"It's got to be there."

Dan held up both hands. "I know. I'm going to look now."

"Mama, I *need* my sleeping bag."

Shelley stroked Aiden's hair and looked to Dan. They'd planned on using sheets for their bed, but Aiden had insisted on bringing his Spider-Man slumber bag.

"Stay calm. I'll be right back." Dan dashed out the door. The wind took it and hurled it back against the porch wall.

"Wow, we'd better shut that," Shelley said. Dan had reached the station wagon and was opening the passenger door and peering into the backseat, where they'd buckled the kids. Had Aiden's sleeping bag gone in there with him? If they didn't find it, they'd have one upset little superhero tonight.

Maybe a distraction was in order.

"Come on, kids, help me put the food in the refrigerator. See? They have a real kitchen here. We'll put things away so..." She let it trail off as she swung the refrigerator door open. No light came on, and she didn't feel the familiar blast of cool air from inside. She reached out and stuck her hand in, then touched the top shelf. It was room temperature.

"Or maybe we'll leave it in the cooler for now," she said. "But we can unpack the cereal and stuff in that box." She set Emma down and marched over to a carton of food that didn't need refrigeration.

"Oh boy, marshmallows!" Aiden grabbed the plastic package and hugged it to his chest. "Where do we put them?"

"*Hmm.*" She opened an upper cabinet. It looked clean and had several inverted mugs and a stack of plastic bowls

inside. "I think way up here, so Emma can't get into them."
Or mice, she thought. She wondered if the owners had been
out here yet this season. The place didn't look dirty, so
she decided to believe they had cleaned at least once this
spring.

The door crashed open again, and they all jumped. Emma
began to cry. Shelley rocked her back and forth. "*Sh,* now."

"Did you find it, Daddy?"

"'Fraid not, buddy." Dan set down the diaper bag and a
toy truck. "This was all I found. But don't you worry. We'll
find you something to sleep in."

Aiden's face crumpled. "No! I need my Spider-Man."

Dan looked helplessly at Shelley.

"Sweetie, we'll work something out," she said. "Dan, the
refrigerator's not on."

"Probably just unplugged. Let me take a look."

Emma continued to fuss as Dan shifted the pile of gear
on the floor.

"Daddy, what will I sleep in?" Aiden wailed.

"Take it easy, Aiden. Just step back now so I can pull the
fridge out."

Shelley watched anxiously as he tugged on it. The
appliance looked older than either one of them—what if it
had outlived its useful life? She supposed they could get
by with the cooler if they had to, but preparing their food
would be a lot easier if they had the refrigerator.

Dan leaned in behind it. "That's it."

"You mean it's just not plugged in?"

"Right."

Shelley huffed out a deep breath. At least one thing went right.

The refrigerator began to hum. It seemed too loud—more like a vacuum cleaner. Maybe it wouldn't be so noisy when it was back against the wall.

Dan emerged a moment later with cobwebs in his hair.

"Oh, you're all dusty," Shelley said. "Why don't you go outside and brush off?"

Emma was still fussing when he came back in without the cobwebs.

"Can you take her?" Shelley asked. "I really want to get this stuff put away."

"All right, but you'd better wait a while to put anything in the fridge," Dan said. "Give it a chance to cool off in there."

Shelley handed Emma over. "Okay. Don't let her climb those stairs, will you? They're not baby-proof."

"Got it." Dan smiled down at Aiden. "Come on, buddy, why don't you bring your backpack, and we'll go see where we're going to sleep."

Aiden hoisted his pack and followed his father into the living room. Two seconds later, a piercing shriek came from Emma.

CHAPTER SIXTEEN

Dan hurried back into the kitchen, cuddling Emma and saying, "It's okay, it's okay. Calm down, baby."

"What happened?" Shelley asked.

"There's a mounted deer head in there, and it scared her."

"Really?" Shelley stepped to the doorway and looked around. Sure enough, over the sofa hung a glass-eyed buck that had had a date with a taxidermist. "Oh man, I didn't even notice that before. How could I not see it?" She turned back to the kitchen, shaking her head.

Emma was still sobbing into Dan's neck, and he was rubbing the little girl's back.

"I don't know. I guess you were too busy looking out at the lake, like I was."

"You got that right. The three of us were all in there before, and nobody noticed it."

Dan nodded. "How about if you hold her while I set up the playpen? Then at least we'll know she'll stay put while we get things squared away."

That made sense, so Shelley took Emma back. By the time Dan had the playpen set up in the living room and had found the pad and Emma's favorite blanket, the little girl was yawning.

"Can you cover up the—you know—whitetail?" she called to Dan.

"With what?"

"I don't know. A towel or something?"

She heard him go up the stairs and back down again. She hoped he didn't just drape a white sheet over the deer head. That might scare Emma worse than the buck. Finally Dan came to the kitchen doorway.

"All set. I used that big towel with Winnie-the-Pooh on it."

"Good. I can't see us going swimming anyway." She looked down at Emma. "There, honey, time for your nap." She doubted they would get Aiden to sleep this afternoon, as wound up as he was, but Emma went down readily and curled up with her stuffed bunny.

Shelley tiptoed up the stairs and found Dan and Aiden in one of the bedrooms. The walls had no Sheetrock—just the backs of the siding boards between the studs—and there was no ceiling. The partition between the two bedrooms ended about six feet above the floor, and they could look up at the bare rafters. They'd have to be quiet when the children were sleeping, as every sound would carry.

"Not too bad, huh?" Dan asked with a grin. "I'll bring Emma's playpen up here tonight. I guess Prize will have to have her bed up here too."

Shelley nodded reluctantly. She wouldn't want the dog alone downstairs in a strange place—not that they could keep her from following Aiden up here. She walked over to Aiden's bed and straightened his pillow.

"We found some blankets in the cupboard, and Aiden's going to camp with those," Dan said.

"That's good," Shelley said, smiling at Aiden. "That's the way to rough it." She'd take a look later and see if there were any extra sheets in there.

"Daddy said we make do with what we have," the little boy said solemnly.

Aiden looked so grown up as he spoke, and so like his father, that Shelley smiled. "That's right. We're real Mainers. 'Use it up, wear it out, make do, or do without.'"

Aiden blinked up at her with a puzzled frown, and she laughed. "Can you guys make our bed in the other room, and I'll start supper?"

"Aw, I want to go in the boat," Aiden said. "Daddy, can we?"

Dan looked out the small window and grimaced. "I don't know, buddy. It's really windy out, and see how the sky's getting all dark now? I'm afraid it's going to rain."

"You don't want to be out in a boat when it rains," Shelley said firmly.

"Can we at least go down and look at the boat?" Aiden whined, his big blue eyes fixed on his father.

Dan glanced at Shelley, and she frowned.

"Uh, well, maybe we should get the big bed made up first, and then we'll go take a look, okay?"

Aiden let out a howl. "Then it will be raining, Daddy."

Shelley sighed. "All right," she said to Dan. "Take him out. At least it will be quiet in here for a while. But you'll help me later, right?"

"Absolutely," Dan said.

"Thanks." Shelley said. "Get going. I just hope the stove works."

The electric range seemed to be in working order, and Shelley quickly put some water on to boil for macaroni. Aiden loved the kind that came out of a box, and she'd warned Dan that the meals would be simple this weekend. She found basic utensils in the drawers and cupboards— nothing fancy, but she'd expected that. Most people took castoffs to their summer cottage, didn't they? There was no dishwasher, but again, she hadn't anticipated having one. It just meant they'd have to do every dish by hand. She was glad she'd thrown in a package of paper plates.

When she had put the kitchen to rights, Shelley set the table and strapped Emma's booster seat to a chair. The light coming through the window had dimmed steadily. It was only four thirty, and she knew it was the approaching storm, not dusk, that was bringing the darkness.

Just as she took the macaroni off the burner, Dan and Aiden burst through the door.

"Mama, it's raining!"

"*Sh*," Shelley cautioned. "Don't forget, Emma's sleeping."

"*It's raining, Mama*," Aiden repeated in a stage whisper.

Dan flipped down the hood of his sweatshirt. "The wind's really howling now."

Rain spattered against the window and drummed loudly on the roof.

"Are you wet?" Shelley asked.

"No, we just took the first few sprinkles," Dan said, "but it's getting cold out there."

"It's none too warm in here." Shelley rubbed her arms.

"Yeah, Mama, we're cold." Aiden squeezed up against her side and reached up to hug her fiercely around the waist, burrowing his head against her hipbone.

"Maybe we can build a fire in the fireplace," Dan said.

Shelley looked at him apprehensively. "You think it will be all right?"

"Phil said we could, and there's some firewood stacked on the porch."

"I know, but..."

"I'll check the flue and the chimney first."

Neither of them said any more about the scare they'd had at home in December, but Shelley shivered just thinking about the near tragedy. "Okay, but be really careful."

"I will."

"What about the kids? We'll have to watch them every second."

"There's a screen that fits over the front," Dan said. "You can see through it, but I think it's solid enough to stop them from falling into the fire."

"Okay," Shelley said uncertainly. "Supper will be ready in ten minutes," she added as Dan and Aiden headed for the woodpile.

Unfortunately, Emma's playpen sat only six feet from the fireplace. The noise Dan and Aiden made bringing in the wood and building the fire woke her.

Dan brought her to the kitchen and held her out to Shelley. "Sorry."

"Oh, it's all right." Shelley was resigned to a flawed weekend by this time. "Can you change her and put her in the booster seat? I'll get some macaroni ready for her, and we can all sit down and eat."

The macaroni was a hit. Somehow, Shelley had forgotten the frozen vegetables she'd planned to serve with it, but they had a bag of packaged salad, and for dessert she brought out cupcakes.

"Marshmallows," Aiden cried.

"Maybe later, honey," Shelley said.

Doing the dishes was a major undertaking, but at last the kitchen was clean once more. She hung up her dish towel and trudged into the living room where Dan was playing with Emma and Aiden.

"Keep the two of them busy while I go up and fix the bed, okay?" Her back ached, and she wanted to make sure she had a place to crash as soon as possible.

Upstairs, the thrumming of the rain was a roar on the roof. *Lord, please let it slack off before we head for bed*, she prayed silently. The kids would never sleep with that din overhead. She took their sheets from a duffel bag and shook out the first one. From downstairs, she heard laughing and thumping, and then Emma screamed.

"What's the matter?" She tore out onto the landing and tripped on one of Aiden's water shoes. She stumbled and caught herself on the peeled log railing. Her ankle turned, and she flinched. It didn't feel serious, but she needed to take her own advice and be more careful. At least she hadn't hurtled down the stairs and injured her knee again.

Bending over to rub her ankle, she called, "Dan, what's going on?"

Over Emma's wails, he replied, "Oh, it's that stupid deer again. Aiden pulled off the towel by mistake and Emma saw the deer."

Shelley limped down the steps, clinging to the railing. "Can't we do something with it? Can you take it down?"

"Maybe." Dan walked over to the sofa and stood scrutinizing the mounted deer. "If I *can* get it down, where will we put it? It's too big to go in a closet."

Shelley wasn't even sure there *was* a closet in the cabin. But he was right—it looked huge, with its branched antlers spreading proudly.

Emma stood in the playpen, holding on to the side and crying piteously. She stared up at Shelley with tears running down her face.

"Mama! Mama!"

Shelley hurried down the last few steps and hobbled across the room to get her. "Well, do *something* with it. I'll take Emma into the kitchen."

Aiden stood in the middle of the floor, swinging the plastic bat back and forth.

"Stop that, Aiden." Shelley stooped to lift Emma. Just as she straightened with the toddler in her arms, a *pop* sounded, and the lights went out. A deafening roar of thunder burst above them, and both children screamed.

CHAPTER SEVENTEEN

O h, Justin, I'm so happy to hear from you, but I don't
think this is a good time for me to be on the phone."
A roar punctuated Diane's sentence.

"Wow, Mom, is that thunder I'm hearing?" Justin
asked.

"Yes, and the lightning's having a field day. I think it's
quite close. Sorry, honey, but I think I'd better call you back
in a little while."

"Do that," Justin said.

He was gone, and Diane set the receiver back in the cradle.
She wondered if cell phones had the same drawbacks as
landlines when it came to electrical storms. Best not to risk
it, she decided. Instead, she scurried around unplugging small
appliances.

Rocky lay on his cushion, trembling, and he whined as
Diane passed him.

"Oh, you poor thing." She went to her knees and stroked
his head. "I don't blame you one bit, fella." She patted him
for a few minutes, trying to think of other things she should
do. "I'm going to get up and find my flashlight," she told
him. "You stay here."

She hoped the power didn't go out, but just in case, she wanted to be prepared. She rooted out the flashlight from the basket of sundries on the bottom shelf of her nightstand. In the kitchen, she set it in the middle of the table where she could find it easily. Next, she ran two large kettles full of water so that she'd have enough to give the dog a drink and wash up if she had to do without the pump. The thunder continued to roll overhead.

"I think I'll light a candle or two," she said, partly to Rocky and partly to herself. "Then if we do lose power, we'll still have a little light in here."

She lit two scented jar candles in the living room and coaxed the dog to join her there. "We might as well be comfortable."

She stretched out on the sofa, and Rocky settled on the rug beside her. Diane let her hand hang down so she could pat him intermittently. Rocky seemed calmer now. She closed her eyes and tried to think about her mystery plot, but every couple of minutes a bolt of lightning flashed, followed by a crash of thunder. She wondered how Shelley and Dan were doing with the kids at the cabin. Maybe the storm would go out to sea and bypass them at the lake.

After half an hour, she realized the lightning was only an occasional, halfhearted flicker and the thunder had drifted off. It sounded muffled. The rain still pattered on the roof of her cottage, but it no longer drummed as though trying to beat holes in the shingles.

She sat up and looked at Rocky. He was asleep, and she grinned.

"If you're snoozing, it must be over. And, hey—we still have our lights! Thank You, Lord."

She went to the phone in the kitchen and dialed Justin's number.

"Hi, Mom. Is the storm gone?"

"Pretty much. It was a wild one."

"I hope you had your lawn chairs put away."

"Yeah, I did." Diane put the teakettle on as she talked. "So, how are you doing?"

"Oh, I'm fine. This course is pretty hard, but I really want to pass."

"I'm sure you'll do well."

"I hope so," Justin said. "So tell me about the book signing. I didn't get to talk to you last weekend."

Diane sighed and opened the cupboard to get a teabag. "Not so hot. I only sold six books, and that's counting the two Beverly and Dr. Spangler bought."

"Dr. Spangler? Is that the vet?"

"Yeah. Leo. It was sweet of him to drive all the way up there."

"I met him last time I came to visit, didn't I?" Justin asked.

"Yes, I think you did. He's nice, but . . ."

"But what?"

"Oh, I don't know. I'm just kind of blue right now. I sort of got stuck on my story line, and then I had that crummy turnout for the book signing, and now it's rainy and cold, you know?"

"Sounds like you need to get out and have some fun. Take your mind off the dreary stuff. Is Leo a good prospect for a diversion?"

She chuckled. "Oh, honey, I don't think so. As a matter of fact, he left a message on my phone last night, and I haven't called him back yet."

"Oh? What did he want?" Justin asked.

"He wants to go out for lunch sometime. I'm not sure what to say. I mean, I like him, but...well, not *that* much. I don't want to encourage him."

"Couldn't you just go out to eat with him as friends?"

"Nnn..."

Justin laughed. "Aw, come on, Mom. I thought there was a little chemistry between you two when I was there. You ought to at least give the guy another chance."

The teakettle puffed out a cloud of steam, and Diane grabbed it before it could build up much of a whistle. She was surprised at Justin's encouragement. Maybe he was just trying to distract her from her dismal book sales.

"Well, we went out before, but I just don't feel the urge to spend a lot of time with him."

"That's okay. But I don't want you to be lonely. What about Shelley, across the street? Maybe you can do something with her."

"Shelley and her family are camping this weekend, but I did promise to go by Margaret's gallery tomorrow, and I'd like to visit Mr. Wheeland too, and maybe Augie Jackson."

"There you go. I think you should do that. Go and visit Margaret and at least one other person tomorrow."

"Okay." Diane couldn't help smiling, though she knew visiting would eat into her writing time. "Thanks. I feel better just from talking to you."

"Well, think how great you'd feel if you had lunch with Leo."

"Oh, you!"

He chuckled. "All right, I'll let that rest. But you *did* say he was sweet."

Diane thought that Justin was the sweet one. The fact that he cared about her emotional health showed her how much he had matured. By the time they hung up, her spirits had taken a decided upward turn, though any stray thought of the book signing and book sales in general still left her a bit deflated. Her solution for that was to head back to the computer, now that the storm was past. Even the rain had let up. Rocky, to her relief, had settled in on his cushion for a good long snooze. Maybe she could get some solid work done tonight.

⋆　　⋆　　⋆

Beverly was surprised when the phone rang. She looked up, realizing the storm had abated. Rain still pattered against the window, but the lightning seemed to have stopped.

"Beverly," her father called up the stairs. "Phone for you."

She walked quickly down to answer the house phone. Maybe she should have a landline extension installed up in her office. Her father didn't want a cell, and sometimes she had trouble keeping a good connection inside the house on hers.

"Hi, Beverly, it's Maddie."

"Oh, hi. How's the work on the exhibits coming?"

"We've been dealing with the refreshments and speakers and a million other details, so we haven't done much more on the exhibits this week. I'm sorry I didn't get that prayer book to you yet."

"No problem," Beverly said. "I could pick it up at church on Sunday."

"All right, if you don't mind. My weekend is maxed out."

"It's fine."

"Hank Roux seemed eager to learn more about it," Maddie said.

"Thanks—I think I'll give him a call as soon as I've had a chance to look it over," Beverly said. She hung up wondering whether the book was a new clue or a wild-goose chase. But she and Diane would never forgive themselves if they didn't follow through on it.

*　　*　　*

Shelley awoke Saturday morning to the steady drumming of rain on the cabin roof. Dan was already gone, and she heard muffled sounds that led her to believe he had brought in more wood for the fireplace.

The bedroom was chilly, but she bounded out from under the covers and dressed quickly in jeans and a sweatshirt. Her ankle gave her only a small twinge of pain.

When she turned around to look for her hairbrush, the mounted deer head that Dan had hung on a nail in their bedroom wall, for lack of a better place, was staring at her. Shelley flinched and turned away, but she could still see it behind her in the mirror as she brushed her long hair.

"Get a life," she muttered to the deer as she headed for the bathroom.

Dan was crouching before the fireplace, wielding the poker. He looked up as she came down the stairs. "Hey. How are you doing?"

"Okay, but it looks like we won't be able to do any of the things we planned today."

He frowned. "Yeah, swimming and hiking are definitely out."

"I'll start the coffee."

Shelley headed for the kitchen, but Dan called, "There's no power."

"Oh yeah." She turned back, her shoulders drooping. "How are we going to make breakfast?"

"You could heat some water over the fire, I guess."

She sighed. "Well, there's juice and cinnamon rolls. I hate to open the fridge to get the juice, though."

"Not much we can do," Dan said.

"How long do you suppose it will take to get the power back?"

"No idea."

She trudged to the kitchen and rummaged through the cupboards. Every pan looked old, and some were dented. One of them had the telltale carbon stains that told her it had been used on a fire or a camp stove. Surely the owners wouldn't mind if they put it over the fire to heat some water.

She took it to the sink and turned on the faucet. A little water trickled out, then the stream stopped. She stared at it and sighed.

From the doorway to the living room, she called to Dan, "Guess what."

"What?"

"No water either."

"Oh yeah." He shrugged apologetically. "The pump's electric. I was figuring to haul some buckets from the lake to flush toilets and all that. I don't know as we want to drink it, though."

"Great," Shelley muttered.

"Hey, didn't we bring some water bottles? Maybe you can use a couple of those for coffee."

That lifted her spirits a little. She'd insisted that Dan pick up a twenty-four-pack of bottled water for the trip.

"Good thinking." A minute later she carried the pan of water into the living room. "Here we go. This pan looks bad enough that I don't suppose they'll care if we use it for this."

Aiden had come downstairs in his pajamas and was huddled in a chair with Prize, wrapped in a wool blanket and staring out the window at the choppy lake.

"Look, Mama. Big waves."

Shelley gave Dan the pan of water and went to stand beside Aiden's chair. Whitecaps studded the surface of the lake as the wind churned it into froth.

"Wow! Yeah." She didn't know what to tell him, so she stood there with him for a couple of minutes watching the wild scene. Finally she ruffled his hair. "Are you hungry?"

He grinned up at her. "I'm so hungry I could eat a monster truck."

"Well, I guess that's better than just eating a monster."

He giggled. "Can we have pancakes?"

"Uh..." Shelley glanced at the fire burning in the fireplace. "I think that would be a little hard to do this morning, but we've got a few things that are already cooked. Come on. I think this is a cinnamon roll morning."

"Oh boy!" Aiden dropped the blanket and padded after her to the kitchen.

Time after time Shelley was hindered by the lack of electric power and water, but she managed to put a passable breakfast on the table. Dan took Prize out on the leash for a few minutes, using the umbrella to keep himself mostly dry, but the little dog came in soaking wet and shook droplets of water all over the kitchen.

Shelley gritted her teeth and called to Aiden, "Come get breakfast."

They all sat down to rolls, bananas, and juice. Shelley had brought ground coffee, but with the pan of water and a jar of instant she found in a cupboard, Dan was content. He was just starting on his third cinnamon roll when Emma began to wail in the room over their heads.

Shelley stood. "I'll get her. At least the rain has slacked off enough so that we can hear her."

She trudged up the stairs and into the children's room. Emma was standing up in the playpen, weeping. She raised her arms toward Shelley and sobbed pitifully.

Shelley picked her up and cuddled her close. "Mama's here. You don't know where you are, do you?"

Five minutes later, with Emma changed and dressed, Shelley lugged her downstairs. Dan came in carrying an armful of firewood with Aiden on his heels carrying two sticks.

"Helping Daddy, are you?" she asked.

"Yes, and we found some stuff, Mama."

"What kind of stuff?" Shelley glanced at Dan.

"There's a closet on the back porch with some camping gear in it." Dan dumped his load of wood in a crate at the edge of the hearth.

"Yeah." Aiden's eyes shone. "There's 'nocklers and tin dishes and a compass."

Dan smiled. "I thought I'd call Phil and ask if we can use some of it. Aiden wants to use the binoculars to look at things on the lake. And there's a sleeping bag in a plastic cover. I thought maybe he could use it."

"Yeah. So I can really camp." The little boy's chin was set just like Dan's when he was determined to do something.

"Well, go ahead and call—if you can get through. I don't know if you'll get service. I've got to feed Emma."

Shelley heard quite a bit of noise from the living room as she tended Emma and cleaned up the kitchen. When they had finished and she carried Emma into the other room, the fire crackled in the fireplace with the woven wire screen in place before it. Aiden and Dan were engrossed in draping two wool blankets over a couple of chairs and a wooden clothes rack.

"What's all this?" she asked.

Dan looked at her and grinned. "Phil said it's okay to use the stuff, and Aiden wanted to make a fort. I couldn't see any harm in it."

Shelley considered that. If the rain continued, this would be a long day. Maybe the distraction of the camping gear would be worth the effort to clean it up later. "All right, I guess. Did Phil say Aiden could use the binoculars?"

"Yes, but don't worry. He's going to be careful, aren't you, buddy?"

"Yup. Where's my bedroll?" Aiden looked around and spotted the sleeping bag. He flopped on it, stomach first. "Look, Mama!"

Shelley laughed. "I see."

"I need to set up my bed in the fort."

"Okay. Maybe your trusty sidekick can bring down Emma's pen." She looked up at Dan.

"Sure," Dan said. "Oh, and Phil's sorry we got such a bum weekend. He's going to call the power company and make sure they know we don't have any juice."

"Good." Shelley had wondered if they were the only ones without power, and whether anyone would know about it to come and fix the problem.

Aiden was inside his blanket fort now, and he peeked out at her between a flap of blanket and the seat of a rocking chair. "She can come in my fort. Emma, wanna come play?"

Emma stared toward his voice, her mouth wide.

"Come on, Emma," Aiden coaxed. "You can sit on my sleeping bag. Mama, can I bring my pillow down?"

"I think that would be fine," Shelley said.

Dan smiled at her. "Thanks, Shell. I'll go get the pen."

Chapter Eighteen

Diane! Welcome." Beverly hadn't expected anyone to come out in this weather. She opened the door wide. "Come in. You can leave your umbrella out there, though."

Diane chuckled and set the dripping umbrella down on the porch. She stepped inside, and Beverly held out a hand for her wet raincoat. "Let me take that."

"Thanks," Diane said. "I think the rain is actually letting up some now, but it hasn't quit yet. I've been wanting to talk writing with your dad, and I needed a break. It seemed like the perfect day for a cozy visit."

"That's great. He'll be happy to see you, I'm sure. I just made some coffee and I was fixing him a mug. Can I get you one?"

"That sounds good."

Beverly nodded. "Terrific. Go on in to his library and I'll bring it right in."

She went to the kitchen and added another mug to the tray she was fixing. Mrs. Peabody had stayed home this morning, nursing a cold, so Beverly was planning a light lunch of sandwiches and leftover vegetables and molded salad. But she'd hoped to run today.

Rain was no deterrent to Beverly when it came to her exercise regimen, as long as there was no lightning. But she hesitated to leave her father alone in bad weather.

She took the tray into the library. Her father and Diane were settled in cozy armchairs, laughing when Beverly entered.

"Ah, coffee. Thank you!" Father took his mug and set in on his coaster. Beverly passed the tray to Diane, and she took hers.

"Won't you join us?" Diane asked.

"Well..."

"Diane was just telling me about some of the tortured ideas she's come up with for titles for her future books," Father said.

Diane chuckled. "I am so bad at thinking of titles. It's even worse than trying to find the right character name. And just when I think I've found the perfect phrase, I realize it's the name of a best-selling book I heard about a few months ago."

Beverly smiled. "Won't your editor help you?"

"Yeah, she probably will, if I don't think of something good. But my online writers' group tells me that if the 'committee' ends up naming the book, you never know what you'll get."

"It might be something good." Father's eyes twinkled as he raised his mug to his lips.

"I suppose it might. I'm afraid it will be something I hate, though, so I keep trying."

Beverly glanced toward the window. "You know, I think the rain has stopped for a while. Would you mind if I took a quick run? I've been itching to go all day." She glanced toward her father, and Diane seemed to understand her concern.

"Sure," her friend said. "Go ahead. I thought I'd stay half an hour or so, if your dad can stand me that long. Then I'll get back to work."

Her father feigned shock. "Half an hour? That's nothing! We'll hardly have time to discuss one book."

Beverly went up to her room and changed quickly into her fleece and running shoes. Diane was a blessing in so many ways. The friends Beverly had made here in Marble Cove had helped both her and her father in ways she'd never expected.

She ran along the sidewalks on some of the residential streets. It was a route she didn't take often, but on a wet day she preferred it to the beach. She managed to skirt most of the puddles and got in a light workout in twenty minutes. Back home, she took a quick shower. Diane was just emerging from the library when Beverly came down the stairs.

"Time to go already?" Beverly asked, a little disappointed.

"I suppose I'd better," Diane said, walking with her to the kitchen. "It's easy to get distracted from my work. Sometimes I do it on purpose."

Beverly nodded. "I do the same thing."

"Say, have you heard from Jeff?" Diane asked.

"No, not since he left on assignment." Beverly frowned. "You know, it's been almost two weeks since he was last here."

"He hasn't called you in that long?"

"No. And I've left him a couple of messages. He left a camera bag here, and I thought he might need it. But he hasn't called back." She searched Diane's face for reassurance.

"You're worried about him," Diane said.

"A little, yes. And I haven't been able to talk to anyone about it. Father wouldn't understand."

"Why not?"

Beverly sighed. "Before Jeff left, we had a little disagreement. Not a fight or anything, but..." She hesitated.

Diane gave her wrist a gentle squeeze. "Enough to bother you now, and you wonder if it's bothering him too."

"Yeah, that about sums it up. At first I thought he'd call in a day or two. Then I started to wonder if maybe he was more upset than I'd realized. See, he wants an exclusive relationship. I told him... Well, Diane, I just didn't feel ready to commit. Not yet."

Diane nodded sympathetically. "Don't rush it. Not until you're sure."

"Thanks. It helps to hear you say that, but... I don't want to drive him away either."

"Yes, I understand."

"Still, I thought he'd call about the camera bag, even if he didn't want to talk to me. He could have called at night, when my cell phone is off, and left a message. But he hasn't.

Is he angry with me or is he just out of the service area for his phone?"

Diane eyed her thoughtfully. "Do you think he might be in real trouble?"

"I don't know. I hate to even consider that, but..."

"You think he might be hurt."

Beverly shrugged. "It's possible. The places he goes to get pictures—some are very remote."

"Do you know which magazine Jeff is working for?"

"Yes."

"Are you worried enough to call the magazine?" Diane asked. "You could use the camera bag he forgot as an excuse. They might know something."

Beverly grimaced. "I'm not sure I'm ready to do that. I mean, if he's all right, I wouldn't want him to think I'm checking up on him."

Diane nodded. "Well, I'll be praying for Jeff. And for you. God can resolve this—nobody's better at straightening out relationships."

"Thanks." Beverly smiled. "It's good to get another woman's perspective sometimes."

"Yup." Diane patted her shoulder. "Okay, I'm going to go home and get to work. Anytime you want to talk, you can call me, though."

"I'll remember that." Beverly got her raincoat for her. "Oh, and Maddie Bancroft called last night about the prayer book. I'll try to get it tomorrow."

"Wonderful. Let me know when you have it."

"I will, and don't forget your umbrella."

She shut the door behind Diane and sighed. Their talk had made her realize how much she cared about Jeff. He had become a close friend—one of her closest—and more. What would she do if he never came back? Tears filled her eyes at the thought that she might have pushed him away with her coldness and uncertainty.

Jeff was a man of action. He also liked people more than she did, but he wanted to know where he stood with them.

In silence, Beverly leaned against the door and closed her eyes. *Dear God, protect Jeff, wherever he is. Keep him from harm. And please, help me to sort out my feelings for him and to know how to react to him. I . . . I care about him, and I don't want to drive him away. Please give him an understanding heart, and help me not to be so fearful. I know he's a good man.*

*   *   *

When she left the Wheelands' house, Diane decided to make a quick trip to the Mercantile. She didn't need to do a complete grocery run, but she was out of milk, and she could grab a quart there and carry it home. The rain had let up, and she considered walking, but that would only prolong her binge of procrastination. She hurried to her driveway and got her car.

At the store, she parked as close to the door as she could get in case it started pouring again while she was inside. She hurried in and went straight to the dairy case. The choice of milk sizes, brands, and fat contents was limited, but she found a half gallon of one-percent and carried it to the counter. In line just ahead of her at the checkout stood a familiar figure. Diane glanced to the side to see if she could slip unobtrusively into another line. But it was too late— Leo Spangler turned and caught sight of her, his smile breaking out immediately.

"Diane! Great to see you."

"Hi, Leo. Thank you." She hesitated, realizing she had to give him some sort of response to his lunch invitation. Justin's words rang in her head—*you ought to at least give the guy another chance.* "Uh...I got your message, and I was planning to call you back later."

"Oh, okay." He moved forward a step as the shopper ahead of him advanced. As he lifted a few items from his basket, he kept glancing uncertainly toward her.

"Might as well save myself the trouble, since you're right here." She must have sounded cheerful, because he paused and smiled tentatively. "I'd be happy to have lunch with you. Uh—maybe tomorrow?"

"Sure." Leo's high-beam smile returned. "That's great. After church?"

"Yes, let's meet then."

A few minutes later, Diane got into her car and let out a big breath. "Was that so hard?" she asked out loud. She flipped down her visor and looked at herself in the mirror. The drizzle had wilted her hair, and she hadn't put on makeup that morning, but Leo had still seemed glad that she'd accepted. She had to admit, a guy like that had some potential.

★　★　★

Shelley watched Dan go up the stairs with fresh eyes. Somehow, in five minutes Aiden had lifted all their spirits. It struck her that she had the same power. In fact, she might even be able to wield more attitude magic than Aiden.

It's up to me to turn my attitude around, she thought. *If I get all grumpy and complaining, Dan won't be happy, and the kids sure won't.*

She turned Emma loose at the opening of Aiden's "fort," and the little girl crawled inside, squealing with delight.

"Hey, Mama, where's Emma's bunny? We can pretend we caught a bunny, and he can live in the fort with us."

Shelley smiled, glad he wasn't planning to roast Emma's bunny over their campfire.

"I'll get it."

She found the bedraggled stuffed toy and set it outside the blanket doorway. "Okay, there's a wild rabbit just outside the gate to the fort."

Aiden peeked out and grinned, eyeing the bunny. "Come on, Emma. We have to catch him."

Prize's black nose appeared in the crack, and she gave a little woof.

"*Sh*, Prize," Aiden said. "You'll scare the bunny."

Shelley walked to the window and picked up the binoculars Aiden had left in the chair. The rain had abated, but the cabin's eaves still dripped, and the lake was a rough sheet of gray. She hoped the weather would clear so they could explore the area. With a little sunshine, she was sure this weekend would be everything they'd hoped.

And if not?

She looked around at the crackling fire and the cozy blanket fort. She supposed they could move their s'mores party to this afternoon, rather than wait until evening. She'd ask Dan what he thought about having it when the children got up from their naps.

If it was still wet out. She wasn't giving up yet on the possibility of better weather later in the day. She and Dan spent the remainder of the morning playing with the children and doing everything they could think of to get ready for another night without electricity.

She made preparations for the evening far in advance. She might not have a kitchen range, but Dan set up Phil's camp stove on the porch, and she was sure she'd be able to cook there more easily than over the fireplace. Maybe they could have their candlelight dinner after all.

"Whatcha doin'?" Dan asked when he came to the kitchen and found her packing their lunch sandwiches into their picnic basket. "It's still raining a little."

"I know, but we can pretend, can't we? I know Aiden can, so I figured we could too. Maybe after their naps, we can make our s'mores. And I thought maybe we could take a pretend hike in here—or outside if the rain stops completely—and tucker them out a little."

"Hey, I like that idea." Dan gave her his lopsided smile and moved in for a kiss. "Thanks for not getting upset."

Shelley smiled up at him. "Well, I was tempted to throw a fit, but that wouldn't help things, would it?"

"Not a bit."

She nodded. "So we might as well make the most of it. We probably won't get two days away from home again for a long time."

He turned to look out the window. "Looks like it's not too bad out right now. Does Aiden have a jacket?"

"Yes."

"Well, if he and I take Prize out, maybe Aiden can get a closer look at the lake. We may get a little soggy, but I really want him to at least be able to stick his hand in the water."

Shelley laughed. "Go ahead. The leash is over there near the back door. Let me get Emma and distract her, though, so she won't fuss when you go out."

"Oh yeah," Dan said with a sheepish smile. "I forgot to tell you—she needs a diaper change."

Shelley laughed. "Well, that will make a distraction." She kissed him again. This was what they'd wanted—time together, relaxation with the kids, and no pressure to fill orders or get Dan off to work on time.

She stood on tiptoe and whispered in his ear, "Maybe tonight, if the kids go to sleep at a decent hour, we can have our special anniversary dinner."

"I'll make sure they're tired." His grin faded. "But I don't want you to have to cook dinner, especially if the power's still off."

"We can't go out and leave the kids. We'll get by."

Dan's eyes lit. "I could run into town late this afternoon, maybe take Aiden with me, and bring back some take-out food. How do you feel about Chinese for dinner tonight?"

"That sounds lovely."

★   ★   ★

Margaret applied a final sliver of deep purple paint to the quahog shell shape in the corner of her new painting. It wasn't so much a shell as the suggestion of a shell—the vague shape and exaggerated color of the quahog.

Business had been slow at the gallery on this gloomy Saturday, and she'd decided to paint between customers. Rarely was she glad for uninterrupted time at the gallery, but today it had paid off.

She stood back and squinted at her canvas. Not bad, she thought, but could she really trust her own judgment? She'd started two hours ago, and somehow, the composition had come together in a fluid, sweeping manner. Against the varied gray-blue background she had placed unstructured images that planted hints of seaweed and shells and a current of swirling water. If the viewer looked hard, he would find a shy starfish lurking behind a lump that could be a rock. Toward the top, the water curled and folded on itself—an impression of waves. Definitely not her usual production.

She smiled. Would this be her debut piece? She had several possibilities now—this, the tide pool, and the one focused on Old First's steeple. Any of the three paintings would qualify. She would get some outside opinions. If this one wasn't good enough, she could go with a safer, more tranquil and traditional scene.

But something inside her stirred when she looked at this unexpected painting. It unsettled her just a bit, and yet that wasn't necessarily bad. It gave her a feeling of anticipation. It revealed all the secrets going on beneath the water when the wind stirred only the surface.

"*Sea Breeze,*" she said pensively. "That's what I'll call it."

She brought over the other tide pool painting she had started. She still needed to do some work on it. She liked it, but next to the more abstract one it looked tame. Of course, she hadn't painted in the boy yet. That would make a big difference. She hoped she could do a good job—she didn't usually put people in her paintings, at least not close up. She knew she could draw faces, but could she bring the little boy to life in acrylics?

Margaret set the painting aside and began to clean up her studio. It was high time she got home.

The phone rang, and she hurried to answer it.

"Hey," Allan said. "Are you ready to come home? It's looking like rain again, so I thought we could swing over and pick you up."

"Thanks," Margaret said. "And if you have a minute, I'd like your opinion on something. Promise not to say you hate it."

Allan chuckled. "All right. If I'm not crazy about it, shall I just say that it's *interesting*?"

"Yes," Margaret said. "That will be fine."

★   ★   ★

The thunder and lightning rolled in over Marble Cove again just after sundown. Beverly jumped at the first loud boom and hastily closed her computer program. She pushed back her chair and was rising to go and check on her father when the electricity went out.

A little light still came through the windows, and every few seconds a flicker of lightning illuminated everything in an instant of startling clarity. She made her way slowly to the top of the stairs.

"Father?" she called.

"Right here in the library," he replied.

"I'm going to grab my flashlight," Beverly said. "I'll be right down."

"Can you get mine too? It's on the bottom shelf of my nightstand."

She went to her own room first, and with light in hand forayed into her father's and found his as well. She paused at his bedroom window to look out at Newport Avenue. The streetlights were out. In fact, she couldn't see any lights at all except for a soft glow from the Littles' kitchen window. Fred and Cindy must have lit a lantern.

When she returned to the library, Father thanked her. "Good thing we already ate supper."

"Yes," she said. "Can I get you anything? I hope this is a short-term outage. I'll call the power company to report it, but it looks as though the entire street is dark."

"It's early," he said. "Maybe we could light the Coleman lantern so we can read for a while. I guess your computer's down."

"It is. I could work on my laptop, but I think I'll stop for tonight."

"Right. Well, where's the lantern?"

"It should be in the hall closet. The box is up on the top shelf."

She had to take a chair into the hall from the kitchen to reach it, but she had no trouble finding the lantern. She was relieved to see that it was the newer, battery-operated type, not the old one she remembered from childhood that involved fuel and mantles and, for some reason, pumping a little handle.

A crack that had to be lightning striking close by startled her and she nearly dropped the lantern. Hauling in a deep breath to steady herself, she climbed cautiously down from the chair.

She carried the box to the dining room table and opened it. Knowing her father as she did, she wasn't surprised to find the instruction pamphlet still inside. She studied it briefly by flashlight and then turned on the lantern. Its brilliance made the room seem almost as bright as in the daytime, but when a flash of lightning made it even brighter, she knew her observation was a matter of perspective.

She went back to the hall and set the lantern down. If she didn't put that chair away now, one of them would probably trip over it later. She picked it up and took it to the kitchen, relying on the rays of light that followed her from the lantern.

Well satisfied, she went back to retrieve the lantern and was headed for the library when someone knocked on the door.

Her heart jumped at the loud pounding of the antique knocker, and she turned around with a gasp to stare at the door. Just because the electricity was off, she told herself, there was nothing to be frightened of. It was just so unexpected, that was all. Probably Diane or Mrs. Peabody.

Thunder boomed, and she walked quickly forward, carrying the lantern. The visitor knocked again, and she called, "I'm coming!"

She turned the knob and started to open the door. The wind pushed it against her, and she let it swing wide.

In the circle of light cast by the lantern, with rain dripping off his hooded plastic jacket, stood Jeff.

CHAPTER NINETEEN

Jeff! Come in!" Beverly stood back to let him enter and set the lantern down. "I was so worried about you! Did you get my messages?"

"Not until today. I'm sorry about that."

"Let me take your coat." The sight of him had sent a shock of relief over her, and her pulse raced madly.

"I don't think you want it in your closet," he said. "It's dripping."

"I'll hang it in the shower." She made herself take a deep breath and opened the closet to get a hanger. "Are you all right?"

"Yeah, I'm fine, thanks." He carefully slid out of the rain jacket and handed it to her.

Beverly took it. To her surprise, her eyes filled with tears. "I'm so glad to see you."

His features softened. "Same here. I thought about you a lot." He touched her cheek gently. "I was afraid I'd completely blown it with you."

"No, not at all." She felt some warmth come into her cheeks and looked away. "I don't want to leave you standing in the dark while I take care of this. There's a flashlight on the dining room table."

"I'll get it." Jeff moved off toward the dining room.

She held the lantern high and a moment later saw the paler beam of the flashlight. She took his coat to the downstairs bathroom and hung it over the showerhead.

Jeff met her again at the door of the dining room.

"I was just getting the lantern for Father when you arrived," she said breathlessly. "The power went out a few minutes ago, and he wanted to go on with his reading."

"By all means, let's take it to him."

Beverly led the way and Jeff followed.

"What is it, Beverly?" her father asked. "Do we have company?"

"Yes. Jeff is here."

He stepped forward and turned off the flashlight. "Good evening, Mr. Wheeland." He held out his hand.

Beverly's father shook it. "Good to see you again, Jeff. Have a seat."

"Actually, I wondered if he was hungry," Beverly said. She turned to Jeff. "Have you eaten?"

"No, I drove straight here, but—"

"We've got leftovers. Come on, I'll fix you a plate. Leave the lantern for Father, and we'll use the flashlights."

"I hope they get the lines fixed before eight o'clock," her father said. "There's a wildlife documentary I want to watch tonight. You'd probably like it, Jeff."

"I probably would," Jeff said. "Have you called the power company?"

"Oh, that was next on my list," Beverly said.

"I can do it if you want, while you rustle up those leftovers you were talking about."

In the kitchen, Beverly checked the coffeepot. "It's still fairly hot. Want a cup?"

"That sounds good." Jeff sank down at the small kitchen table, and Beverly got him a mug.

"The chicken alfredo's probably cold, but I can heat some on one of the gas burners."

"Oh, don't open your refrigerator," Jeff said. "This outage could last a while."

"It's all right. I'll be quick. Oh and here's the number for the power company." She took the promotional magnet from the front of the refrigerator and handed it to him.

He took out his cell phone and made the call while she worked. Ten minutes later she set a plate of warmed-over dinner before him and sat down opposite him. He had stood one flashlight on end so that the light shone off the ceiling.

"I'm sure we have a few candles somewhere," Beverly said. "I should probably look for them."

"This is fine. The power company says there are trees and limbs down due to the storm, but that it's isolated and they're working on it."

"Well, that's not too bad," Beverly peered at him in the dim light.

"I wouldn't hold my breath, seeing as how the storm's not over," Jeff said with a chuckle.

She looked toward the window. "Maybe not, but the thunder certainly isn't as loud as it was a little while ago."

As if to support her words, lightning flickered, but it seemed weaker and more distant than the earlier flashes. Several seconds passed before she heard the rumble of thunder. "Maybe it's blowing out to sea," she said hopefully.

"Well, thanks for the dinner. This is very good."

Beverly chuckled. "I'll tell Mrs. Peabody you said so."

The overhead light blinked and then came on, making her squint. The refrigerator began to hum, and the microwave oven's clock flashed 12:00 at them.

"Hey, there you go!" Jeff cried gleefully. "I shouldn't have been so skeptical."

"Hooray!" Beverly jumped up. "I'll go check on Father. And we can zap that coffee now if it's not hot enough."

Before she could cross the kitchen, her father appeared in the doorway.

"This is more like it," he said. "So, Jeff, I guess we can watch that documentary. It starts in about fifteen minutes."

"Great," Jeff said. "If you don't mind, I'd like to talk to Beverly for a few more minutes first."

"Sure, sure."

"Can I get you anything?" Beverly asked.

"No, I'm fine. Take your time, Jeff." Her father turned and ambled back toward the living room. A moment later, she heard the television go on.

Jeff smiled at her ruefully. "I hope I wasn't too short with him. I really think we need to talk."

"You weren't, and . . . " Beverly swallowed hard. "I think you're right." She resumed her seat. "Jeff, I owe you an apology."

He shook his head. "No, I'm the one who was unreasonable, and I'm sorry. I shouldn't have pushed you. You've been through a lot, and ... well, I'm crazy about you, but I know we all have times when we need some space. I should have understood that, and there's no excuse for getting upset about it."

Her heart melted and she smiled at him. "Thanks. I'm at fault too. I overreacted to what you said. I mean, it's natural to want to see progress in a relationship. And when I thought about it carefully, I realized I want to go forward. I just think I may need to move more slowly than you would like."

He reached for her hand. "That's okay. Really. While I was away, I had a lot of time to think." He chuckled. "I left here in such a hurry, I didn't realize I'd forgotten my camera bag."

"Oh yes." Her impulse was to jump up and get it, but his tone kept her in her chair.

"Well, guess what," he said. "I left my phone charger in the bag, but I didn't really need that camera, so I figured I'd pick it up when I came back. I didn't think about the charger being in there for about three days—until I needed it."

She shook her head. "I never looked inside. I kept leaving you messages and wondering why you didn't call me."

"Now you know. I stopped at a phone store this morning on my way and bought a new mobile charger, and that's the first time I was able to retrieve the messages. Beverly, I'm so sorry."

"I was getting a little worried, I admit."

"Were you?"

His plaintive smile brought home her anxiety and the depth of her relief.

"Yes. More than a little, to be honest. I didn't want to admit it at first, but I was."

"Well, I probably should have called you right away. Instead, I figured I'd take care of business and then come up here. I'm sorry I kept you wondering for a few more hours."

"You're forgiven. But if I'd known you had no way to use your phone for the last two weeks, I would have been a basket case. And Diane would probably have called the Coast Guard."

He laughed. "Diane?"

"I finally told her what was going on. I didn't go into detail, but I needed to talk to someone, and to have somebody objective tell me I'm not crazy."

"Diane would be a good person for that."

"Yes, she certainly is. She's very practical. She even suggested I call the magazine if I was too worried, because you were probably checking in with them. If I'd known about the phone situation, I might have."

"Well, for at least half of the time I was gone, I probably couldn't have gotten service where I was anyway," Jeff said. "But listen, I'll keep you better posted next time I'm out. Would that help?"

"Yes, I think it would. Thanks." She looked down at their clasped hands and felt a new serenity that she'd never felt with him before.

Jeff made a wry face. "For the first few days I didn't want to bother you, and to be honest, for a while I felt as though you probably didn't want to hear from me."

"No, that's not true." Her conscience nudged her a little as she recalled her dread at seeing his name on her caller ID. "Well, sometimes I've been a little nervous to talk to you. But that's only because I didn't know what to say. I think..." She gazed into his eyes. "I think the more we talk, the easier it gets. I'm not entirely comfortable with—with 'us' yet, but I'm feeling better about it now that you're back."

"Good. Maybe we can keep making progress." He squeezed her hand. "I'd like to continue this conversation, but I think I should go watch the program with your dad. Do you mind?"

Beverly smiled. "I think he'd like that. I need to reboot my computer and do a little more work." It would be cozy to know Jeff was just a few yards away while she worked, to hear his muffled voice and her father's from the library.

"Beverly, I don't want to scare you off by being too intense again, but I *like* you. I'd rather be with you than just about anyone else on earth. And it would be nice to know if...well, if it's not too much to ask..."

A wave of tenderness brought tears to her eyes and a lump to her throat. She inhaled deeply and looked up at him. "I care, Jeff. I care...deeply."

He smiled but said nothing.

"I'm not sure I'm ready to make a commitment," she said uncertainly.

Jeff nodded. "That's all right. I can live with that, as long as you can think of possibly—when you're ready—moving on from here."

"I think that's a good idea," she managed. "Forward, but slowly."

"Yes."

Jeff leaned over and brushed her cheek with his warm lips.

She nodded. "Oh, wait a minute. We have custard pie."

Jeff laughed. "How about you bring me a piece in the other room? Your dad's probably thinking I'm missing the best part of the show."

"He's being very patient," Beverly said, amazed that her father hadn't forayed into the kitchen again. She'd better put the teakettle on for him now that the power was restored.

"Well, I can be patient too," Jeff said. "Contrary to what you've seen in the past." He touched her cheek and left the room.

★   ★   ★

Shelley lit the candles on the kitchen table when she heard Dan drive up in front of the cabin. As he opened the door, she turned off the lantern. He came in using his flashlight and carrying a bag. Delicious smells wafted to Shelley.

"Oh, tell me you got sweet-and-sour chicken," she said.

"I did. That and some beef with broccoli. Fried rice, egg rolls. Did I forget anything?"

"I don't think so."

He set the bag down, reached inside his jacket, and pulled out two pairs of wooden chopsticks in paper holders. "Ta-da."

Shelley laughed. "Perfect." She hugged him and snuggled against him for a moment, then pulled away. "Hey, your jacket's dry."

"Yup. It didn't rain the whole time I was gone."

"Great. Maybe tomorrow we'll see the sun." She turned to the table and began removing the containers of food from the bag.

"Kids all settled down?" Dan asked.

"Both sound asleep. Even Prize quieted right down." She grinned at him. "Thanks for doing this. All of it—the cabin and everything."

He shrugged. "I wondered if you wished we'd stayed home. We could have had a nice dinner out tonight."

"If they have power in Marble Cove," Shelley said.

"True."

"Well, I'm glad we came," she said. "There were moments, but I think this weekend has been good for all of us."

Dan pulled her into his arms again. As he was kissing her, the overhead light flickered and stayed on, too bright by far.

"Well, look at that," Dan said. "There must be real electricity between us."

She laughed. "The power company has terrible timing."

"Let's turn the lights off and keep the candlelight," Dan said.

"Really?"

"Sure. Why not? And then if you want to, after we eat we can wash all the dishes you want, and you can have a hot bath to boot."

"Oh, and we can make coffee the easy way," she said.

"Yeah. And flush the toilet without buckets."

She kissed him again. "Happy anniversary. And thank you."

CHAPTER TWENTY

After the church service on Sunday, Maddie Bancroft met Beverly in the aisle as they moved toward the door. She held out a shopping bag.

"Beverly, here's that item we discussed." Maddie smiled at Beverly's father. "Hello, Mr. Wheeland."

"Hi." He nodded toward the bag Beverly now carried. "Is that the book Beverly was telling me about? I'm anxious to see it myself."

"That's the one. If you can tell us anything about it, we'd be happy to hear it." She turned back to Beverly. "I wrapped it in tissue paper and put it in a padded envelope to protect it."

"Okay, thanks," Beverly said.

Maddie smiled. "I almost said, 'Handle with care,' but I know I don't have to tell you that. Just remember it's on loan, and the owner wants it back in the same condition he gave it to us in." She frowned as if puzzling over her syntax. "Well, anyway, you know what I mean." She lowered her voice. "He's not particularly sentimental about Thorpe or Old First, but he wants to preserve the book. I expect he'll sell it later."

"That's too bad," Beverly said. "Does he think it belonged to Thorpe?"

"Not a hundred percent, but he said it's possible. Ask him about it."

"I'll do that, and we'll certainly be careful. Thank you for letting us have a look at it."

"You're welcome." Maddie laughed. "I've been a little frazzled, wondering how we'll protect all the artifacts. Knowing this one's with you will ease my mind a little since you're so responsible."

Beverly didn't comment, but she wondered if that was her image in Marble Cove—the responsible one. Instead, she said, "The committee does have a great obligation to take care of those fragile items."

"Oh yes, and I'm trying to get some of those glass cases to display them in. The library is going to lend us one, but only for the actual week of the celebration. If you think of anyone else who might have one, let me know."

"All right."

"The library's really nice," Maddie went on. "It's like a table with a glass top, and you can lock the lid, so the items inside will be secure. If we could get a couple more of those, we'd be all set."

Beverly nodded, realizing how much trust Maddie was putting in her and her friends, allowing them to take the book out of her sight and actually handle it.

"I'll keep my ears open," she said.

"Great." They had reached the door, and Maddie said, "We'll see you." She turned to shake the pastor's hand.

After greeting Reverend Locke, Beverly and her father went out to her car. She wondered if the minister had any idea what she was carrying. She doubted it. Since he was so interested in Jeremiah Thorpe, he probably would have mentioned it if he'd known.

When they got home, Beverly carried the package inside feeling a bit nervous about the prayer book. Perhaps she ought to wait until the other women could be with her to look at it, but she knew her father was anxious to see it. She would see her friends later, but she doubted they'd have time to do much today since everyone was so busy.

They ate lunch together, and her father settled in his library. Beverly carried the padded envelope in there, and her father eyed it with anticipation.

"Is that the antique prayer book? I'm eager to see it."

"All right." There was no helping it now. Beverly had told him about the possibilities the little volume held, and she couldn't deny him the chance to see it. "Are your hands clean?"

Her father frowned. "Yes."

"Well then, you can open it." Beverly passed it to him. "Maddie was quite anxious that we not damage it by rough handling."

"Ha. We'll have none of that. But let's go out to the table." He sat down in the dining room, opened the envelope, and slid out the tissue-wrapped book.

"I'm going to wash my hands." Beverly went to the bathroom and washed, then carefully dried off with a clean towel. She wouldn't be surprised if Frances or Maddie asked her later about her procedures for handling the artifact.

When she got back to the dining room, Father was bent over the small book, turning the pages slowly.

"Well, it's certainly old. It doesn't have Thorpe's name conveniently inscribed in the front, though, or anything like that."

"Diane and I need to go see Mr. Roux and find out exactly what he knows about it," Beverly said. She sat down beside him and leaned in.

"It's fascinating," Father said. "Look at the old typeface. Hard to read, after what we're used to."

"We've been spoiled." She scanned the page before them. "May I see the title page, please?"

Her father gently turned back to the beginning, and she read the imposing title: *Book of Common Prayer and Administration of the Sacraments, and Other Rites and Ceremonies, According to the Use of the Church of England: Together with the Psalter or Psalms of David, Pointed as they are to be sung or said in Churches.*

"That's quite a mouthful," Father said.

"Yes, especially with half the S's printed as F's." She smiled at the line, "fung or faid in Churches."

"Wonder how many people have held this book," he mused.

"I expect a great many over the last three hundred years and more."

"Yes."

Beverly flipped a few pages. "Did you see anything written in by hand?"

"You mean doodles?" He smiled. "No, they probably thought back then that it would be wicked to write notes in a prayer book."

"Maybe." Beverly continued turning the pages until she came to one blank sheet at the back of the book. Except that it wasn't blank. Someone had penciled in some words—or symbols. It was hard to read the faded inscription. "Look. There's writing on this page. What do you make of it?"

"Huh, didn't see that." Her father leaned in close. "Someone did doodle, after all."

Gingerly, she picked up the book and brought it closer to her face. "Maybe a magnifying glass would help." Beverly's excitement grew. "It's faded, but we ought to be able to..." She stared, baffled, at the writing on the paper. "That's odd." She held it out to her father. "What do you see?"

He squinted at it. "Is it in English?"

"Good question."

"Well, they're definitely letters. But they all run together. Looks like mishmash to me. Or..."

"Or a code," Beverly said.

"Yes, that thought did cross my mind."

She frowned over the symbols. "There are no spaces or punctuation. Maybe it's just an old way of writing."

Father shook his head. "Doesn't seem so to me, but I'm no expert. Most of the letters don't make words."

"*Hmm*. Too many consonants." She looked at the book's cracked binding. "I don't think I could make copies without damaging the book. I'd have to open it up flat."

"Don't do that."

She sighed. "You know what? I'm not going to look too closely at this or try to figure it out until my friends see it. If it's a puzzle of some sort, they should get in on the fun too."

Her father looked a little disappointed, but he straightened and nodded. "I suppose that's fair. Let me know what you find out."

"I will."

"It wouldn't surprise me a bit if that was something Jeremiah Thorpe penned himself. He was a clever man, if half the stories about him are true."

"Yes, he must have been, but we've no reason to believe this was his." Beverly took one more look at the mysterious writing and gently closed the book. She reached for the white tissue paper and folded it around the volume. "All right, back in the envelope you go." She hoped the four friends could work on it soon—her curiosity might distract her from her own work.

⋆   ⋆   ⋆

Diane pulled into the parking lot at the Landmark Inn on Sunday afternoon. Leo was waiting on the front porch, smiling. She walked up the steps toward him, looking around as she went and inhaling the fresh ocean breeze.

"They have such a beautiful view here," she said.

"Yes, and I think Victoria has repainted again." Leo stood beside her for a moment, watching gulls swoop in over the rocky shore. "Hungry?" he asked.

"Ravenous."

"Let's go in then."

Victoria Manchester, the owner, met them at the dining room door with a big smile.

"Hello. Welcome back to the Landmark."

"Thank you," Diane said, peering past her. "Looks like you've done some redecorating in the dining room."

"Yes, I'm very happy with it. Thanks so much for your help when I needed it—and I can assure you both that things are running smoothly now. You'll find the service excellent."

"I'm sure we will," Leo said, smiling.

"Beverly Wheeland has been singing your praises," Diane told her.

Victoria laughed. "The fan club goes both ways. Beverly has done a terrific job on my promotional materials and my bookkeeping program. Two of you today?"

"Yes," Leo said.

Victoria led them to a table near the big windows overlooking the shore and handed them menus. "Your waitress will be right with you. And I'll make sure she knows you get the family discount."

"Oh, you don't need to do that," Leo said.

"I insist." Victoria smiled and walked back to the entry, where more customers were waiting.

"I really like what she's done in here," Leo said, gazing around at the nautical antiques and artifacts hanging on the walls and the rafters. Among them were oars, lobster buoys, and an old block and tackle.

"That ship's wheel looks authentic," Diane said, nodding toward the piece in the center of the room. It was mounted on a raised platform with a rail around it, suggesting part of a ship's deck.

"Nice," Leo said. "Oh, and look." He gazed toward the far wall, where a framed half model of a schooner was mounted. "If that's an old one, it's worth a fortune. I read up on them a bit after I saw one at an auction."

"Do you go to auctions often?" Diane asked.

"Not often, but maybe two or three a year. I enjoy it. Don't always buy much." He shrugged. "I like anything to do with veterinary practice, and I picked up some antique surgical instruments at one. If I see something I like, I bid on it."

"It sounds like fun."

He raised his eyebrows and smiled. "Shall I tell you the next time I'm going?"

Diane hesitated only a moment. "Sure. If it's not too far away." Already she was wondering if she could fit something like that into her next book. A country auction might lead to all sorts of mysterious happenings in fiction.

"Great. I'll keep it in mind." Leo opened his menu. "Now, what are we going to have today?"

Diane looked over the possibilities. "The special is a cup of chowder and a lobster roll. That sounds really good to me."

"Yeah? I was thinking maybe I'd have the deep sea scallops."

"That sounds good too." She chuckled. "Thanks for bringing me here, Leo. I've intended to get out and do more, but I've been pretty much chained to my desk."

"How's the book coming?"

"Oh, not bad." She grimaced. "Slowly, if I'm truthful. But it is progressing. You know what's funny?"

"What?"

She shook her head ruefully. "Some days I am so sick of this story, I just want to be done with it and get on to the next one. For some reason, it seems as though the next one will be easier. And more fun."

"Maybe your brain is just playing tricks on you."

"That's what I'm afraid of. I'm a champion procrastinator."

"Surely not."

Diane smiled. "Oh yes."

"Well, anytime you need a pep talk—or a stern reprimand—give me a call, and I'll oblige."

"Great."

The waitress came over with a pitcher of water. Diane decided to be adventurous and join Leo in ordering the scallop plate. She opted for iced tea, while Leo asked for coffee.

Diane sat back in her chair and realized she was having a good time, and she wasn't nervous. Maybe she was past that with Leo. He seemed as though he could be a good friend—someone to talk to or to go out with now and then for a change of pace.

After their entrees came, they continued to talk casually about their dogs and their work. Leo didn't have the intensity of an ardent suitor, and that relieved the last layer of Diane's stress. Maybe they could just be friends—for now, anyway.

"I saw in the paper that there's going to be a Cary Grant week next month at the theater. They're going to show a different one of his movies every afternoon for their matinees."

"Oh, fun," Diane said. "What's your favorite Cary Grant movie?"

Leo shrugged. "Maybe *North by Northwest.* I always did like Hitchcock. Although *Gunga Din* is interesting—very different from his others."

"I haven't seen that one," Diane said. "I think *Father Goose* is my favorite."

"Oh yeah, I like that one too." Leo smiled. "Want to go?"

"Sure, it would be fun."

He nodded. "Great. I'll watch for the schedule so we'll know what's playing when, and we can pick one we both think we'll like."

Half an hour later, they separated between their cars in the parking lot. Leo gave her hand a squeeze.

"Thanks for coming, Diane. I really enjoyed this."

"Me too," she said. "The scallops were delicious, and I had a good time talking to you."

Diane drove the short distance home humming to herself. When she parked in the driveway, Rocky started barking inside the house.

"Oh yes, I'm sure you're eager to get out," she called with a laugh as she fumbled with her keys. She'd let him out briefly between church and her meeting with Leo, but Rocky would be ready for a long walk on the beach now.

She unlocked the door and he pranced around her, yipping joyfully. She laughed and patted him. Rocky sat down and wagged his tail with enthusiasm.

"Let me get changed," she said. "It'll only take a minute."

As she quickly put on jeans, Bogs, and a sweater, she wondered briefly what Justin would say now. Smiling, she grabbed her phone and the leash. She might just call Justin while she and Rocky enjoyed the beach.

⋆   ⋆   ⋆

"Glad you're back, Shelley." Margaret gave her a big hug. "Come on in. I know you weren't gone long, but we missed you."

Shelley walked into Margaret's kitchen and greeted Diane and Beverly. "Hello, ladies. Thanks for inviting me over."

"Well, it had been a while since we were all together," Diane said. "We just felt like we needed to catch up."

Beverly smiled at Shelley. "So how did the weekend go? Did you get the same storms we did?"

"And how." Shelley grinned. "We made the most of it, though. We had a lot of fun, although we had to stay in the cabin until this morning. At least the sun came out and Dan and Aiden got to have one good boat ride before we had to pack up and come home."

Margaret poured lemonade as the others found seats around the table. "I'm glad Dan let you come over. I promise we won't keep you long though."

"He was sweet about it," Shelley said. "We'd only been home an hour when you called, but Emma's sleeping, and I had one big load of laundry done already and another in the washer, and I'd cleaned out the cooler."

"It must have been a challenge, keeping the kids occupied," Diane said.

"Yes. We didn't get to swim or hike like we'd planned, but we had a fireplace, so we got our campfire. Aiden built a fort in the living room, and he and Emma and Prize had a grand time of it."

Margaret smiled and took her seat. "That sounds fun for them. What about you and Dan? Did you celebrate your anniversary?"

"We did." Shelley's cheeks went pink and she smiled. "The electricity was out all day yesterday, so Dan went out for takeout and we had our candlelight dinner after the kids were in bed."

"That sounds nice and romantic," Beverly said. "We lost power here too, if it's any consolation."

"I did wonder, until we got home and all the digital clocks were flashing at us." They all laughed. "So, Margaret, how are your preparations for the art fair going?"

"Not too badly." Margaret smiled in satisfaction. "I'm going to have enough paintings to display, and I have a couple of new ones you're all welcome to drop in and see at the gallery any time this week."

"I can't wait," Diane said.

"Well, they're very different," Margaret told her. "Both started with some inspiration from Aiden, but they came out poles apart."

"From Aiden?" Shelley's face lit. "I'll have to tell him."

"Yes, remember when he gave me the shell? Well, that and what he said about the starfish got me to thinking, and I'm pleased with the results."

"I'll drop in tomorrow and take a look," Beverly said.

"Me too, if it's not raining," Shelley added, and they all chuckled.

"I've had enough rain for the entire season," Diane said, shaking her head. "So has Rocky."

"Margaret, have they given you any chores to do as artists' ambassador?" Beverly asked.

"Oh yes," Margaret said. "I've had quite a few phone calls, mostly from artists who are new to the fair this year, wanting information. Of course, I'm new too, so several times I had to call someone else and then get back to them. And I've been to two organizational meetings."

"You've been busy," Diane observed.

"Yes, but Allan and Adelaide have filled in the gap for me, not to mention you gals."

Diane looked at Beverly with raised eyebrows. "So, did Maddie bring you the prayer book today?"

"She did. Father and I looked at it briefly, but I haven't really done anything with it, and I didn't have time to do any Internet research. But I did call Hank Roux and made an appointment with him for Diane and me to talk to him about it tomorrow night—if that's okay with you, Diane."

"Sounds perfect," Diane said.

"Good. And if either of you can go..." Beverly looked expectantly at Margaret and Shelley.

"Not me," Margaret said, "though I envy you."

"Better count me out," Shelley said. "It's going to take me a while to catch up on my schedule."

"Well, I wish you could go, but Diane and I understand. And I brought it today so that Margaret and Shelley could see it." Beverly took the padded envelope from her tote bag. She eased the tissue-wrapped book out and folded back the paper.

"Wow, that does look old," Shelley said.

"Yes." Margaret leaned in close. "What do we know about it?"

"Next to nothing," Diane said. "Mr. Roux got it in a box of stuff at an estate sale."

"There was an old hymnal in the same box," Beverly said. "It's not nearly as old as this prayer book, but the hymnal did say Old First in the front—or rather, First Church of Marble Cove. And there was a booklet about the church that Frances said was printed in 1970. I want to check with Mr. Roux and see if they were in the same box when he bought them. If so, that might help tie the prayer book to Old First."

Diane nodded. "It wouldn't be conclusive, but it would be a start."

Shelley glanced at the kitchen clock. "Well, I'd better skedaddle if I want Dan to be as cooperative next time I need a break. Can we look at that again when we have more time?"

"Sure we can," Beverly said. "There are a couple of things about it that I'd like to discuss. But maybe Diane and I will get more information from Mr. Roux."

"Let's meet again after the art fair," Diane suggested.

"That sounds good to me," Margaret said. She hated to be the one to postpone the sleuthing, but with all she had going on right now, that would probably be best.

"No problem," Beverly said serenely.

"Margaret, thanks so much." Shelley stood and carried her empty glass to the counter.

Margaret walked with her to the door. "Don't forget to stop by the gallery with the kids if you can. Aiden might like to see those new paintings too."

"Thanks. I'll do that. He'll be excited when I tell him you used his shell."

"Oh yes, he'll be able to see that shell plainly in my tide pool painting. It's more obscure in the other one."

Shelley laughed and gave Margaret a hug. "Can't wait to see them."

CHAPTER TWENTY-ONE

On Monday morning, Margaret unlocked the gallery and put her things away in the back room. Her new abstract painting sat on the easel in her studio, and she studied it carefully. Did she really dare exhibit it as her premier piece at the art fair?

She carried the canvas out into the front room, where the light was better, and stood it on one of the tables. She snapped on the track lighting above it and stepped back a few paces to gaze at it. Slowly, she smiled. The painting might not have a lot of structure, but its colors and forms combined in a way that made her happy.

The bell on the door jangled behind her, and she turned to greet her first customer of the day. A woman perhaps a little older than Margaret entered, looking about curiously. She was very short, and her straight brown hair was cut short, with bangs. She wore a matching navy blue skirt and jacket with a pearl gray blouse—a very conservative outfit for a woman browsing a gallery in a coastal town.

"Hello," Margaret said. "Welcome to the Shearwater."

"Thank you." Her low voice surprised Margaret. The woman didn't smile but gazed all about. She walked over and stood before one of Louellen Lumadue's paintings, which depicted a dilapidated barn where a colony of swallows was nesting. She squinted at it for several seconds, then moved on to one of Margaret's lighthouse paintings, but gave it only a glance.

"Feel free to look around," Margaret said.

"Thank you."

Margaret went to the refreshment table and took the carafe out of the coffeemaker. She took it to the restroom to fill it. When she returned, the woman had zeroed in on the new painting and stood staring at it.

"Oh, I'm sorry," Margaret said. "I only brought that one out to view it in this light. It's not even framed yet."

"Are you the artist?"

"Yes. I'm Margaret Hoskins." She set down the carafe, prepared to shake hands or answer questions, but the woman only continued to stare at the abstract painting. Margaret began to feel uneasy. The rules for the art fair stated that her debut piece must not have been exhibited anywhere prior to the fair.

"How much is it?" the woman asked.

"Oh well, you see, it's not for sale."

The woman turned and blinked at her. "But it's in a gallery."

"I know. I'm sorry, but as I said, it's one I just finished and I brought it out here to look at it, not to display it for sale."

"I'll give you a hundred dollars. You don't have to frame it."

It was Margaret's turn to stare. "I—well—no, I can't do that. I'm entering it in the Port Clyde Art Fair this weekend.

I can't sell it now." She didn't mention the fact that the woman's offer was insultingly low.

"Will you sell it after?"

"I might." The somber little woman was making Margaret nervous. "Excuse me. I was just about to make some coffee." She poured the water into the coffeemaker, keeping an eye on the customer. She wished the woman would leave, but she stayed rooted to the spot before the abstract. Perhaps Margaret could draw her interest to another painting.

The door opened and the bell jangled again. Evelyn Waters came in grinning. "Good morning, Margaret."

"Hello, Mayor Waters."

The petite woman in navy glanced at Evelyn and at last moved on to study another painting.

Evelyn said, "I spotted a vase in here last week, and I want to buy it for a gift. If you still have it, that is. It was green pottery. Very lovely lines."

"You must mean this one." Margaret guided her to one side of the room, where the exquisite vase sat on a doily atop one of Allan's tables.

"That's the one," Evelyn said.

"I'd be happy to box it and wrap it for you if you wish."

"That would be wonderful. How about if I pay you now and pick it up on my lunch hour?"

"Terrific," Margaret said. The door opened, and she leaned around one of the dividers just in time to see the odd customer making her exit. The abstract still sat where Margaret had left it, but she realized she needed to get it out of sight before anyone else saw it. She wouldn't want other people to think she was exhibiting it now.

"Who was that woman?" Evelyn asked.

"I've never seen her before," Margaret said. "She was interested in one of the paintings."

"Maybe she'll come back later. I hope I didn't run her off."

"I don't think so." Margaret walked with the mayor to the checkout counter. "I get a lot of people in who look and then go away and think about it. Some of them come back later."

"Like me," Evelyn said with a laugh as she took out her credit card.

In an odd way, Margaret felt the strange woman had validated her new painting. Of all those in the gallery, the abstract was the one that caught her eye. And she might not be a big spender, but she had immediately offered to buy it. Perhaps the painting was a good choice for her debut piece. She hoped everyone at the art fair liked it as much as that woman had.

★   ★   ★

Shelley's doorbell rang and she looked out the window. Her mother-in-law's car sat in the driveway, and Shelley's heart sank. Even though she'd caught up the laundry from the trip to the cabin and put away all the gear from it, the house was far from ready for Frances' scrutiny.

"Aiden, go get dressed," she said, snatching Emma up off the floor. "Meemaw's here." On her way to open the door, she plopped Emma in her playpen, grabbed a couple of toys off the linoleum, and tossed them in after her.

By the time she reached the door, Frances had pressed the doorbell again. Shelley dredged up a smile and flung the door open.

"Frances! Hello."

"Good morning, Shelley." Frances' gaze raked the length of her, and Shelley was very conscious of her old slippers, jeans, and baggy pullover.

"Come on in. What can I do for you today?"

"I haven't talked to you since you got back, and I just thought I'd come see how you all survived the weekend. Did you get that awful electrical storm at the cabin?"

"We sure did. Can I get you a cup of coffee?" Shelley snatched Dan's empty mug and a crumpled napkin off the table and carried them to the counter, where she grabbed a dishcloth.

"Sounds good." Frances sat down at the kitchen table, frowning at the crumbs on the surface.

Shelley hurried over and wiped the tabletop, trying to keep her smile in place. "We had a really good time with the kids. I'm sorry we changed plans on you at the last minute, but it was good for us to have some family time."

"Uh-huh."

Emma let out a squeal for attention, and Frances winced but turned toward her. "Well, young lady, did you have fun too?" Frances asked in an exaggeratedly polite tone.

"Did she ever," Shelley said. "She and Aiden loved the cabin. We had to watch her around the stairs, but she did fine."

At that moment, Aiden came skipping into the kitchen wearing only his undershorts and swinging a green T-shirt over his head.

"Mama! Is this what I'm supposed to wear?"

"Aiden! No! Yes!" Shelley shook her head. "Yes, put that on, but go in your room and do it." As he turned and rocketed toward his room, she called, "And don't come back until you're completely dressed!"

She turned sheepishly to face Frances, who sat staring after Aiden, her eyebrows raised.

"My, it's awfully late for him to be getting dressed, isn't it?"

Shelley smiled, but she felt like screaming. "He slept late, and I let him eat in his pj's. Let me get your coffee."

"Well, if you're too busy here . . ."

"It's always busy here," Shelley said, in what she hoped was a gracious tone. "But I'd love to sit down with you for a couple of minutes." She went to the coffeemaker. Enough coffee was left for a cup for Frances and about half a cup for herself.

"Thank you," Frances said. "Do you have any creamer?"

"Oh—uh—let me check." Shelley hadn't fully restocked the refrigerator since their weekend away, and she was pretty sure they were out. A quick glance confirmed her fears. "I'm afraid it's just milk today. Two percent."

Frances grimaced. "Well, if that's all you have."

"It is. Sorry." Shelley placed the jug on the table. "I'll need to get groceries later. So, how are things going with the Founder's Day preparations?"

Frances' face went sour. "Not too badly, I suppose, but that Maddie Bancroft! I don't understand that girl."

Emma let out another squeal, and Shelley went over to pick her up.

"What did Maddie do?" She wasn't sure she really wanted to know, as she and Maddie had become friends of sorts, but she'd rather talk about Maddie than her own lack of housekeeping skills.

"Oh, she's let Beverly Wheeland borrow one of the artifacts we have on loan. Can you beat that? Borrowing something from the owner and then letting someone else take it away from the church!"

"*Hmm.*" Shelley had a feeling she knew which item Frances was talking about, and this topic might not be so painless after all. "Well, I'm sure Beverly will take good care of it. She's a very conscientious person."

"I suppose so. But Beverly wants to show it to her father and her friends. I mean, what's the point of exhibiting it if everyone's already seen it?"

"I wouldn't worry about that," Shelley said. "Beverly probably just wants to learn as much as possible about it so that you can tag it correctly for the exhibit."

"Maybe so." Frances sipped her coffee. "But still! People entrust their heirlooms to us. We shouldn't let them go out of our possession—the committee's possession, that is."

Shelley sat down and pushed her coffee mug out to the middle of the table so Emma couldn't reach it.

"I wouldn't mind if they looked at it over at the church," Frances added.

"I'm sure they'll be careful." Shelley smiled brightly. "Would you like a scone? I made them last night for the Cove, and I had some extras."

"Oh, are they those blueberry ones I tried once? I did like those."

"Yes, I have blueberry, and I'm trying out raspberry. Maybe you'd like that as well."

With Emma on her hip, Shelley got up and went to the cupboard to get out the containers of extra scones.

Aiden ran into the kitchen, this time wearing his jeans, shirt, and sneakers, with his dog bouncing right behind him. "Mama! Prize and I want to play outside."

"All right, but stay in the side yard."

"Okay." Aiden rushed to the door and opened it. Prize dashed past him, and Aiden looked over his shoulder. "Hi, Meemaw."

"Well, hello, young man. How about a kiss?"

Aiden reluctantly shut the door and went to give her a brief embrace. Prize began to whine on the other side of the door, and he hurried back to open it.

"I really should be going," Frances said, leaning to look out the window. "And I'd love to take some of those raspberry scones with me."

Shelley smiled. Just as she closed a zipper bag around the paper plate of scones, the phone rang. "Oh, excuse me, Frances."

"Go ahead," Frances said. "I've got Emma." She did glance at her watch, though, and Shelley picked up the receiver determined to make the call short.

"Lighthouse Sweet Shoppe."

"My name is Amy London," her caller said. "Is this Mrs. Bauer?"

"Yes, this is Shelley Bauer."

"Great. Your husband Dan gave me your card when he was here working on the wiring with Mr. Stover last week."

"Oh, how nice," Shelley said. Dan was turning out to be one of her best promoters.

"Well, I had mentioned how we wanted to get the wiring and painting all finished before my parents' twenty-fifth wedding anniversary party, and now I'm ready to start looking for a caterer. I'll need a cake and finger food—punch too. Dan said you might be able to do something like that."

"Oh yes," Shelley said. "How wonderful that you're hosting a party for them. Might I come see you and bring some of my menus and samples? We could talk about what you want, and you could see if you think I'd be a good fit for the event."

"Yes, that would be terrific." Amy gave her the address and telephone number. She lived about twenty minutes away on the other side of Frances and Ralph.

Shelley made a quick decision and excused herself for a moment. "Frances, this sounds like possibly a big job for me. Would you be able to babysit tomorrow morning for a couple of hours?"

Frances beamed at her. "I'd love to. Thank you." She beamed down at Emma. "Did you hear that, cutie? You're going to come visit Meemaw tomorrow."

Shelley quickly set up the appointment and hung up the phone.

"Thank you so much, Frances. That woman said she wants sandwiches, finger foods, and a special cake for an anniversary party in a few weeks."

"You did such a good job on Ralph's birthday party," Frances said. "You'll do fine, I'm sure."

Shelley tried not to let her jaw drop at the unexpected praise. "Well, thanks very much." She reached to take Emma. "I know you need to run, and I'd better get Aiden in and clean him up so we can go get some groceries. I'm glad you dropped by."

Frances smiled. "So am I."

Shelley walked to the driveway with her and stood with the children, waving, as Frances pulled out. "Thank You, Lord," she whispered. She smiled to herself, thinking of all the things that simple prayer covered—the potential job, the visit with Frances that had turned out quite pleasantly, and the fact that Frances seemed to have forgotten about the antique prayer book.

★   ★   ★

Beverly picked up Diane at six o'clock on Monday evening and drove to Hank and Elsie Roux's house. On the way, she told Diane what little she had learned so far about the prayer book.

"Do you think we'll ever be able to say for sure whether it belonged to someone at Old First?" Diane asked.

"I don't know, but there's something else. I would have showed you yesterday at Margaret's, but Shelley was in such a hurry, I decided not to bring it up then."

"What is it?"

"When I first brought the book home, Father and I looked at it. There's a page in the back that was blank originally, but someone wrote on it. We couldn't make out the writing. At least, we couldn't make sense of it. I'll be interested to hear what you think when you see it."

"Now I'm intrigued."

Beverly signaled to turn in at Hank's driveway. "I thought maybe I wouldn't mention it tonight unless Hank or Elsie brings it up. If they never noticed it, let's just keep it to ourselves, okay?"

"Sure," Diane said.

"Thanks. If they did see it, they might have some ideas as to what it is. But if they didn't, it might make them want to keep it and puzzle over it."

Diane chuckled, "Which is exactly what *you* want to do."

Beverly felt her face color. "I don't want to hide anything. I just want the four of us to have a fair chance to unravel this little mystery."

"Understood."

Elsie Roux met them at the door and took them to the comfortable living room. Hank joined them and shooed the children out.

"Thank you so much for allowing us to borrow the prayer book." Beverly held the padded envelope on her lap, but didn't take the book out.

"No problem," Hank said.

"Have you found out anything?" Elsie asked. "Where it came from or how old it is?"

"Not yet." Beverly looked at Hank. "We hoped you could tell us the location of the estate sale where you found it."

"It was the old Donaldson house in Willow Corners."

Diane slipped a small notebook from her purse and jotted a note in it.

"Do you know anything about the family?"

"No. The man had died, and his kids were selling stuff off last summer. I saw a little book about Old First in there, and I gave them two bucks for the whole box."

"Can you believe that?" Elsie brushed back her blonde hair. "There were some other books in it too."

"Yeah," Hank said, "I took out a few that didn't have anything to do with church. There was a bird book and an old cookbook. Elsie wanted that."

"Were there any names in them?" Beverly asked.

"Don't think so." Hank looked at his wife.

"No, not in the cookbook, anyway." Elsie shrugged. "I can show it to you. It's from the fifties, I think. I like old stuff, and I like to cook." She got up and went into the kitchen.

"You know, I showed that prayer book to the owner of an antique shop up in Rockland."

"You did?" Beverly stared at Hank. "What did he say?"

He laughed. "That it was old. He said it wasn't his area of expertise, but he did some looking online. He said they made a lot of them the same for a long time, and it could be from colonial days."

"Wow," Diane said. "Anything else?"

"He offered me twenty bucks. I said no, I'd hang on to it for a while."

"Well, we are going to take super good care of it," Beverly said.

"I asked if it might have to do with Old First, since some of the other books that came with it did. He said it might, but there was no way to tell. And it was by far the oldest thing in the box. A lot older than the hymnbook, for instance."

Beverly nodded. "That's pretty much what we thought too. Is there anything else you can tell me about it?"

"I don't think so. I just thought it was kind of cool, and that the church might like to show it with the other old things at Founder's Day."

"I'm sure they will," Diane said. "It's nice of you to lend it."

Elsie bustled back in with one of her eight-year-old twins following her. "Here's the cookbook and the bird book that were in the box."

She handed Beverly the cookbook, and gave the other volume to Diane. They both looked at the front and back endpapers and leafed through the pages.

"Very interesting," Diane said, holding the bird book out to Elsie. "This one says 'John Donaldson' on the flyleaf."

"He was the guy who used to own the house," Hank said.

"I don't see any writing in this," Beverly told her, "except some notations beside a few of the recipes." She smiled. "Apparently Mrs. Donaldson liked this Lady Baltimore cake recipe."

"I noticed that," Elsie said. "She wrote 'very good' beside it. I'm going to try it!"

Beverly and Diane soon took their leave, declining coffee.

"Sounds like we pretty much have free rein," Diane said once they were back in the car.

"Yes, and the family that owned the prayer book lived close enough to have attended Old First."

"I wish we could jump right into it," Diane said.

"Me too, but we'll have to wait until after Memorial Day."

"That doesn't mean we couldn't do some online research this week."

"You're right. I'm sure Margaret and Shelley wouldn't mind." Beverly glanced over at her. "Do you want to take it?"

"I think you should keep it," Diane said. "I really, really need to work on my book, and if I had that prayer book in my house, it would be the perfect reason to procrastinate."

"All right, if you're sure you don't mind."

"I don't."

Beverly headed for home, eager to take the prayer book out again and study the old volume.

Chapter Twenty-Two

Margaret arrived at the art fair Saturday morning an hour before the official start of the setup time. Only a few committee members were on hand, instructing a crew of men and teenage boys who were setting up tables and display walls. Some of the heavy work had been done the night before, but much remained to be accomplished.

Margaret was able to drive to her spot, though she would have to move her car after unloading. The streets and two adjoining parking lots would be closed to vehicles for the weekend. All of the artists had received instructions to unload and then park at least three blocks away, to allow close parking for patrons.

She barely finished getting her own table, folding chair, display racks, and easels in place before the hour was up. A girl who looked to be high school age came sauntering along the sidewalk and peering at the placards that told which artists would be located in each spot.

"Mrs. Hoskins!"

"Yes. May I help you?"

The girl's face lit in a delighted smile. Margaret thought how pretty she was when she smiled. Her fine features and short, dark hair gave her an almost elfin look.

"I'm Jenna, and I'm your helper for the day."

"Oh, you must be one of the volunteers," Margaret said, extending her hand.

"Yes, our whole art club from school is helping today. I'm glad I got you. I love nature paintings."

"Why, thank you." Margaret clasped her hand for a moment, amazed that the girl knew anything about her. "I just have a few more things to do, but I need to move my car."

"I can stay here while you do that and watch things," Jenna said.

"Thanks. That would be a big help." Margaret gestured to the four canvases she had yet to hang. "Do you want to put those up? There are two more hooks on the display board, and I have those two freestanding easels."

"Sure," Jenna said. "I'll be very careful."

"I'm sure you will. I'd like these two paintings on the easels, please." Margaret touched the frames of her new abstract and the more realistic tide pool painting, her two latest endeavors. The Old First painting would go on the wall with several others, she'd decided. It fit in with her seascape and lighthouse paintings. She hesitated, then indicated the abstract. "This is my debut piece, so we want it in the most prominent position."

Until that moment, she hadn't made her final decision as to which painting she would feature as her primary piece, but now she was committed.

Jenna studied it, frowning. "It's different from the others."

"Yes." Suddenly, Margaret felt the old uncertainty return. She watched Jenna's face.

"But I like it," the girl said.

Margaret exhaled her pent-up breath. "Thank you. I'll take the car down to the parking lot. I should be back in about ten minutes."

"Okeydoke."

When she returned to her display, Jenna was talking to a middle-aged woman wearing a large straw hat.

"Here's Mrs. Hoskins," Jenna said.

"Oh, hello." The woman turned to Margaret. "I'm Tabitha Lane. We spoke on the phone last week."

"Yes, of course," Margaret said. She had made a list of all the entrants who had contacted her so she'd remember to touch base with each of them today. "Nice to meet you."

"Thanks. I'm having a little trouble with my display space. I arrived to find the artists on either side of me had encroached a bit, and I can't fit my table in to the area that's left."

"Oh dear. Let me come along with you, and we'll see what we can do."

Margaret was able to smooth things out with the neighboring exhibitors, and she'd no sooner gotten Tabitha settled than another artist approached her for help with a wobbly table leg. Margaret was able to round up one of the handymen on the crew to assist with that and hurried on to greet Barry Towers and his wife.

"I'm so glad you made it," Margaret said to Barry. "How are you feeling?"

"Not too bad." He gestured toward the padded rolling chair he'd brought. "I brought a comfortable seat. If the day's too much for me, I'll take a break, and my wife will hold down the fort."

"Wonderful." Margaret chatted with the couple for another minute or two and helped Mrs. Towers lift the two heaviest of Barry's framed paintings into place.

"Thanks so much," Mrs. Towers told her. "I was afraid he'd overdo setting up, and that would ruin the whole day."

"Not a problem," Margaret assured her.

A gangly boy of about fifteen approached hesitantly. "I'm looking for Mr. Towers."

"That's me," Barry said.

The boy exhaled in relief. "I'm your helper. Sorry I'm late." He stuck out his hand. "My name is Kyle."

Margaret decided she could leave the couple in Kyle's hands, since they had only a few more paintings to hang. She got back to her own space just as the general public was allowed to enter the pedestrians-only area.

Jenna jumped up as she approached. "Oh, Mrs. Hoskins, I'm so glad you're back."

"Please call me Margaret. Is something wrong?" She tried not to puff as she caught her breath.

"No, but several people have stopped by wanting to talk to you about your art. I think you should stay here, and I'll run and help the next people who need something."

"That's very kind of you, Jenna, but since I'm the official artists' ambassador, it's sort of my job to help with all these little last-minute things."

"That doesn't seem fair. You need to be able to show off your work."

Margaret smiled. "Thank you, dear. I hope things will slow down now that most people are set up and we're open to the public."

She sank down into her canvas chair. The crowd was thickening, and people were ambling along, studying the various exhibits and lingering to talk to the artists. A middle-aged couple stopped to look at Margaret's abstract painting.

"I *like* that," the man said.

"Do you?" asked his companion. "I think I prefer this one." She pointed to Margaret's painting of the little boy at the tide pool. "Or one of those impressionist-looking ones we saw back there."

The man smiled at Margaret. "Are you the artist?"

"Yes." Margaret smiled and held out one of her business cards. "I'm Margaret Hoskins."

He looked at her card. "Oh, you have a gallery."

"Yes, it's the Shearwater, in Marble Cove."

"I don't think we've ever been there," the woman said.

"If you had, you'd remember," Margaret assured her. "These paintings are all of Marble Cove." She swept her hand through the air to include all of the works hanging on her display backdrop.

"Oh yes," the man said. "That's the Orlean Point Light, isn't it?"

"That's right," Margaret told him.

He scrutinized the different views of the lighthouse through his wire-rimmed glasses. "Sure, we've been there."

"Have we?" The woman squinted at one of the lighthouse paintings. "I suppose so." She shrugged and moved on to the next booth.

The man winked at Margaret and tucked her card into his shirt pocket. "Best of luck today. I may be back."

"Thanks for stopping." Margaret wouldn't hold her breath waiting. If his wife didn't like something, she wouldn't let him buy it to hang in their house. Besides, there were hundreds of other people to talk to.

Several browsers commented on her lighthouse paintings. People who had seen Orlean Point in person waxed especially nostalgic over it. One woman caught her breath and pointed to one of them. "Look, Linda. The birthday card my brother sent me has that same lighthouse on it."

"That was probably one of my paintings," Margaret said with a smile.

The woman checked the price tags on several paintings and took one of Margaret's cards.

Jenna asked if she could get Margaret a drink or run errands for her.

"I have several bottles of water in that small cooler," Margaret said, pointing beneath the table. "Would you like to get one for each of us?"

The crowds only increased as the morning passed. About ten o'clock, several people Margaret recognized from the fair committee meetings strolled slowly along, making the rounds of the booths. When they reached Margaret's table, Rosalyn Neely smiled at her.

"Margaret, these are our judges. They'd like to see your debut piece."

Margaret stood and smiled at the three people wearing beribboned badges.

"This is it, right here." She went to stand beside the abstract shell painting.

The three judges eyed it critically and scribbled notes on clipboards. Meanwhile, Jenna stood by uncertainly, holding the water bottles.

"Very nice presentation," murmured the female judge. Her gaze swept over Margaret's entire display.

The other two judges also looked over the additional paintings.

"Ah, Marble Cove," one of the men said. His neat gray mustache twitched in a smile as he looked over her views of the lighthouse and Old First.

"Yes," Margaret said. "I live there."

"How fortunate for you. I'm Richard Leland."

Margaret recognized his name—he was an artist from New York who summered in Maine. His paintings were quite sought after.

"Oh, what a pleasure to meet you." She shook his hand. "I've admired your work for some time. I believe

I saw some of your paintings last summer in Boothbay Harbor."

"Yes, I keep some in a gallery there."

He seemed pleased that she knew that and had noticed his work.

The other male judge, a younger man with long, dark hair tied back in a ponytail, noted, "The single piece you entered for judging is not your usual style."

Margaret nodded. "I've tried a few different things lately. I thought I'd enter this one and see how it was received."

"I like that," Leland said. "Not playing it safe."

"Well, a lot of people like my other paintings, but I have an adventurous streak," Margaret said with a chuckle. "Some days I just want to get my feelings on canvas, rather than what I actually see."

The two men nodded, and the three judges all studied the abstract for a moment.

"Well, are we ready to move on?" asked the woman.

Rosalyn Neely led them to the next artist's booth. Margaret exhaled, and Jenna put a water bottle in her hand.

"Good job, I'd say," Jenna said with a grin, "but what do I know?"

Margaret laughed. "Thanks. I'm glad I was here when they came around."

Matt Beauregard was the next acquaintance to stop by her booth, with his wife and young daughter in tow.

"Great to see you, Margaret," he said. "We decided to come enjoy the fair."

"It's a beautiful day for it." Margaret glanced up at the cloudless sky. "I'm so glad we didn't have to move it indoors."

"Much nicer this way." He turned to include his family. "You know Suzy, but I don't think you've met my wife Amanda."

"Hello," Margaret said.

"It's so good to meet you." Amanda took her hand. "Matt's told me a lot about you, and I love your paintings."

"Thank you." Margaret bent down to speak to their little girl. "Hi, Suzy. Are you looking forward to summer vacation?"

"Uh-huh."

Amanda laughed. "She has two weeks of school left. She can hardly wait."

"Is this new?" Matt was studying her abstract painting.

"Yes. It's something I did just for the fair. I'm not sure if it's a success or not, but I thought I'd do something different."

"For the critics?" Matt asked.

"Well, partly, I suppose. But I'll admit I wanted to do something that was very different from the scenes I do for you—though I love doing them. I enjoyed painting in a different style, and I've had some favorable comments this morning."

"I hope it does well." He stepped closer to her display board. "Some of these are mine, I hope."

Margaret smiled. "Yes, two of the ones I did for you are hanging." She pointed them out to him—views of the lighthouse from different vantage points and in different lighting. "The other two are hanging in the gallery this weekend so our walls aren't totally bare."

"Excellent," Matt said. "I absolutely love the one with the lobster boat. And I'll be in to see you Tuesday."

"Great." They chatted a little more and then the Beauregards moved on. Even though Margaret hadn't expected Matt—the traditionalist—to like her abstract, she felt a little disappointed. Would she ever be completely satisfied with her work unless someone praised it to the skies? And even if that happened, would she doubt their sincerity, or their judgment of art?

Chapter Twenty-Three

M argaret wondered what people thought of her prices. She'd marked the abstract higher than any of the others. When she decided on the amount, she'd thought herself rather daring, but no one had seemed to think it was too high. Of course, not many would be rude enough to say so.

A few other artists sent their helpers to ask her questions, but Margaret was able to stay at her booth for the next couple of hours, and she thoroughly enjoyed talking to all the art lovers. The first day of the fair was going well. About twelve thirty, Allan and Adelaide arrived, carrying a picnic basket and soft drinks.

"Well, hello," Margaret said, realizing she was hungry. "How are things at the Shearwater?"

"Going great," Allan said. "We sold a pottery vase this morning. Diane is there now, and Beverly's going to relieve her later, so we don't have to be back until four."

"Fantastic." Margaret turned to her helper. "This is Jenna, and she's been helping me all morning. She's saved me a lot of headaches. Jenna, this is my husband Allan and my daughter Adelaide."

Jenna greeted them both cheerfully.

"Would you like to take some time off?" Margaret asked. "I'm sure we have enough food in that basket to share with you if you'd like to eat with us, or you can take a break."

"If you don't mind, I'd love the chance to look at the other exhibits," Jenna said. "I can pick up a hot dog while I'm away."

"All right," Margaret said. "Take your time."

For the next hour, in between greeting more browsers, she talked to Allan and Adelaide while they ate and told them in detail of her morning's adventures.

"Did you win a prize, Mom?" Adelaide asked.

Margaret smiled. "I won't know until Monday, but the judges were here this morning looking at the painting. They were very nice."

A group of women stopped at her display to study her paintings, and Margaret rose to talk to them.

"I absolutely love this painting," one of the women said, pointing to the lobster boat picture promised to Matt Beauregard.

"Well, I have good news and bad news," Margaret said, reaching for one of her cards and a brochure about the giclée prints they offered. "The bad news is that the original has been purchased by Lighting the Way Greeting Cards. But we're offering prints of that and several of my other paintings. The good news is that the prints are much more economical than the paintings. If you're interested, here's more information about the prints. They're limited edition, numbered and signed. Some people find it a good way to get the art they want at a very affordable price."

"That sounds like a good idea," the woman said, perusing the brochure. She and her friends lingered a few more minutes.

In the meantime, several other people stopped by and commented on her paintings, especially the abstract. When the crowd thinned a little, Allan said, "Well, I guess you got your answer about that new painting. People seem to like it."

"Yes, I've had some very good comments on it," Margaret agreed. "I might try doing some more along that line."

Adelaide came over with a cookie in her hand. "Dad, can we look at the other artists?"

"Sure, honey. I wouldn't miss it." He looked at Margaret. "Maybe you could walk around with us when your helper comes back?"

"Maybe for a little while, but I'm making lots of new contacts by being here when people look at my work."

She left Jenna in charge for about half an hour, but couldn't bring herself to stay away longer. Allan and Adelaide strolled about for some time, then came back to sit with her for a while before they headed home.

By the end of the day, Margaret was tired but content. She had sold one painting—a lighthouse view not in Matt's lineup. A great many people had shown interest in her work, both the traditional and the abstract. She gave out several dozen cards and brochures.

They closed up at five o'clock, with all the paintings put safely in the artists' vehicles to be rehung in the morning.

Margaret thanked Jenna and drove home alone. The gallery was closed when she passed it, which was as it should be. She wondered how Diane and Beverly had made out that afternoon.

Allan had supper ready—chicken stew in the slow cooker.

"This is wonderful," Margaret told him, "coming home to a hot meal and knowing I can relax and get a good night's sleep."

"You don't have to do a thing tonight," Allan assured her. "Adelaide and I have the dishes covered."

While they ate, Margaret told them about a few more encounters she'd had after they left the fair. Allan reported that her friends had sold one of Bernadette Lassiter's necklaces but had also had some serious inquiries about paintings and prints.

"Sounds like we had a good day here," she said.

"Only one necklace, Mom." Adelaide frowned at her. "That's not much."

Margaret chuckled. "Lots of days I don't sell anything at the gallery. And I did sell a painting at the fair."

"Yes," Allan said. "That's not bad at all." He smiled at Margaret, who was trying to hide a yawn behind her hand. "You'd better turn in."

*   *   *

Finishing up her solitary supper in the kitchen, Diane was surprised to hear a quiet knock on her back door. She went to the window first to see if she could identify her caller before opening the door. Dan stood on the step, gazing anxiously toward the street.

She threw the door open. "Dan, come on in. What's up?"

"I'm hiding," he said sheepishly. "Didn't want Shell to see me pop over here."

"Oh?"

"Tuesday's her birthday, and I'm taking her out to dinner, but I figured you and Beverly and Margaret would want to know."

"Ah, yes. Thank you very much." Diane nodded slowly. "We were going to get together soon to talk about the old prayer book. Did Shelley mention that to you?"

"Yeah. She says it's awesome."

"Well, I'll talk to Beverly and see if we can set up something for Tuesday morning or afternoon. Nothing fancy, just a little recognition."

"Sounds good. Thanks, Diane. Oh, and this is twenty-nine for her. Not sure if that's important or not."

"Not as tricky as next year," Diane said with a laugh. "May I offer you something to drink?"

"Better not. I'm supposed to be closing up the garage for the night. See ya!"

He left as quickly as he had come. With a smile, Diane dashed to the living room window. Rocky barked and followed her. Dan sprinted across the street and to his yard. He pushed Aiden's tricycle into the garage and lowered the door. A moment later, the light in the Bauers' garage went out.

"He's a good guy and a good neighbor," she said out loud.

Rocky woofed and stuck his nose into her palm.

"Oh yes, Rocky." She stooped to pat his head. "You're a good guy too."

*　　*　　*

On Sunday morning, Margaret again headed out early while Allan and Adelaide were getting ready for church. Margaret hated to miss services, but for this one-time event, she'd made an exception to her usual commitments. The bright weather continued, and the tourists thronged the fair. Several people took Margaret's card and brochure, and she directed dozens to the Shearwater Gallery.

A different high school student, Perry, was her aide that day, but Margaret found she needed him less than she had Jenna. She was called away less often now that they were into the second day of the event, and she spent nearly all of the time at her own booth meeting art aficionados.

One woman returned several times, and Margaret was sure she was focused on the Old First painting. At last the customer introduced herself and explained that she lived in Sunrise Shores, a condominium development in Marble Cove.

"I love this view of the old church," she said, "but I think for my living room I'd like an autumn scene. I don't suppose you ever paint to order?"

"Yes, I do," Margaret said. They spent several minutes discussing exactly what the woman wanted for a focal point of her room and the colors she'd used in decorating.

After some time, the woman smiled at Margaret. "I feel so comfortable with you—as though you see things the same way I do. I'd like to commission an autumn foliage scene from this same spot, with Old First Church in the background, the same as it is in this painting."

"I'd be happy to do that for you next month," Margaret said. She quoted a price, and the customer agreed to it and wrote Margaret a check for a down payment.

Two other patrons were waiting to talk to her when the woman walked away. It was tempting to start thinking about how she would execute the foliage painting, but that would have to wait. Margaret took a deep breath and turned to them with a smile and a quick silent prayer of gratitude.

About an hour later, she took a short break, leaving Perry at her booth while she visited the restroom and stopped by a couple of the other artists' displays to see how they were doing. When she returned, a dark-haired man was talking to Perry. When Margaret neared him, she saw that he had a streak of white at each temple. Around his neck, a pewter cross hung on a chain.

Margaret stepped forward.

"Oh, here's Mrs. Hoskins," Perry said, with a smile at Margaret.

"Hello." The man waved toward the abstract painting. "I was interested in this painting. Your helper tells me it's being judged, so you can't sell it yet."

Margaret shrugged with a smile. "Well, I'm allowed to sell it, but it has to remain on display for the remainder of the show—that is, until tomorrow at five o'clock."

"I see." The man turned back to gaze at the painting, frowning. "I can't help imagining this hanging over my desk at the office. It's striking."

"Thank you," Margaret said. "What sort of business are you in?"

"I'm a podiatrist."

She nodded, watching his face. He didn't mention the price, and she figured he'd looked at the tag before she arrived. "Will you be at the fair tomorrow?"

"No, I have to get back to Portland." He turned away from the painting at last. "I'm going to think about it. If I want to buy it, I'll come back before I leave today."

"Of course," Margaret said. "Why don't you take one of my cards, so you'll have my contact information?" She handed him one of her business cards, and he tucked it in his pocket.

"Thanks. Now, if this wins a prize, does the price stay the same?"

She laughed. "Yes. I wouldn't change it on you. And if you do decide to buy it, we could arrange for you to pick it up at my gallery in Marble Cove later, or to have it shipped to you if you'd prefer it."

He nodded. "Okay. Good to know. I may see you later."

So close, Margaret thought as he walked away. She saw him stop at the next exhibit and speak to the artist.

"Wow, he really sounds like he wants it," Perry said at her elbow.

"Yes, he does. But he might see something he likes just as well down the row. I won't count on it until he comes back and pulls out his checkbook."

★   ★   ★

Diane typed slowly to the end of a sentence and scanned back over the last paragraph she'd written. Not bad. She'd put in several hours of good, solid work on the book Monday morning. That would have to do for now. She saved her file and stood, stretching. Rocky rose from where he'd been lying on the rug and stretched too.

She laughed. "Come on, Rocky. You've been good this morning. Let's go out for a quick walk before I run off for the day." A glance at the time told her she'd have to leave in thirty minutes to pick up Shelley and Beverly for their outing to the art fair.

Allan had suggested the women go today, the final day of the event. Margaret might be feeling a little blue, he'd reasoned, especially if she didn't place in the competition. And she might welcome some friendly faces and extra hands when it was time to pack up everything. That could be a bittersweet moment, Diane reflected.

She and Rocky headed down to the beach for a few minutes. She hated to call him back after such a brief outing when he'd be shut up alone for several hours afterward.

"We'll have a good, long romp when I get home," she promised him.

Quickly she changed into her favorite slacks and a comfortable print knit tunic that looked a little fancier than what she wore around home. She made sure Rocky had plenty of water and patted him for a moment.

"Be good!"

Shelley was ready, and Dan waved to them from the porch, where he held Emma. Aiden frolicked about the yard with Prize, shouting, "Bye, Mama! Bye, Miss Diane! Have fun!"

Diane and Shelley were still laughing when they pulled up at the Wheeland house and Beverly climbed in.

"How's everything going this weekend?" Diane asked her.

"Fine." Beverly arranged her purse and a tote bag on the backseat and buckled her seat belt. "Jeff has gone back out on assignment."

"Oh, for how long?" Shelley asked.

"Only a week this time. And he promised to call when he's able."

"That's good," Diane said.

"Yes, I admit I was worried last time."

Shelley turned in the front seat to look at Beverly. "It's almost like when sea captains were gone for months and months, and their wives had no idea where they were or if they were all right."

Beverly laughed. "Not quite that bad—and he took his phone charger this time. You've got a great imagination, Shelley."

"Yes, you ought to write stories," Diane said.

"I'd never have time for that. Sometimes I do make up stories for the kids, though, when they're bored with the same old storybooks. Oh, did I tell you about the cool event I'm catering next month? It's a twenty-fifth anniversary party."

"No, you didn't," Diane said. "That sounds wonderful."

"I took some samples of my best desserts over to the lady, and she loved them," Shelley said. "And guess how she heard about me."

"Through your Web site?" Beverly asked.

"No, through my husband!"

Diane and Beverly laughed.

"Terrific," Diane said.

"Yeah, Dan's been great. He brags about me all the time. And the woman who hired me for this party was one of their customers for the electrical firm."

"Maybe I should hire him to promote my book," Diane said.

Beverly chuckled but then said earnestly, "It's like I told you, Shelley—word of mouth is the best advertising. And if this woman's friends like the food at the party, it will probably lead to more jobs."

"That's what I'm hoping."

When they reached the art fair, Diane let Shelley and Beverly out close to the display area and then went to park farther away. She picked up a flyer giving the layout of the artists' stations and strolled along toward Margaret's booth. She kept seeing gorgeous exhibits that she longed to linger over, but that would come later. It took her about ten minutes to find Margaret's spot, and she was gratified to see that several people were clustered before her stand.

"Oh, great, Diane's here," Shelley said as she approached.

Margaret turned to her, smiling broadly. "Thank you so much for coming, all of you." She beckoned to the teenage girl sitting by her table. "This is my helper Jenna. She was assigned to me Saturday, and she asked to be with me again today. Can you imagine?"

"Yes, I most certainly can," Diane said.

"These are my friends," Margaret said to Jenna. "Shelley, Beverly, and Diane."

"We won't expect you to remember all of our names," Shelley said.

Jenna laughed. "It's nice to meet you. Working with Mrs. Hoskins has been great. She's taught me some things about art just through the conversations we've had."

"I'll bet," Beverly said. "What do you think of her paintings?"

"I love them—especially the lighthouses."

The friends looked over Margaret's display.

"I do like this one immensely," Diane said as she stood before the tide pool painting. "And I can see echoes of it in the abstract. They're both good, Margaret. I think I'd pick this one if I were going to have one in my house, though."

Margaret smiled. "I've had a lot of comments on both."

Shelley gasped. "Is that Aiden?"

"I forgot you hadn't seen it since I put the boy in," Margaret said. "It's not exactly Aiden, but you could say that Aiden was my inspiration."

Diane gazed at the little boy's freckled face, set in an intense expression as he reached into the water. "He does look a lot like Aiden—maybe a year or two from now."

"It's beautiful," Shelley said wistfully. "May I take a picture of it, Margaret? I'd like to show Dan."

"Of course you can. And if it doesn't sell today, he can drop by the gallery and see it anytime." Margaret excused herself to speak to some of the browsers.

"Has Margaret sold any paintings?" Beverly asked Jenna.

"At least one. And she told me that yesterday someone commissioned another painting of Marble Cove—similar to that one." Jenna pointed to the view of Old First. "The lady wanted it with autumn leaves instead of summer, I guess."

"Awesome," Shelley said.

"That will be gorgeous." Diane nodded as she gazed at the painting and imagined the trees garbed in vibrant orange, yellow, and red.

When Margaret was free, she confirmed what Jenna had told them. "And a lot of people have shown interest in the gallery and the prints," she added. "I thought my abstract was going to sell, but the man who talked to me about it yesterday never came back."

"Did you give him your card?" Beverly asked.

"You bet I did." Margaret smiled. "I feel as though this weekend was well worth it for me. Even if I don't sell anything else today, the contacts are invaluable."

"Excuse me. Is this painting for sale?" a man asked.

They all looked toward the speaker. A man was standing squarely in front of Margaret's abstract painting.

CHAPTER TWENTY-FOUR

Margaret walked over to greet the new customer. He was eyeing her debut piece and he looked very interested. Margaret had seen that glitter in the eyes before when a gallery customer was about to say, "I'll take it!"

She chatted with him for a good ten minutes, trying not to wonder what her friends were doing behind her back. The man had silver-gray hair, and he wore a powder blue polo shirt and khaki slacks.

"My name is John Wilson," he said. "I collect in a modest way. I like to buy artists who are just emerging."

"That's very flattering," Margaret said. The fact that he'd told her his name encouraged her. He must be serious about the painting.

"Well, I'm not a real expert, but I fancy I have a good eye," Mr. Wilson said. "And I buy what I like. Tell me how you came to paint this."

As the tourists shuffled past, Margaret recounted how Aiden had presented the shell to her. "Both of these paintings were inspired by that gift," she said, gesturing to the tide pool scene as well.

Mr. Wilson looked back and forth between the two. "Yes, I see the shell in that one, and here." He pointed to a curved smear of golden brown and white.

"That's right."

"Two very different paintings, with one inspiration and one theme."

Margaret felt a surge of pleasure that he understood what she'd done.

"Cute boy," he added.

"His mother is here too." She smiled at Shelley, and Shelley gave a little wave.

The man smiled and turned back to the abstract. Other people swarmed Margaret's booth, and she began to feel she should break away and speak to them, but Jenna and Diane stepped up to engage some of the browsers in conversation, and she saw Jenna give a woman one of her business cards. At last Mr. Wilson gave a firm nod.

"I'd like to buy it."

Her heart jumped. "Wonderful. It has to remain on display throughout the fair, since it's being judged. Would you be able to pick it up late this afternoon?"

His smile faded. "I live in Boston, and I have to head out soon. I have a commitment this evening. Could I pick it up next month? I'll be returning to Maine near the end of June..."

"Yes, you certainly can," Margaret said. She handed him one of her cards. "May I display it in my gallery in Marble Cove until you do? With a 'sold' sign, of course."

They soon reached an agreement, and the man wrote out a check while Margaret's friends and Jenna continued to greet other customers. When he left, Margaret glanced at it and whispered, "Thank You, Lord," before she put it into the pocket on the front of her blouse and buttoned the flap securely. It was the largest price she'd ever gotten for one of her paintings.

"Margaret, I'm so excited for you," Beverly said softly.

"Thank you." Margaret gave her a quick squeeze and accepted hugs from Diane and Shelley. That made two paintings sold over the weekend, and a third commissioned. "And the man who bought it didn't quibble about the price," she said.

"Should we mark 'sold' on the tag?" Jenna asked.

"Good idea."

They chatted for a few more minutes, while Jenna got a marker and boldly wrote SOLD over the price on the tag. More customers kept stopping at the booth, and it became obvious that Margaret needed to concentrate on them.

"This has got to be the biggest crowd we've had," Jenna said. "You can hardly walk through the aisles between the booths today."

"Margaret, how about if we go look around for a while and come back when you're not so busy?" Beverly asked.

"Unless we can help by staying," Diane added.

"I guess that's a good idea for you to look around now," Margaret said. "Jenna will help me."

"We brought a cooler," Shelley told her. "Maybe we can all eat lunch together."

"Well, the noon hour is usually a very busy time," Margaret said, "but we'll see how it goes."

Diane ambled about the pedestrian area with Beverly and Shelley. Several times she was tempted to make a purchase, but then asked herself, "Where would I put it in my little cottage?" That inquiry kept her from spending much money, though she did pick up a couple of handmade cards.

They were headed back toward Margaret's booth when Jenna came toward them through the crowd, anxiously scanning the shoppers' faces. When her gaze met Diane's, she smiled in relief and hurried toward her.

"I'm so glad I found you! The judges are going to make their presentations, and Mrs. Hoskins hoped you'd be with her."

"Of course." Diane turned to be sure Beverly and Shelley had heard, and they all hurried back to join Margaret.

"Oh, great, Jenna found you," Margaret cried when she saw them. "I'm a bundle of nerves."

"How do they do this?" Shelley asked.

"They go around and hang the ribbons on the winners' frames," Margaret said. "There are several categories—oils, acrylics, watercolors, and subject categories like landscapes, still lifes, portraits, and so on. And, of course, Best of Show. After all the awards are handed out, they'll make a general announcement over near the city hall, but they like to go around and put the ribbons right on the paintings rather than handing them to the artists. That way, the people can go around afterward and see which paintings have the ribbons."

"I like that," Beverly said.

Jenna kept watch, standing on tiptoe to see over people's heads. At last she turned and announced, "They're coming!" She wriggled in behind the others at the back of Margaret's allotted space, out of the way but close enough to hear and see everything.

Sure enough, Diane could see the group of dignitaries moving slowly down the row of exhibitors. They stopped two booths away.

"That's Thomas Carey's booth," Margaret said softly. "I hope he gets something. He does such lovely portraits of children."

"Oh, I think I saw those," Beverly said. "There was one of a little girl in a hayfield that was just adorable."

The clutch of onlookers around the judges let out a collective "ooh" and began to applaud.

Diane squinted. "Looks like a blue to me, but I can't be sure."

Margaret, who was several inches shorter, nodded in satisfaction. "I'll stroll over later and see, after the hoopla's died down."

Suddenly the judges were forming up before Margaret's debut painting. The head judge looked toward Margaret and nodded, then turned to face the crowd. "Margaret Hoskins, Debut Painting, *Sea Breeze,* second place."

The onlookers erupted in applause, and Margaret caught her breath. The judge held up her hand. "Not finished, folks. Margaret Hoskins, in the Abstract category, *Sea Breeze,* first place."

The clapping was sprinkled with a few whistles and shouts of "Yay," and "Congratulations!"

The judge with the ponytail stepped up to pin a blue ribbon to the frame on Margaret's abstract, and a red one on the other side.

Margaret clapped a hand to her cheek, overwhelmed by the rush of emotion flooding her. "Oh my."

Diane slipped her arm around Margaret and hugged her. "Well deserved."

Margaret stepped toward the judges. "Thank you. Thank you so much!"

Richard Leland grasped her hand. "An intriguing piece, Margaret. I'd like to see more from you in this vein."

"I think you will," Margaret said, a little breathless.

"I see it's been sold," said the female judge. "I'm not at all surprised. Best of luck to you."

As they moved on to the next recipient, Margaret hauled in a deep breath. "Well. I don't know what to say."

Shelley laughed and threw her arms around her. "Say 'Praise the Lord!' and celebrate."

"Thanks, Shelley."

"Congratulations," Beverly said, giving her a shy squeeze.

Jenna moved in for a quick hug too. "I knew it was a great painting, Mrs. Hoskins."

★   ★   ★

Diane pulled the cooler from beneath the table, and soon they sat down to eat. Margaret had several interruptions as other artists came by to congratulate her and talk shop, while the tourists kept on strolling through. Diane tried to keep an eye on her, and she noted that Margaret did manage to eat half a sandwich and drink a bottle of iced tea.

When the rest of them had finished eating, Shelley helped Diane clean up the food wrappers and drink containers.

"We thought we'd go down to the lighthouse for a short visit," Beverly told Margaret. "We'll be back well before four o'clock, though, so we can help you pack up."

"That sounds perfect."

"Would you like one of us to stay?" Diane asked.

"No, go ahead. I think the crowd is starting to thin. Jenna's here if I need anything, and they've only called on me to do an artist ambassador's chore once today."

They piled into Diane's car, and she headed for the picturesque little lighthouse at Marshall Point.

"I love this one," Shelley said. "It's the one they put in the movie *Forrest Gump.*"

"I've never seen it in real life," Diane confessed. "I can hardly wait."

The lighthouse itself was smaller than the lighthouse at Orlean Point. They couldn't go inside it, which Diane had expected, but the Marshall Point Lighthouse Museum, in the old lighthouse keeper's house, welcomed them. Diane scanned the exhibits on local history eagerly. When they'd finished browsing there, the well-stocked gift shop drew them in. Diane was immediately attracted to the book display.

"They've got your book," Beverly said with satisfaction.

Diane smiled and reached out to touch the cover of her mystery on the rack. Two more copies nestled behind it. "That's really nice."

"You should ask if they'll let you sign them," Shelley said.

"Oh, I don't think I'd dare do that." Diane wondered if authors really did such brazen things.

"I'm sure the staff would at least like to know you were here," Beverly said.

"Yes. Come on." Shelley reached for a copy of the book, grabbed Diane's hand, and pulled her toward the counter. "I'll do the talking."

One of the two women waiting on customers smiled at them. "May I help you?"

Shelley held up Diane's book. "Yes, I wanted to tell you that the author of *The Lighthouse Goes Dark* is here in the store. This is Diane Spencer."

The woman's eyes widened. "Oh, I love that book!" She looked eagerly to Diane. "Is there another one coming out soon?"

Diane felt her cheeks grow warm. "Well, uh, yes. Not *soon*, exactly. I'm still working on it, but I'm—I'm getting there."

"Wonderful! We'll certainly stock it."

"Do you ever let authors sign their books here?" Shelley asked.

"Occasionally, but you can see how little space we have." The woman gestured toward the cramped sales area. "But, Ms. Spencer, we'd be delighted if you wanted to sign the ones we have in stock now."

Diane shot a glance at Shelley, who beamed at her in triumph.

"That would be . . . lovely. Thank you."

It took her only a minute to sign the three books, and one of the customers, having overheard the exchange, grabbed one as soon as Diane placed it back in the rack.

"I just love mysteries," she said. "Would you mind adding a personal note? To Heather?"

"I'd be glad to." Diane wrote the inscription and handed the book back to the woman.

"Thank you so much. Do you live in Maine?"

"Yes, I do," Diane said.

"I'm from New Jersey," Heather said. "We're only here for a few more days."

"Wonderful. Enjoy the rest of your stay."

Heather made her way to the counter, and Diane exhaled.

Shelley laughed. "Did I make you nervous? Sorry. But it's like Beverly says . . . word-of-mouth advertising. You can bet that woman will tell all her friends she met the author."

Diane patted her shoulder. "Thanks. Maybe I should hire you as a publicist." She began to browse the other books. Beverly had wandered to the other end of the shop and was looking over the selection of lighthouse memorabilia, and Shelley's attention was snagged by a hanging display of stuffed lobsters, seals, and moose.

Diane picked up a colorful children's book. "Oh, isn't this cute? *A Maine Alphabet*. The pictures are darling."

Shelley peeked over her shoulder. "Aiden would love that."

"I'm going to get it for him," Diane said on impulse.

"Oh, you don't have to do that," Shelley protested.

"I know, but I want to. The next time he comes over, we can read it together, and then I'll let him take it home. He can read it to Emma."

"They'll love it. Thanks, Diane," Shelley said.

Beverly came over, her eyes gleaming. "Look what I found in the card rack." She held up two greeting cards with Margaret's paintings on the front.

"Oh, that's fantastic," Shelley said. "She'll be so pleased to know you found them here."

Beverly went to the checkout to purchase the cards. When she was done, she came back to Diane and Shelley. "I told them about Margaret, and I wrote down her name for the manager. I wish I had one of Margaret's business cards with me. They might be interested in carrying her prints here. Her lighthouse paintings would be perfect for them."

"I've got one of her cards," Diane said. "I picked it up at her booth this morning." She fished it out of her purse and gave it to Beverly.

"Thanks. Be right back."

Outside, Beverly positioned Diane and Shelley with the lighthouse in the background and snapped a photo. Only under protest did she let Diane take one of her and Shelley. Soon they were in Diane's car, heading back to the art festival.

"You know," Beverly said, "if we had something like that at Marble Cove, it would draw in a lot more tourists."

"You mean a museum?" Shelley asked.

"Maybe. Remember how we've talked about a tasteful gift shop near the lighthouse. It could have some historical displays. I don't know if there's enough memorabilia associated with the Orlean Point lighthouse for a museum."

"True," Diane said. "We never really pursued those ideas, but it might be something to think about again in order to raise some money for the maintenance of the lighthouse."

"And that one has several people working in it," Shelley added.

Beverly nodded. "Anything that adds jobs in Marble Cove is good. But I'm not sure the town would want to spend money for the start-up costs. A new building and all of that."

"Let's think about it," Diane said. "Maybe the Crow's Nest or the Hermit Crab would consider a small annex near the lighthouse, if the town would allow it. Maybe something seasonal."

When they got back to the art fair, Margaret was waiting anxiously for them, and the crowd was much smaller.

"Everyone's gone over to where they're making the announcements," she explained.

"Well, let's walk over there," Beverly said.

"All right."

"I'll stay here," Jenna offered.

The four friends strolled between the other art displays to the outskirts of the throng around the city hall steps, where the chairman of the festival committee, Rosalyn Neely, was standing with a portable microphone. She read through the list of winners for each category of artwork.

"I know you've all been waiting for this one," she said at last, smiling at the people. "Every year we choose one painting as Best of Show. Our winner this year is Thomas Carey, for his watercolor portrait *Ashleigh in Blue.*"

Diane shot Margaret a glance to see if she registered disappointment, but her friend was grinning and applauding with the rest of the crowd.

"He deserves it," she said.

Several people came by to speak to Margaret in the next half hour. Diane, Shelley, and Beverly, with Jenna's help, packed up everything but the artwork, easels, and display board. They even took down Margaret's table and folded the tablecloth.

"As soon as it's officially over, you can bring my car up," Margaret said, handing her key ring to Diane. "Then we'll get everything loaded, and off we go."

"You can put some things in my car if it will help," Diane told her. "In fact, we could carry a load down there now. It's not that far. When we came back from the lighthouse, I was able to park fairly close."

Soon she and Shelley were toting a couple of boxes and Margaret's small cooler to the parking area where Diane had left her car. The table would have to wait until they could drive in.

By the time they got back to Margaret's booth, Diane was tired, but she knew that Margaret must be exhausted after the three-day event.

Beverly strode out to meet them on the sidewalk. "See the couple talking to Margaret?"

Diane looked toward their friend's display area. A middle-aged man and woman in casual clothing were deep in conversation with Margaret, and the man was holding what appeared to be a checkbook.

"They're buying Margaret's tide pool painting," Beverly whispered.

"The one with Aiden in it?" Shelley wailed softly.

"That's the one. Sorry."

Shelley shrugged. "It's not like I could afford to buy it."

"And I'm sure Margaret could do a painting that looked more like Aiden," Diane said.

Shelley nodded, smiling. "I'm glad I took a picture of it. He'll be so excited when I tell him."

"I think Margaret's very pleased with her sales this weekend and the contacts she's made here," Diane said, watching as Margaret lifted down the painting for the couple.

"It was nice to see her get some recognition from the local art community too," Beverly added. "Maybe she'll be more confident in her abilities now."

"Hey, it looks like she's letting them take the painting," Shelley said. "That must mean the show is officially over."

Diane glanced at her watch. "Yes, so I'll go get the car."

"Better wait a few minutes until the pedestrians clear out," Beverly said.

Of course she was right. Diane realized she was eager to get home to Rocky and her unfinished manuscript, but a few more minutes wouldn't matter.

They carefully took down Margaret's artwork and boxed it. As they dismantled the display board, Beverly said, "Now that this is over, we all need to take a look at the antique prayer book. Do you think we can get together soon?"

"How about in the morning?" Margaret asked. "Before I go to open the gallery."

"Do you think you'll be up to it?" Diane looked at her in concern. This was what she had hoped for, to slip in the celebration of Shelley's birthday, but she didn't want Margaret to overdo.

"Yeah," Shelley said. "If I were you, I'd want to sleep in tomorrow. Not that my kids would let me!"

Margaret smiled. "Thanks, but I'm feeling pretty good. As long as I fall into bed on time tonight, I think I could manage a half hour before I go to the Shearwater."

"Why don't you all pop over to my house for breakfast, then?" Diane suggested. "Maybe Shelley can slip across the street and leave the kids with Dan."

Shelley frowned. "Well, he'll probably have to leave by seven."

"Maybe Adelaide can watch them," Margaret said. "I've hardly spoken to her for two days, but if she's free, I'm sure she'd like to."

"And if she can't, just bring the kids. We'll work it out," Diane said.

Beverly nodded. "Sounds good. I should be able to get out without disturbing Father."

Margaret beamed at them as she slid one of the painting boxes into the back of her car. "Thanks for offering, Diane. Sounds like we'll all be there."

★   ★   ★

Just as she got out of Diane's car in her driveway, Beverly's phone rang. She waved to her friends and pulled it from her pocket. Jeff. She smiled and put the phone to her ear.

"Hi, Jeff."

"Hi. How did the art fair go?"

"Great. Margaret won the abstract category and took second in the debut category. And she sold a few paintings. I think it was a good weekend for her."

"How about you?" Jeff asked.

"I'm good. How's your work going?"

"Great. I went out on a lobster boat today."

"A lobster boat? Is that a new assignment?"

"Yes. An editor I've worked with before called me and asked if I could get some photos to illustrate an article about the fishing industry. It was a hurry-up job, but I enjoyed it. The boat's crew was amazing. I met some real characters, I'll tell you."

"Sounds interesting."

"It was." He paused. "Beverly, I miss you."

She stopped on the walkway and looked toward the water. The sun was low behind her and cast long, golden rays over the cove. *It would only look like that for a minute,* Beverly thought. Margaret could capture that distinctive shimmer.

Maybe she would ask her if she had a painting with the sunset rays shining on their little slice of the ocean.

She realized she was smiling. Instead of the churning stomach and tightening in her chest that Jeff's calls had brought on in the past, she felt relaxed and secure, as though this was the appropriate ending for a day spent with friends.

Into the phone, she said quietly, "I miss you too, Jeff."

CHAPTER TWENTY-FIVE

Beverly was the first to arrive at Diane's the next morning. Rocky leaped about her and barked, and Diane lunged for his collar.

"I'm sorry, Beverly. Let me hitch him outside."

"Not a problem," Beverly said, but she was glad the dog wouldn't be in the room when she unwrapped the antique prayer book. If anything happened to it, she'd have to answer to both the owner and the committee.

"Now, Shelley has no idea we're celebrating her birthday," Diane said. "She's bringing cinnamon buns. I couldn't say no—she'd have been insulted. But the cake is in the fridge."

Beverly gave a little moan. "Cake *and* cinnamon buns?"

"I know, but what could we do? And I've got the gift all wrapped in my bedroom."

Shelley came next, carrying a large plastic container. Diane flung the door open.

"Where do you want this?" Shelley asked.

"I'll take it." Diane took the container. "Come on in."

Beverly made a mental note to run her longer route when she took her jog later. Shelley's sweets were just too good— let alone the surprise cake.

"Hi, Beverly," Shelley said with a grin.

"Is Adelaide with the kids?" Diane asked.

"No, Dan actually didn't have to leave as early as usual. They finished the job they were working on last night, and the new one that they start today is a lot closer."

They went into Diane's small, bright kitchen, where the odors of coffee and something else added to the temptation.

"What are you cooking?" Beverly glanced toward the stove and saw that the oven light was on.

"It's a breakfast casserole. I don't usually do a big breakfast, but today's special. Fruit cup, casserole, and Shelley's cinnamon buns." She gave Beverly a significant glance.

Beverly hugged her stomach and gave another moan. "That sounds like three breakfasts, but I can hardly wait."

The doorbell rang.

"There's Margaret," Diane said as she hurried back to the entry.

"Were the kids up when you left?" Beverly asked Shelley.

"Aiden was, but Dan was okay with it. I left them eating their Cheerios and talking about what video they were going to watch until I get back." She laughed as she peeled off the top of her container and set it aside. "I really think Dan enjoys cartoons as much as Aiden does, especially when they watch them together."

"There are worse things," Beverly said.

Margaret bustled in and set a bottle of flavored creamer on the table. "There's my contribution. Good morning, girls."

"Hi," Beverly said. "I guess I'm the only one who didn't bring anything."

"You brought the reason for this meeting," Diane reminded her.

"Yes," Margaret said, "and we're all eager to see it."

"All right, shall we look at it first, before we get the food out?" Beverly asked.

"It will probably be safer that way," Diane said. "And we can talk about it while we eat."

"Yes, and when I have to leave, I won't miss too much," Shelley put in. "I don't want to have to go before you've shown it to us."

"Let's go in the living room," Diane suggested, since the kitchen table was already set for breakfast.

They all took seats, Beverly and Margaret on the sofa, and Shelley and Diane in chairs close by. Beverly opened the padded envelope and gently removed the wrapped volume.

"Of course, Maddie warned me to be careful without really warning me."

Shelley laughed. "Naturally."

"Well, I don't blame her really. We *are* responsible for returning it in as good condition as she gave it to us." Beverly laid back the tissue and set the little book on the coffee table.

All of them gazed at the crackly old brown leather.

"Were you able to find out how old it is?" Diane asked.

"Not exactly, but I did some research online. I didn't want to jump ahead of the group, but I thought a little background information would be useful."

"Great," Margaret said. "What did you find out?"

"Well, as you can see, the title page has a lengthy title." Beverly opened it and held it so the others could see. "I looked up this title, and I learned that the Book of Common Prayer, as it's called, was first published in 1549. But this one isn't that old. Several revisions were made. The 1662 version became the standard. I believe that's what we have here."

"Yikes," Shelley said. "That thing is over three hundred years old?"

"I think it is," Beverly said. "Of course, there were many printings after 1662, so we don't know exactly what year it was printed. But Old First was founded a hundred years later—in 1762. If this book belonged to Jeremiah Thorpe or one of his congregation, it was probably printed in England sometime before the church was founded. That's as close as we can come for now."

"It's good to know," Diane said.

"Yes, and it tells me Maddie's absolutely right about handling it with care." Margaret looked around at the others. "Do you think we should wear gloves?"

Beverly winced. "Father and I held it in our bare hands. We did make sure our hands were clean first."

"You're probably fine," Diane said, "but we should handle it as little as possible, right, Margaret?"

"Yes. Have you looked all the way through it, Beverly? I don't see any inscription on the title page or opposite it."

"I did leaf all the way through it." Beverly was a little relieved to move on to another topic. "I didn't see anything unusual in the book. Father and I were speculating that people wouldn't write in their books or Bibles as much then as we do now."

"That's right," Margaret said. "They would probably only have one prayer book for their entire lifetime, and they treasured things like that."

"I did find one verse underlined," Beverly said, gently turning to it. "Here we go. Psalm 17:15: 'As for me, I will behold thy face in righteousness: I shall be satisfied, when I awake, with thy likeness.'"

"That's an odd verse," Margaret said. "Are you sure that's the only one?"

"Yes. And as I said, I don't think the owner wrote anything in the book—until you get to the very end." Beverly gingerly turned the leaves until she exposed the one at the back that had been blank. "On this page alone, someone has written something. I think it's a message, but I couldn't make it out. Father and I wondered if it was in English."

"Could it be Old English?" Margaret asked.

"I don't think the book goes that far back," Beverly said.

"A foreign language, then?" Shelley gazed at her hopefully. "French, maybe? When did the Normans conquer England?"

"That was back in 1066," Diane said, "but I suppose there were a lot of people in England who spoke French in the 1700s."

Beverly hesitated. "Take a good look. The order of the letters doesn't really make sense to me. And there are no spaces or word divisions. The letters don't seem right for words—at least not in English. The infrequency of vowels, for instance."

The others leaned in without touching the book.

"Hey!" Shelley looked up at her again. "Is it a code?"

"I don't know." Beverly smiled. "If it is, then maybe we have another clue to figure out."

Diane sat back in her chair. "This gets more and more intriguing."

Shelley glanced at her watch. "I hate to cut this short, but we'd probably better eat. I'll have to leave in fifteen minutes or so."

"Okay," Diane said. "Let's move back into the kitchen."

Beverly closed the book gently and nestled it in the tissue paper. Rocky was still outside, but just to be safe, she slid it into the envelope.

Over the table, the four continued to discuss the mysterious writing in the prayer book.

"What's your best guess?" Margaret asked Beverly. "You've had the longest to think about it."

"I think it may be a cipher of some sort."

"Is that the same as a code?" Shelley asked.

"Not really. A code generally uses words to replace other words, or symbols to replace words or phrases. For instance, the Secret Service would use code words for the president's name and those of other prominent people, and for places."

"Right," Diane said. "So if they said the teddy bear was in the garden, that might mean the president was in his office, something like that."

Beverly smiled. "Yes. But a cipher replaces individual letters. And often it's more complicated than just substituting one letter for another. The words are rearranged on the page, or interspersed with meaningless letters to confuse people trying to solve it. Sometimes the final, enciphered message is set off in groups of five letters, as if it were all five-letter words."

"I've read a little bit about that," Diane said. "It can be pretty hard to solve if you don't know what type of cipher they're using."

"Yes, it can. But one thing that puzzles me is that we didn't find anything like this in Thorpe's letters."

"True," Margaret said. "This book may not have any connection to Jeremiah Thorpe. Because if he used a cipher frequently, why didn't he use it in the letters to his wife, or on the hidden map?"

"Maybe his wife wasn't in on it," Shelley suggested.

"That's a thought." Diane looked around at all of them. "It could be something he began doing after her death."

"Or it could be that someone else entirely wrote that in the prayer book," Margaret added.

"Good point," Beverly said. "We just don't know who owned this book. And if the cipher is not as old as the book, it was probably done in an entirely different system than it would be if it were written in the 1700s."

They sat in silence for a few seconds.

"Well, I think we should try to figure it out," Shelley said at last.

"So do I," Beverly said. "I didn't mean to discourage you from that."

"No, but you had to tell us what we're up against." Margaret stood. "Anyone want more coffee?"

"I really have to go," Shelley said. "If you all think of something, be sure to let me know later."

Beverly shot Diane a panicky glance. "Hold on."

Diane's wall phone rang. "Oh, excuse me just a second." She picked up the receiver. "Hello?"

"Hi. It's Dan."

"Do you need Shelley?" Diane asked. "We're not really done yet." She glanced toward Shelley, who had paused in the doorway at the sound of her name.

"No, that's why I called. My mom is here, and she'll stay for a little while."

"Great. Hang on a sec." Diane covered the receiver with her hand. "Shelley, Dan says Frances is at your house, and she'll stay with the kids if you want to stay here a few more minutes."

"Well..."

"There's one more thing we'd like to show you," Beverly said quickly.

"Okay. Tell him I said thanks, and I'll be home in fifteen minutes or so."

Diane relayed the message and hung up with a smile. "We'd better get right to the last order of business."

"Yes," Margaret said. "Today is a very important day."

Shelley looked suspiciously from one to another of her friends. "What are you guys talking about?"

Diane turned to the refrigerator. "This." She leaned in and pulled out a frosted layer cake. "Happy birthday, Shelley."

Shelley gasped.

Beverly and Margaret went to hug Shelley as Diane set the cake on the table.

"Wow!" Shelley swiped a tear from her cheek. "You guys are good at surprises. And after that huge breakfast."

"I know," Diane said. "Maybe we should just let you take it home and enjoy later with the kids." She caught Beverly's eye and pointed toward her bedroom.

"We know you have a family celebration later," Margaret said. "So we thought we'd throw this in here."

Beverly disappeared and returned a moment later with a wrapped package.

"Here you go, Shelley. From all of us."

"Oh, you guys!" Shelley sat down again, her face turning red. "You're not going to sing, are you?"

Diane laughed. "You'll probably get enough of that later."

After a little cajoling, she opened the package. She held up a beach glass necklace in graduated shades of green. "Oh, I love it. Did this come from your store, Margaret?"

"Yes, it did."

Shelley picked up a small envelope and slid a gift card from it. "Oh, Captain Calhoun's! Thanks!"

"That's so you and Dan can go out some night," Diane said. "And let me know if you need a sitter."

"Thanks so much! But don't let me take that whole cake home!"

The four settled down with token slices.

"So, Beverly, what do you recommend we do next about the prayer book?" Diane asked.

"If the book belonged to us, I'd want to take it to an antique book expert. But it doesn't." Beverly looked around at the others. "Hank told us that he took it to a dealer in Rockland, but he didn't learn much."

"And the dealer wasn't a specialist in seventeenth-century books," Diane said. "I think we should show it to someone else who deals only in books."

"That's what I thought," Beverly said. "If we took it to Portland, or even Boston, we could get a more complete report."

"But it wouldn't be right for us to do that," Diane said with a frown.

"Not unless Hank and Elsie okayed it, and we have to give this back to the committee soon," Beverly said. "I'm sorry to say that I don't think we could photocopy that page without damaging the book, no matter how careful we were."

"We'll take some digital photos, like we did for the letters," Diane assured her.

"Well, I need to get over to the gallery," Margaret said regretfully.

"And I've got to go home."

"Take the cake," Diane said. "Maybe Frances will eat a piece."

When Shelley had left, Diane turned to Beverly. "Can you stay and take those photos now? I can spare some time this morning."

Beverly nodded. "Great. Then I'll print out copies of the photos when I get home for each of the four of us."

"Sounds good." Margaret stood. "Good-bye, my dears. Diane, thank you so much for having us in. And Beverly, thank you for doing the research."

They saw her to the door, and Diane looked wistfully at the prayer book. "I don't suppose it could be just an anagram?"

"Nothing that simple, I'm afraid," Beverly said, "but we could put it into the computer and see if it would 'unscramble' it, just for drill."

"Well, come on. What are we waiting for?" Diane led the way to her desk.

Beverly held the prayer book carefully. This adventure was far from over. She was glad to have a little time with Diane. She reflected how unlikely this scene would have seemed to her a year ago. Her life had changed so drastically in last twelve months that she barely recognized herself. New home, new job, new friends.

The three friends she'd found in Marble Cove had blessed her richly. Beverly had never felt so close to a group of women before. The support and encouragement she got from them was something she had never experienced.

Part of the pleasure came from knowing she was giving to them, as well as receiving.

Now they had a challenging mystery to solve. A year ago, Beverly would have doubted they could do it. But they'd laid to rest the mystery of the lighthouse. She felt now that it was entirely possible they could solve this one too, and help save the beautiful old church.

"Okay," Diane said, sitting with a pen poised over a notepad. "You read the letters off and I'll write them down. Then I'll look and see if I agree with you."

Beverly smiled. If anyone could solve this intriguing mystery, she thought to herself, it was her and her three dear friends.

About the Author

Susan Page Davis is the author of more than forty published novels. A Maine native, she now lives in western Kentucky with her husband Jim. They have six children and eight grandchildren. Susan is a past winner of the Carol Award and the Inspirational Readers' Choice Award, as well as Heartsong Presents Favorite Author of the Year.

A Conversation with Susan Page Davis

Q. This is your first book in the Miracles of Marble Cove series. Which of the characters is your favorite, and why?

A. I love them all, but Beverly, who is the featured character in this book, is perhaps my favorite. She's had a bit of trauma in her life, and she isn't always as sure of herself as she seems. But she's learning to trust her friends and her Lord. I admire her self-discipline and talents, but I like her for her insecurities and the way she handles them.

Q. What was the most challenging/rewarding/enjoyable scene in the book to write?

A. The scenes where Beverly awkwardly interacts with Jeff almost hurt to write. I found myself longing to speed up the reconciliation. I think that was the most challenging. The most enjoyable were the cabin scenes with Shelley's family.

Q. You were raised in Maine. How do you think that affected your approach to writing this book?

A. Some things were easy—I know where things "are" in the story, and how the air smells on the Maine coast and what birds and plants my characters are likely to see. But I had to remember that not all the readers know those things, so I have tried to bring it to them.

Q. What is your writing process?

A. First I brainstorm, using the basic idea for the mystery and characters' journeys. I outline the story in detail and do a little research to make sure my plot twists will work the way I want them to. Then I write the rough draft. Sometimes I go back and change things as I go. When the complete draft is finished, I go over the whole thing to make sure it's consistent and clean it up where needed. Then my husband reads it (he's a former news editor). Then it goes to my book editors and they send me any revisions they feel are needed or would enhance the story. Sometimes this includes adding new scenes or putting in incidents to foreshadow something that will happen in the next book. For instance, in *Setting Course*, I added a few minor characters who will reappear in Book 13. I make those changes, and then the editors go over it again. Finally, there's a "galley" version for me to check for any typesetting errors or other last-minute small changes.

Q. When you're not writing, what other activities do you enjoy?

A. I like reading, needlework, genealogy, and logic puzzles. I also like to travel and visit historical sites.

BAKING WITH SHELLEY

Maine Needhams

½ cup (1 stick) butter

¾ cup unseasoned mashed potato with ½ teaspoon salt
   well incorporated

2 (1-pound) packages confectioners' sugar

2 (7-ounce) bags flaked coconut

2 teaspoons vanilla

½ (2½-by-2½-inches) block of paraffin (This is the wax
   used to seal jam and jelly jars.)

1 (12-ounce) package chocolate chips

4 unsweetened chocolate squares

Using double boiler, melt butter over boiling water. Add the
salted mashed potato, confectioners' sugar, flaked coconut,
and vanilla. Blend thoroughly and turn into a buttered jelly
roll pan. Spread evenly, then set the pan in the refrigerator
to cool. When hard, cut into small squares.

Dipping Chocolate

Place paraffin in a double boiler over boiling water to melt. Add both kinds of chocolate and allow to melt. Stir well to mix ingredients. Dip cooled candy squares in the chocolate mixture, using a toothpick or a skewer. You may need to reheat the chocolate mixture, so it stays thin and excess chocolate drips off easily. Place dipped candies on waxed paper to cool and then refrigerate to keep.

Makes four to six dozen pieces (depending on size).

From the
Guideposts Archives

This story by Ida M. Saenz of
San Antonio, Texas, originally appeared in
the November 2008 issue of *Guideposts*.

My five-year-old daughter Teresa came into my bedroom Sunday morning. "Mommy, are you going to church with me and Daddy?"

I groaned. I'd woken up with every muscle and joint aching—another flare-up of my rheumatoid arthritis. I didn't want to get out of bed, let alone go to church. "Oh, sweetie, I don't feel well."

"Church might make you feel better," Teresa coaxed. "I'll pray for you and maybe God will heal you like the leopard!" I knew she was remembering a Sunday school lesson about the leper. "Okay, I'll come," I sighed, wishing I *could* be healed.

My husband Joe insisted we sit up near the front. He and Teresa got into the service. But I couldn't focus on anything except the pain gripping me.

Midway through, a couple slid into the pew directly in front of us. I'd never seen them before. I would have remembered the woman's striking blonde hair. Visitors, I figured. "Welcome," I said during the greeting, leaning over the pew. "Are you new to the area?"

The blonde gazed into my eyes. "We're here to visit a friend," she said. "She's having a hard time. We want her to know everything is going to be all right." At that exact instant an enormous sense of peace settled over me. I felt healed. Not in my body—the pain was still there—but in my spirit.

I looked for the woman and her husband as soon as the service ended, but they were gone. I asked our pastor if he'd seen the couple. He looked at me, puzzled.

"She'd be hard to miss with that blonde hair," I prompted.

"But, Ida, that pew was empty," he said. "No one was there."

I knew better. Someone *had* been sitting there. Someone healing.

Read on for a sneak peek of the next exciting book in
Miracles of Marble Cove!

Pressing On
by Camy Tang

Diane Spencer breathed in the tangy scent of the sea air. This was a perfect end to her day.

She headed down the beach, her dog Rocky racing ahead of her along the sands and chasing seagulls. The June day was still bright despite the waning afternoon.

Rocky tore ahead of her, chasing some seagulls, his golden coat almost gleaming in the sunlight. It wasn't until the second ring that Diane realized the shrill sound she was hearing wasn't from the gulls, but from her cell phone. She saw her daughter's name in the caller ID and answered quickly. "Hello, sweetheart. How are you doing?"

"Hi, Mom. I'm fine. Things in the firm have finally started slowing down a bit."

Jessica talked about some of the stresses she had with a case she'd been working on, but it was obvious from the lilt in her voice that she still loved her job as an associate at her prestigious law firm in Boston.

"But Mom, now that the case is over, I can take a few days off work," Jessica said. "How about I visit you for a few days?"

"I would love that." But even as she said it, Diane's stomach tightened at the thought of all the work she had to do in addition to having her daughter here.

"And, Mom..." Jessica now sounded unsure. "Would it be okay if Martin came with me?"

"He would be more than welcome. He can sleep on the foldout couch." Diane couldn't help being intrigued by this chance to finally meet her daughter's boyfriend. Granted, Jessica had said she'd been so busy for the past six months that she'd barely had any time to spend with Martin, let alone bring him to meet her mother. But Diane thought it was high time they met, especially since Jessica had been to see Martin's family at Thanksgiving. "When will you both arrive?"

"Not for another week or so. I'm still waiting to clear my days off. I'll e-mail you to let you know the exact dates. Is that okay?"

"That's fine." Maybe the delay would give her time to plow through all the work she needed to do.

"Great. Okay, Mom. I'll talk to you later."

"Bye, sweetheart."

Diane disconnected the call and whistled to Rocky, who abandoned his chase and bounded back to her. She smiled to herself. Jessica was coming to visit. How wonderful. And she'd finally be able to meet Jessica's boyfriend too.

Still, she couldn't help feeling apprehension about him. Would any man would be good enough for her daughter?

Well, she thought, *here's my chance to find out.*

"Diane!"

The voice behind her made her turn before she got too far out onto the sands.

Beverly ran toward her, waving a piece of paper. "I have something for you."

"*Ooh*, a present? I love presents." Diane grinned.

Beverly caught up with her and gave her the paper. "Something like that." She brushed a windswept lock into place. "Maybe a treasure."

It was a printout. Beverly had copied down the encoded message they'd found on the back page of Jeremiah Thorpe's prayer book, not an easy feat since it was a dense paragraph of ornate capital letters in seemingly random order.

"This is typed out. Did you actually input it into a computer?" Diane asked in amazement.

"In a sense. I copied it out by hand on a piece of paper, then scanned it into my computer. I have software that translates my handwriting into typed text. Then I double-checked it to make sure it was accurate and printed out copies for everyone. I wanted to have a copy of the message on my computer in case I found a software program that would decode the message."

"Do you think it could be that easy?"

"I'd love to think so, but..." Beverly shrugged. "How has your day been?"

"Busy." Diane sighed. "I needed to get out of the house and go for a walk in the fresh air."

"Have you been at your computer all day too?"

"I really don't like to complain, because I've been busy promoting my book, and it's a dream come true. But I recently got a lot of requests for blog interviews and guest blog posts—the publicity manager at my publisher set up a blog tour for me."

"A blog tour?" Beverly asked.

"Basically, I write a guest blog for an established blogger to help promote my book. Usually they ask questions and I answer them. So I have lots of little pieces to write for the different bloggers."

"Isn't your second book due soon?"

"No! Just the first three chapters." She laughed. "Don't give me a heart attack like that." But Diane had to admit the thought of the three chapters *and* all the interview questions to answer *and* the guest blog posts to write did seem a bit overwhelming if she really sat and thought about it. Just work on one thing at a time, she told herself.

"Will you be able to do the chapters with all this extra stuff you have to write?" Beverly's face was concerned.

"I'm pretty sure I will. I used to be a reporter, so I'm used to writing short pieces very fast." Diane knew she sounded more confident than she actually felt. If she gave in to her worry, it would only paralyze her and she wouldn't get anything done. "Besides, the research for my second book involves researching ciphers, which is perfect for this cipher." She held up her copy of the message. "The only problem is that my research has come up with dozens of different types of ciphers that it could be. How would we know which one?"

"Well, we know about how old the paper is. It looks to be about the same age as the prayer journal, which would put the cipher in the late eighteenth century."

"So we can limit our search to ciphers created up till then. That'll help a lot because there are a ton of really complicated ciphers created in the twentieth century, especially for wartime."

"This one looks difficult enough," Beverly said.

"I wonder why Jeremiah had this cipher," Diane said thoughtfully. "I'm guessing it's in code because it relates to the treasure from the letters. But did Jeremiah receive this coded message from someone or did he write it, intending to give it to someone? Or was there someone in particular he was trying to hide it from?"

"If other people knew he had a treasure, they'd all want to get their hands on it. I'm guessing there wasn't any one person he had in mind."

"But I think there was one particular person he had in mind when he—or whoever it was—wrote this coded message. He meant for at least one person to find this message and know how to decode it."

"Or maybe this was a message *for* Jeremiah," Beverly said. "It might not have anything to do with the treasure, but have some other reason for secrecy."

"Wet blanket." Diane winked at Beverly. "That takes all the fun out of it."

Beverly laughed, then glanced at her watch. "I'd better go. I need to go start dinner for my father and I'll let you get back to your walk. Bye!"

Diane waved good-bye and headed out toward the beach. The sea breeze ruffled her hair and seemed to clear her mind of stress. She lifted her face to the light, feeling its warmth on her skin, and again breathed in the fresh salty smell, grateful to God for blessing her with her home here in Marble Cove, her friends, her career as a published novelist.

And then she added, *And thank You for the exciting scavenger hunt we've been on, looking for Jeremiah Thorpe's treasure. If it really is still out there, please help us to find it so that we can save Old First.*